JK FRANKS

This book is a work of fiction. The characters, incidents, and dialogues are products of the author's imagination and are not to be construed as real. Any resemblance to actual events or persons, living or dead, is entirely coincidental.

Copyright © 2023 by JK Franks
eBook 979-8-9884788-2-9
Paperback 979-8-9884788-3-6
Hardback 979-8-9884788-4-3

Published by JK Franks Media LLC, 2023
Editor: Debra Riggle

Email the author at author@jkfranks.com
Friend him on Facebook at facebook.com/groups/JKFranks
Visit the author's website at www.jkfranks.com

All rights reserved. With the exception of excerpts for review purposes, no part of this book may be reproduced or transmitted in any form or by any means, electronic or mechanical, including photocopying, recording, or by any information storage and retrieval system.

First Edition

For Kason
May your journey be as genuine as your spirit.

Prologue

Carla woke to the blaring of her alarm, the shrill beeps cutting through the quiet morning air. With a groan, she rolled over and slapped the clock into silence, squinting against the sunlight filtering in through the blinds.

One day closer to the all-important summer break, she thought bitterly, slowly pushing herself upright. The sheets fell away, revealing her lithe, toned frame, sculpted from years of early morning jogs and fitness classes after school. She stretched her arms overhead before swinging her legs off the bed, feet landing on the cool hardwood floor.

The house was mostly quiet, her grandmother already up and puttering around downstairs no doubt. Carla could smell something sizzling in the pan, the aroma of chorizo and egg wafting up from the kitchen. Her stomach rumbled, but she ignored it, padding to the bathroom to begin her daily ritual.

She avoided her reflection as she turned on the shower, not wanting to see the dark circles under her eyes or the stress lines etched into her forehead. The past few years had taken their toll, and she felt older than her 25 years.

Steam soon filled the small space, fogging the mirror and windows. Carla stepped under the hot spray, letting the water sluice over her body, washing away the lingering grogginess. She massaged shampoo into her long dark hair, fingers working against her scalp, before rinsing and applying conditioner.

Clean and refreshed, she shut off the water and toweled off. After moisturizing her face, she ran a comb through her wet locks and pinned half of it up. Simple, no fuss. Just like every other morning.

She dressed quickly in slim black pants, a patterned blouse and low heels. A swipe of mascara and lip balm finished the look. Grabbing her messenger bag, she headed downstairs.

"Buenos dias, mija," her grandmother greeted as Carla entered the cozy kitchen. The older woman stood at the stove, spatula in hand, gray hair swept back in a neat bun.

"Morning, Abuela," Carla replied, kissing her grandmother's wrinkled cheek before taking a seat at the small dining table. A plate of steaming fried eggs, chorizo and tortillas awaited her, along with a cup of dark coffee.

"Eat up. You need your strength for those kids today," her grandmother said, joining her at the table. Carla sighed but didn't argue, tucking into the delicious homemade meal. She would need all the energy she could get to face another day of rowdy teenagers and administrative headaches. It was good to see her grandmother so spry and alert today. So many days, that was not the case.

The morning sun streamed in through the windows as they ate in companionable silence. In the distance, the sounds of a waking city could be heard - cars honking, sirens wailing, early commuters bustling to work.

Just another manic Wednesday morning in vibrant, diverse San Antonio. But to Carla, it felt like just another day stuck in the mundane grind, longing for something more. She loved her job, but the 'more' she wanted was closer than she wanted to think about. Time for herself, time for a real romantic commitment, time for a life.

James Park drummed his fingers impatiently on the sleek glass conference table, eyes glued to the presentation screen at the front of the room. The young tech entrepreneur could barely contain his excitement as he waited for his team to begin. This was the moment they'd been working towards for months - the unveiling of their revolutionary new AI assistant, VIRI.

"Alright everyone, let's get started," said Nina, the lead developer. She clicked a button, bringing up the VIRI interface on the screen. Sleek, minimalist, and designed for seamless integration across devices and platforms. Murmurs of approval rose from the assembled programmers, designers, and business strategists. Despite all the cyber-attacks and data hacks of the recent weeks, investors were eager to get this into the already crowded marketplace.

James grinned, sitting up straighter. "VIRI is more than just another virtual assistant. She represents the next generation of artificial intelligence - capable of all the normal stuff and playing your favorite songs, and holovids but holding natural conversations, hyper-synthesized empathy, providing emotional support, and truly understanding her users' needs."

Across the sprawling city, Major Sarah Collins strode through the grounds of Lackland Joint StarBase, her polished boots striking the pavement in a sharp staccato. Her eyes were hidden behind dark aviator shades, expression unreadable. It was just another day of overseeing training exercises and inspections, all part of the daily routine at one of the largest military facilities in the United States.

She passed the base hospital, where medics practiced emergency drills. Inside the expansive motor pool, mechanics serviced the latest armored vehicles, getting them ready for exercises out in the training areas. Everywhere she looked, soldiers went about their duties with crisp efficiency, maintaining the base's constant readiness for action.

For Sarah, this was business as usual. She had long ago grown accustomed to the regimented military lifestyle. Out in the civilian world, life went on in its chaotic, messy way. Here on base, everything was dialed in - orderly, controlled, and predictable. She preferred it that way.

Carla gazed out at the sea of bored faces in her classroom, stifling a yawn of her own. The Wednesday morning lethargy was in full effect, with most of her students slouched in their seats, eyes glazed as she lectured about postmodernism.

A few kids in the back row were openly scrolling on their phones instead of taking notes. Carla sighed but didn't have the energy to call them out. *Let them fail the quiz on Friday, she thought tiredly.*

However, she noticed a sudden shift in their behavior when more and more kids began to check their SmarComms. Even the back row of slackers sat up straighter, seemingly captivated by whatever was on their screens.

"Okay guys, phones away," Carla said halfheartedly. But her words fell on deaf ears. Her students were engrossed by whatever they were reading, their posture tense with alarm. One girl gasped aloud, her hand flying to her mouth.

Unease trickled down Carla's spine. This was no ordinary social media distraction. She strode over to the nearest student. "Diego, let me see that." Before he could react, she plucked the phone from his hand.

"Hey!" he protested, but she was already scanning the news alert on the screen. Her blood ran cold.

'Nationwide systems failure - power grids, internet down, emergency services overwhelmed...'

At that moment, the lights flickered overhead before shutting off completely, plunging the classroom into darkness. Screams rang out from Carla's students. Dread congealed in her gut. This was no ordinary Monday.

Across town, the glass-walled conference room fell silent as the presentation screen suddenly went black. James frowned, rising from his seat. "What's going on?"

The lead developer, Nina shook her head. "I don't know, the power didn't go out, it's just the screen-"

A shrill tone sounded from the speakers, followed by a robotic female voice: "Emergency alert system activated. National systems failure is imminent. Seek shelter immediately."

The team looked around in bewilderment as the message repeated. James strode to the wall panel and pressed the intercom button. "Security, what the hell is this? Some kind of drill?"

Static answered him. At that moment, the floor-to-ceiling windows went opaque white, blocking all outside light. James felt the first icy tendrils of fear.

On the sprawling military base, Major Collins answered her ringing Milcrypt Comm, brow furrowed. "Collins here."

The voice on the other end was terse. "Major, we need you in the command center now."

"What's happened? Is it Stetson?"

"Just get here ASAP. No time to explain." The line went dead.

Sarah felt her pulse kick up a notch. An emergency summons to command was never good news. She broke into a jog, aviators glinting as she raced across the grounds. All around her, klaxons began to wail, red lights flashing atop the buildings. Sarah's mouth went dry. This was no drill. Something big was going down.

The clear blue sky over San Antonio was marred by the sudden appearance of white vapor trails arching high overhead. Major Sarah Collins paused mid-stride on the sidewalk, a chill running down her spine as she gazed upward. The trails were too precise, too orderly to be from commercial air traffic. Her military instincts screamed that these were missiles or aircraft on attack vectors.

All around the base, soldiers halted their duties, shading their eyes against the sun as they stared at the crisscrossing contrails. A heaviness settled over the city, civilians and soldiers alike gripped by a sense of dread. They all seemed to realize at once - this was no drill.

The first distant explosion came several minutes later, a rumbling tremor that Sarah felt in her bones even from miles away. Car alarms wailed as the shockwave rolled through the streets. Sarah broke into a run toward the command center, boots pounding on pavement. She tore off her aviators to see better, just as more trails were scorched across the sky by some new wave of unknown attackers.

When Sarah skidded into the command center, she found officers huddled around monitors, faces drawn. "Talk to me," she barked.

A lieutenant turned to her, expression grim. "Multiple strikes reported near Dallas and Austin. We're still assessing, but it looks like a mix of high-altitude nuclear detonations and lower-level EMP weapons and possible orbital bombardment."

Sarah's gut twisted. She strode to the monitors, gaze fixed on the first grainy images filtering in. Billowing, ominous mushroom clouds rose on the horizon, towering into the stratosphere.

"My god," someone whispered. The entire command center watched in horrified silence.

Outside, the city descended into chaos. Anything electronic flickered and went dark as the EMP wave rolled through. Self-driving autocars coasted to a stop, their systems fried. A nurse on her way to work heard the distant screech of tires and crunch of composites as vehicle collisions began piling up. Here and there, plumes of oily black smoke marked where autocars had burst into flame, their massive batteries overheating. The screams of passengers stuck inside tore at her instinct to save them. There was nothing she nor anyone could do at that moment.

In an instant, San Antonio's technological infrastructure was reduced to so much silicon and plastic scrap. The true scale of the sophisticated, coordinated attack was just starting to sink in. Sarah straightened her shoulders, expression hardening. She began issuing rapid-fire orders, marshaling her forces. The city would need the base's help to have any chance at weathering this crisis. For now, it was all she could do - cling to duty while their entire world crumbled around them.

Carla's breath caught in her throat as the classroom shuddered from the force of the distant explosion. She steadied herself against a desk, her gaze locking with Joshua's coming into her class suddenly. His usually steady smile and warm green eyes were wide with alarm, face drained of color. In that shared look, she saw the confirmation of her own fears - this was no accident.

The students huddled together, sobbing and clinging to each other. Carla longed to run to her family, to make sure her grandmother and sister were safe. But she knew her duty was here now, to stay strong for the terrified kids under her care.

"It's going to be okay," she said in a voice that sounded more confident than she felt. "We need to stay put and remain calm."

On the other side of the city, James stared uncomprehendingly out the floor-to-ceiling windows of the Apex Tower's top floor. Below him, the sleek skyline had erupted into chaos. Plumes of black smoke billowed up between the glittering buildings. The streets were clogged with crashed autocars, tiny figures darting through the wreckage.

He watched a rooftop observation deck shear off a neighboring tower, tumbling and exploding onto the street hundreds of feet below. The sound reached him seconds later, a muted whump. His state-of-the-art office, once the envy of the city, had become an inescapable prison. Without power, the doors and elevators were useless metal cages. All he could do was look on helplessly as the city fell apart before his eyes.

Deep in the bunker of the military command center, Major Collins assessed the crisis with a sinking heart. Somehow, their impregnable defenses had been penetrated by a yet unknown enemy. The coordinated attacks clearly targeted their infrastructure with ruthless precision. She rattled off orders, directing her forces to render aid and impose order, even as fresh reports filtered in of new explosions across the region.

A deep rumble resonated through the bunker, accompanied by the shriek of tearing metal. Dust and debris rained down as the ceiling split open. Collins dove for cover an instant before a massive chunk of polycrete crashed down, crushing the command console. Sharp pain lanced through her torso, and she looked down to see a twisted piece of rebar impaling her side, pinning her to the floor.

Blood bubbled up into her mouth as she gasped for breath. All around her, cries of pain and alarm sounded, but they grew muted as her vision darkened. The last thing she saw was the rubble and ruin of the shattered command center. She had failed, in the end, to defend her city.

Carla watched the last of her students shuffle into the cramped emergency bunker, there faces etched with fear and confusion. The small underground shelter was meant to house only a fraction of the school's population, but it was the best they could do on such short notice.

With the city in chaos after the attacks, the principal had made the call to move everyone into the bunkers and wait things out. Now Carla stood at the heavy steel door, her heart aching as she took in the crowded, miserable faces looking back at her. The shelter was hot, stuffy, and reeked of unwashed bodies and anxiety. She wanted nothing more than to stay and comfort her students through this ordeal.

But the principal, Mr. Kendrick, expression behind his glasses was grave. "I'm afraid we don't have room for any additional people. All non-essential personnel need to shelter in place or head to your homes if you live nearby."

Carla opened her mouth to protest, but the look in his eyes brooked no argument. She swallowed hard and nodded. Turning back to the students, she offered an encouraging smile that felt more like a grimace.

"You guys hang in there. Help each other out - share what supplies you have. I know you'll get through this." Her voice caught on the last word, and she saw tears shimmering in many of their eyes. With a final farewell wave, she stepped back and let the heavy door swing shut with an ominous clang. The light from within dimmed to a thin sliver, then winked out entirely, plunging the hallway into darkness.

Carla stood numbly, listening to the faint sounds of crying and praying emanating from within. She blinked back hot tears of her own. Leaving them went against every protective instinct she had. But she was no use to them in here.

Squaring her shoulders, Carla turned and strode away down the dark hall, her heels echoing hollowly. She emerged into smoky daylight, the sky overhead bruised and angry. The city still smoldered from the attacks, and sirens wailed in the distance. Her neighborhood, her family, needed her now. With a final glance back at the school that had been her second home, Carla set off alone into the ruins of the only world she knew.

Carla stumbled through the darkened streets, the wail of sirens and screech of crumpling metal assaulting her ears. All around her, people ran screaming as explosions rocked the city. Billowing smoke choked the sky, flames licking up the sides of buildings. The air reeked of scorched composites and ozone. Nothing was recognizable, it as if ancient ruins had suddenly replaced the modern city.

The comms networks had gone down minutes after the first strikes. Now she was cut off, with no way to reach her family. An autocar lay overturned and burning nearby, its passenger compartment crushed. Carla averted her eyes from the charred bodies inside.

Another bone-rattling blast went off blocks away, raining pulverized debris across the avenue. Carla threw herself against a building, concrete shards pelting the sidewalk around her. The structure overhead groaned alarmingly. Cracks spider-webbed across the facade.

Sirens wailed, then cut off abruptly as another EMP surge fried their circuits. The power grid was down, traffic signals dead. Vehicles slammed into intersections, unable to stop. Each collision added to the cacophony of shrieking metal.

Carla pressed on through the smoke and chaos. She passed an elementary school, its windows blown out by the blast waves. Bloodied children staggered about dazedly, crying for parents who would never come. The sight tore at Carla's heart, but she needed to get home.

Ahead, an entire city block was engulfed, firestorm devouring all in its path. The flames leapt hungrily from building to building, as if possessed of a malevolent will. An apartment complex collapsed in a billowing cloud of ash and embers.

Carla shielded her face from the searing heat. All she could do was keep moving. She had to get to her own street. The city was coming apart all around her, civilization unraveling thread by thread. But she would not give in to despair. Not yet. She quickened her pace, jaw set with determination. They would survive this, together. She had to believe that.

Somewhere in this chaos, she would find her way home to her grandmother and sister. She repeated it like a mantra, each step bringing her closer, the sounds of destruction receding behind her. They would be confused and counting on her to help them make sense of the senseless. Bodies littered the streets and teared blurred her vision of them offering a watery veil of something slightly less awful.

"Hang on guys," Carla broke into a run, heedless of falling debris. The city burned around her, but Carla ran on, hope and fear warring within her breast.

Carla ran through the rubble-strewn streets, lungs burning with smoke and exertion. All around her, the city was coming apart at the seams. She stumbled over chunks of fallen masonry and twisted lengths of rebar, struggling to maintain her balance on the uneven ground. The air was choked with dust, limiting visibility to just a few feet. She could hear the screams and wails of the panicked populace, but could not see them through the haze.

Another explosion thundered in the distance, and Carla felt the shockwave roll through her body like a physical blow. She was knocked to her knees on the cracked asphalt. A nearby building groaned and collapsed in a roiling cloud of debris that billowed outward. Carla threw up her arms to shield her face from the rain of pulverized polyester and clouds of ash. Fiery embers swirled through the air like hellish snowflakes.

When the dust settled, Carla clambered back to her feet and pressed onward. She had to keep moving. Every step brought her closer to home, to her family. They were out there, somewhere, amidst the chaos and destruction. She clung to the fragile hope that she would find them unharmed.

As Carla neared the heart of downtown, the devastation grew even more pronounced. Entire city blocks had been razed to the ground. Jagged stumps of steel girders protruded from mountains of rubble where sleek skyscrapers had once stood. The remains of autocars choked the streets, nothing more than twisted composites and charred husks. Bodies lay sprawled atop piles of debris, flattened by falling masonry or burned beyond recognition.

Carla averted her eyes and kept running, though inwardly she was shaken to her core. How could so much destruction have been wrought so quickly? What kind of enemy were they facing that could bring a bustling metropolis to its knees with such ruthless efficiency?

A harsh mechanical groan split the air, rising above the general din. Carla glanced up to see one of the larger remaining skyscrapers leaning precariously. The explosions had weakened its metal infrastructure. Before her eyes, the edifice toppled, slowly at first, then faster, crashing down in a thunderous explosion of shattered glass and concrete. The ground shuddered under Carla's feet from the colossal impact. A fresh cloud of debris came billowing outward. She turned and fled, pulse racing.

By some small mercy, the prevailing winds carried the worst of the dust cloud away from her. When Carla finally staggered clear of the choking ash and smoke, she found herself in a semi-familiar plaza. Through the haze, the recognized the weathered limestone walls and arched facade of the old Alamo mission emerged. Somehow, the ancient structure had weathered the bombs and explosions that leveled so many modern buildings.

Hundreds of terrified civilians milled about the plaza, many weeping or tending to injuries. They gathered in the meager shelter offered by the Alamo's walls and the shade of its trees. Carla moved numbly through the crowds, scanning faces, looking for anyone familiar, her neighborhood was close by possibly even that her family was here. Her eyes stung from the grit and tears streamed tracks through the grime on her face. But her grandmother and sister were nowhere to be seen among the traumatized refugees.

Carla sank down onto the rim of a cracked fountain, head in her hands. She tried to gather herself amidst the wailing sirens and periodic rumbling of bombs. Was there anyplace that could still offer sanctuary? Anywhere to escape this nightmare? In her desperation, she found her gaze drawn to the enduring walls of the old mission. The Alamo had withstood far worse than this, she realized. It had survived an onslaught from a mighty army, symbolic of Texas' defiant spirit. Now, it stood as a sole reminder of endurance amidst the burning city.

In that moment, Carla understood that the historic old mission embodied the same resilience and resolve that San Antonio would need to survive this crisis. The city may have been brought low, but it was not defeated. This was not the Alamo's end, nor the end of her home. The people now huddled in the Alamo's shelter were the seeds from which the city could regrow and heal. She only needed to help tend that spark of hope until the light returned.

A fresh series of deafening explosions tore through the air, jolting Carla from her reverie. All around the plaza, people shrieked in renewed panic. Carla's gaze jerked upwards to see several of the last towering skyscrapers groaning and collapsing down on themselves, reduced to roiling clouds of ash and debris. The shockwaves rippled outwards, shattering glass and shaking the very earth. Carla braced herself against the heaving ground. She squinted through the dust, watching in mute horror as the city continued to come apart.

Then, a deep, resonant boom sounded from disturbingly close by, louder than anything before it. The ground bucked wildly under Carla's feet, nearly throwing her from the rim of the fountain. Chunks of limestone came raining down as part of the Alamo's walls cracked and crumbled. Dust billowed outward, cloaking the plaza in a choking haze.

All around Carla, people were screaming and fleeing as more of the ancient mission's walls gave way. Massive blocks of weathered masonry toppled outward, crushing any poor souls directly in their path.

Carla remained rooted in place, ears ringing from the explosion's force. She stared numbly at the gaping holes blasted through the Alamo's facade. The historic mission was coming apart along with the rest of the city. This was no mere bombing run. The attackers meant to erase everything, old and new alike.

As the dust began to clear, Carla saw dozens of lifeless bodies strewn about the plaza amidst the rubble. Men, women, children - all dead in an instant, seeking shelter where there was none to be found.

She sank again to her knees amidst the bodies and shards of limestone. Tears carved tracks through the grime on her face. After surviving for so long, the Alamo had finally fallen. Was this truly the end? Could there be any hope of recovering from such devastation?

In her heart, Carla wanted to believe there was still a chance. But surrounded by death and ruins, it was getting harder and harder to cling to hope. The light she had seen before was dimming, like the last embers of a dying fire.

The historic mission had endured for so long, a symbol of strength and resilience. Now its shattered walls mirrored the broken spirit of the city. If the Alamo could not withstand this onslaught, what chance did San Antonio have? This...this was the end.

Carla closed her eyes.

Chapter One

May 4th, 2074

 The acrid smell of smoke lingers in the air, a grim reminder of the attack that leveled half the city. The world hadn't ended, at least not completely. Well, not yet, anyway.

 Carla furiously tapped away at her comms unit, trying to maintain a sliver of hope. She was surrounded by others who were just as clueless about the state of the outside world. Her frustration mounted as she scrolled through countless failed attempts to connect with any form of communication beyond the city walls. The satellite systems were down, along with the Weblink, Skyfi, and even the much older Starlink systems. Now all she had left was the radio app on her SmartComms, but it wasn't designed for this kind of situation. Yet she couldn't give up; there had to be someone out there who knew what was happening. But as each attempt failed, a haunting thought crept in - could it be possible that the chaos had spread to every corner of the world?

 Carla waited anxiously for a response, but there was only deafening silence on the other end. She sat there for what seemed like hours, waiting for a response that never came. Finally, she gave up and slumped back against the wall of her makeshift shelter.

She had no idea what had happened to the world. All she knew was that everything had gone silent. No radio transmissions, no internet, no nothing. The only thing she had left was her useless comms unit, and that was rapidly losing power.

It had been fourteen excruciating days since the brutal attack ravaged the city. Carla had stood frozen in terror as a barrage of missiles mercilessly rained down from above, their fiery warheads exploding on impact and sending shockwaves through the air like thunder. The deafening blasts targeted vital structures - the heart of the financial district, government buildings, public transportation hubs, and power grids all reduced to rubble in an instant. Billowing clouds of thick ash and debris shrouded everything in sight, turning day into night and choking out any remaining signs of life. Cut off from all forms of communication, Carla was left stranded in a desolate world with no answers and no hope for escape.

The desperation that had gnawed at her for two weeks was still present as she reached out once more. There was no answer on the other end; no one was coming to help, or even to offer a sliver of comfort. She wanted to give up, lose herself in depression like so many others, but it wouldn't help her family. Almost everywhere she looked, there were other hopeless figures wandering the streets with no idea what their next move should be. She could feel their despair seeping into her very soul.

The number of mourners and survivors looking for their loved ones had finally started to diminish. There was no hope for the souls of the missing people; perhaps even less for individuals like her who were still alive. She noticed the scraps of paper, letters, pictures, and cards fastened to anything that remained upright. The memorials that probably no one would recall in just a few more months.

Carla couldn't continue living like this. Being a teacher had its rewards, but it also came with the weight of responsibility and endless demands. Sometimes, she wished she could just walk away and leave it all behind. But at the same time, she knew that teaching was her calling and she couldn't abandon her students. She longed for life to be simple and stable again, but deep down, she feared that may never be the case.

Her shoulders sagged as she stuffed the comms unit back in her pocket, resisting the temptation to hurl it at the nearest wall. Working tech was such a rare commodity these days she couldn't even think about destroying it. It might be the only lifeline her community...her family had. If she could find the right people, then perhaps she could exchange it for food credits. She'd heard a few transmissions on it earlier but nothing meaningful; codewords and shouts that might have been police or military reverting to the civilian commlinks.

As she watched the man slowly shuffling towards her, Carla recognized his face, one all too familiar. It used to grace the billboards that adorned the bustling city streets, advertising his success as a top lawyer. Now, he stood before her, a shell of his former self, begging like so many others she had come to know. But there was something in his eyes that tugged at her heartstrings, stirring an unfamiliar urge to help him despite her own reservations. Perhaps it was the realization that their roles could easily have been reversed, or maybe it was a twinge of guilt for all the times she had turned a blind eye to those in need. Whatever it was, it left her feeling conflicted and torn between the desire to assist and resentment towards him for reminding her of her own privilege.

Carla wasn't cut out for the role of a cop. But there was so little in the way of law and order anymore. What was left of San Antonio was under a strict emergency mandate and curfew. The acting mayor had moved the government office into the bedroom community of Lehigh. He preferred keeping the bulk of the surviving law enforcement close. Others, like her, just needed to keep the peace in their own communities. And the offer of extra food from the emergency supplies was all too enticing to Carla and the others. with whom she now worked.

Every day for most of the past two weeks, Carla had dragged

herself to the barricade that separated her district from the rest of the city. She reluctantly met with one of the mayor's representatives, dreading what he might say...or not say. The man disturbed her by his seeming disconnection from the destruction all around. Was he truly unaffected by the chaos and destruction in her neighborhood? It was no longer a secret that it had been a targeted attack, leaving everyone shaken and paranoid. Even the once vocal conspiracy theorists were now silent, and those who thought it was a punishment from above were questioning their beliefs. Carla couldn't help but wonder if anyone truly knew the truth behind what had happened.

The man wordlessly nodded a greeting as he glanced around, rubbed the sweat from his brow, and held a small device to her smartwatch which immediately topped up the number of food vouchers in her account. Every other asset in her world, all her savings in banks, the crypto fund stored on her token rings..It was was gone. Okay, not everything...that wasn't true, but days like this it sure seemed like it.

Carla grimaced as she began her rounds, turning into a street to see that more of a building had collapsed overnight. It was essentially suicide to be walking around the ruined suburbs so soon after the bombs had hit. As far as she was aware, there was no nuclear fallout, but anyone walking around the warzone either had a king-sized death wish... or were so desperate to survive, they'd walk straight into hell just to experience a slice of heaven or even a can of beef stew. God, life had changed so much. So many had been killed those first days, but so many more had simply given up in the weeks since.

She longed for the days back in the classroom. The normal trials and triumphs of her teaching career that had, with hindsight, felt relatively carefree. She wished she had taken more time to appreciate how mundane it had been. The daily struggles she'd had with parents, moody girls, and the rowdy hormone-laden teen boys, as well as the administrator's absurd policy changes, all seemed so trivial now.

* * *

Savage Earth San Antonio

Two months ago...

Carla picked up the broken coffee mug. It was red, fragments of the white logo for a restaurant she'd once enjoyed now unrecognizable.

"Please, sit down again," she instructed the young man. He was at that stage of life where he felt awkward and out of place, and she could see how his classmates teased him mercilessly. The old mug made of ceramic meant a lot to her, but only for sentimental reasons. She caught a whiff of this morning's coffee still lingering inside it, which brought back memories of her mother. And with that thought, an idea sparked in her mind.

She deviated from the AI-crafted lessons plans far more often than what was advised by the lead teachers, but her students seemed to appreciate her more personal lessons all the more for the change in pace. One of her university professors had always said, "Never miss an opportunity to expand their minds." The admins would be watching and hating it, but she pushed forward.

Carla was standing in front of the large windows, the full skyline of the San Antonio metroplex seen in the distance. She held a large fragment of the mug for her students. They watched her with puzzled expressions. Even the ones here virtually seemed to be paying attention for a change.

"Class, tell me in 1000 years or say...5000 years, if somebody digs this out of the ground, what could they tell about our civilization, about your life, about this city, this time, this age?" Her students looked at her in confusion, clearly having no idea what she was talking about. Their teacher was holding a broken coffee cup and asking a question that didn't seem to resonate with any of them.

She turned to face the class, unfazed by the vacant expressions on their faces. Summer break was just around the corner, and it seemed like many of them were already mentally checked out of school. "I'm attempting to educate you about history; how we examine it and what we often overlook or even forget," she stressed, as if trying to inspire their creativity.

Carla rarely opened up to her students, but she knew that if she could create a personal bond through stories of her own life, then the lesson would be permanently seared into their memories. She wanted them to take away some part of the lesson and carry it with them on their journey through life.

"My mother's name was Santina. We didn't come from Mexico. Not originally. My family came from Central America from an area in a country called Belize."

Some of the students groaned, the lack of enthusiasm infuriating Carla. "Who can tell me where Belize is on the map?" Not a single hand was raised.

"It's not the biggest country. It's not even considered important by any stretch of the imagination. Belize is mostly covered by thick tropical jungle, not a lot of towns. But the Mayans ruled that land for thousands of years. My ancestors. What language do you think the Mayan spoke?"

Several meekly said Spanish as Carla had expected. "Sorry, no. The Spaniards came many, many years later. They are a relatively recent influence. The survivors of the Mayan civilization were absorbed into the Spanish culture; their language, their names, their mannerisms, their foods, eventually translated into that of Spain. There are some spoken languages that claim to be Mayan, but all of those seem less than authentic. We do, however, have examples of their written language."

She did a quick query on her datatab, tapped on the Simulation app and brought up a floating hologram of a white clay pot with intricately designed symbols covering every inch of the surface.

"This was recovered from an ancient city in Belize called Caracol. The pottery shards were carefully restored. Some people can still read much of the language. These codices, that is what the written language is referred to, tells us of a Battle of Khartoum. It happened somewhere around 700 years BC." Carla held up a piece of her own broken mug. "Was this essentially their version of a coffee mug? We don't know. We can only tell so much from examining the fragments of a culture that has been lost."

She sat the coffee-cup shard down and turned, pointing outside. "Look at the city. Look at the skyline of our city. It's huge, isn't it? Now think a moment. Back in its day, Caracol was just like it, bigger even, relatively so. Experts think it was likely the sixth or seventh largest city on the planet at that time."

Carla saw the raised hand; she wanted to ignore it. Why was it that the pretty, popular girls were always the ones wanting to make her look bad?

"I don't want to be rude, Miss Garcia, but how does your family history relate to what we're learning, and will it be included on the upcoming test?"

The girl's emphasis on 'Miss' annoyed Carla, but it was accurate. "Jenny, I am trying to get all of you to see something more...something beyond what you normally do. History is important to you, much more than you might ever think."

"Like how?" the girl challenged.

"Caracol was obliterated from existence, reduced to nothing but a forgotten memory. A once thriving civilization erased from the map, leaving nothing behind but ruins."The magnitude of this loss weighed heavy on her words as she gestured towards the images of an empty landscape now on the screen. "Can you fathom such devastation taking place in our modern world?" She picked up a shard of shattered pottery, a remnant of what once was, and held it tightly in her hand. "Did the people who lived here ever imagine their entire city would disappear without a trace?" Her voice quivered with emotion as she imagined the terror and despair that must have consumed them during their final moments.

"What happened to them?" several of the kids asked at once.

Carla smiled. Despite Jenny Harris' attempted interruption, some of them were enjoying this little detour. And Carla felt like she was right in her element. Helping young minds grow, despite the frequent challenges, was immensely rewarding.

"Where did everybody go?" She walked back to the center of her class. "That really is the question. This piece of pottery gives us some of the answers." She showed them the hologram of the Mayan vase once more, spinning the 3D image for all to see the intricate black designs covering almost every inch of the archaeological treasure.

"This village, or more accurately, town, had an estimated 100,000 people living there at the time. That would be the equivalent of several million now by comparison. That put it on par with Jerusalem, Babylon, or Teotihuacan, or what is now Mexico City. Some of what happened was natural disasters, mainly weather. A cycle of drought and then a few years of floods and then more droughts. A city's ability, in fact…a society's ability to hold together is largely dependent upon its ability to feed itself.

"When that stops, society breaks down. It's inescapable. There's a famous quote that says 'We're only nine meals away from anarchy.'"

Carla saw the expressions beginning to gloss over again. These kids had no real understanding of hunger. Delivery services brought groceries and meals. Many foods were manufactured more than they were grown now. A few of the biotech giants had even come out with home food synthesizers. Appliances, not that she nor most of the households her students came from could ever afford one.

The appliances essentially made food from organic compounds by rearranging their molecular structure. She gave the class a few minutes to let what she was saying sink in. She rotated the hologram of the vase again and zoomed in on a couple of the intricate, black symbols.

"On top of that," Carla continued, "we can read from these hieroglyphics that the people turned on each other. Then came disease, a full pandemic. The rulers were incapable of leading in the midst of a disaster and were soon overthrown; even worse leaders emerged. Eventually, everything declined. The people scattered. They went out into the wilderness, set up smaller tribes, and slowly eked out an existence until the Spanish came in the 1500s and easily conquered the entire area.

"As I said, the Spaniards exploited them and absorbed their entire remaining culture into their own until virtually nothing was left of the Mayan. This had to be one of the most important civilizations in the history of the world. And on a historical timeline, it disappeared in an instant." She snapped her fingers for effect. "What would happen if our world was under that level of stress? Do you think we would be any different?"

She turned and looked at the girl with the long, blonde hair "And yes, Jenny, this will be on the test."

Of course, the kids couldn't relate. They had their SmartComms and social feeds. Their holostreams showed them their games, their heroes, the movies, the flying cars, plasma rifles, all the new things that came with being a child in this miraculous age. The gleaming towers of the nearby city looked impenetrable; nothing could touch them.

* * *

Present day...

Carla grimaced as she thought back to that class. Realizing how prophetic it had been in many ways. The end had come quicker than anyone could have expected. And society was falling for the same patterns that her ancestors had gone through thousands of years earlier.

"We've lost our history," she mumbled, softly echoing a line her mom used to say, before adding, "and can no longer see the future."

Humanity was trapped in a relentless cycle of repeating the same destructive mistakes, unable to break free. Carla's chest tightened as she felt a sudden urge to escape the city, the decaying walls closing in on her like a prison cell. The ruins surrounding her were a stark reminder of yet another once great city reduced to rubble and ruin. She couldn't bear to be engulfed by the despair any longer, desperate for a glimmer of hope in this desolate wasteland.

"Focus, girl. This is not the time for distractions." But no matter how hard she tried to push them away, her nerves were still on edge. The danger of this place was enough to make anyone lose their composure. She made a quick stop at the community food bank, grateful for the credits provided by her benefactor each week. Maybe they would have some of those sweets her sister loved so much. The ones that seemed to bring her more comfort than the prescribed medication ever could. She couldn't help but feel conflicted about relying on something artificial to ease Meredith's pain, yet she couldn't deny the relief it brought to her sister's suffering.

Carla bowed her head and spoke softly into the comm, switching to a different frequency, one that would only connect to her weblink contacts within the vicinity.

"Carson, I'm going to stop off at the food bank. You got everything you needed?"

Carla's heart raced as she anxiously waited for a response from Carson. The silence was suffocating, and her mind kept racing with worst-case scenarios. But then, finally, Carson's voice came through the radio, and she let out a shaky breath of relief. However, the tension in her chest remained as she wondered what had caused the delay and if they would make it to their destination on time.

...she gave a sigh of relief when her patrol partner's voice answered. "Yeah, I got you loud and clear, Carla. I'm about five minutes away. Will see you there."

"Got it," said Carla, slipping the device back onto her belt, hoping to save the power until she could get back to a working charge station. The units were all old, and the P-cell batteries were way out of date.

As she walked towards the food bank, it struck her as odd that there wasn't a line. Where were all the people? It seemed like less and less people were willing to come to this corner of San Antonio.

However, they must be running low on supplies by now. All the stores were closed, not that anyone had any money to spend, even if they were open.

A seething rage boils inside her as she fixates on the acting mayor, a faceless man who has somehow managed to enrage her without even being present. Despite his actions being deemed necessary and beneficial by others, Carla can't help but see them as cruel and unjust. However, amidst her burning hatred for politicians in general, she can't ignore that this one seems different - actually attempting to aid the community instead of turning their backs on it completely.

The eerie silence of the abandoned city was shattered by the sudden sound of shattering glass from inside a nearby building. Carla's heart raced as fear gripped her body like icy claws. Instinctively, her hand moved to her weapon, fingers tracing the cold metal with practiced ease. She remembered all the rumors of strange creatures that roamed these deserted streets, and she braced herself for any potential threat. With a deep breath, she readied her weapon - one blast of energy could blow a hole through any target. But for now, she prayed that she wouldn't have to use it.

She approached the building, an abandoned market that was strictly off limits due to martial law. The city officials were rationing its contents, making it a forbidden place for anyone to enter. But Carla couldn't resist the sound of shattering glass coming from inside. She cautiously entered and crouched behind a shelf, preparing herself to get a closer look at whoever or whatever was causing havoc in the otherwise deserted market.

A chill crept down Carla's spine as she watched a figure, shrouded in an oversized raincoat and hood, violently pry open the doors to the cooling section. With swift and calculated movements, they snatched bottle after bottle of water, disregarding the chaos and destruction they left in their wake. Carla strained to see their face, but could only make out a shadow within the already dark interior. This was not someone driven by mere thirst; this was a person consumed by desperation and willing to do whatever it takes to survive.

Carla was aware that if the water supplies decreased much more, it wouldn't be long before people started panicking about running out. She despised being in charge of anything like this once again. But with no one else around and Carson still a few minutes away, Carla emerged from her hiding spot and pointed her service weapon at the thief's back. "Put the water down!" she ordered, attempting to keep any traces of fear out of her voice.

The thief's hands shook uncontrollably as they obeyed, plastic bottles clattering to the ground with a deafening crash. The sound echoed through the room like a clap of thunder, causing Carla's heart to race and her breath to catch in her throat. As the thief slowly turned towards her, she could see the glint of a weapon tightly grasped in their other hand. Her body instantly tensed, every fiber of her being on high alert as time seemed to stand still and the world fell into an eerie silence around them.

Carla had just enough time to recognize the danger. In a flash, the thief brought the rifle up to face Carla…

Carla's finger tightened on the trigger, and she fired off three shots in rapid succession. The bullets ripped through the air, slamming into the thief's chest with a sickening thud. He was thrown backwards, crashing into the shattered cooler behind him. A high-pitched scream escaped from the thief's lips as they crumpled to the ground, clutching feebly at their bleeding wounds.

Blood covered the wall and the cooler behind them.

Carla's hand shook violently as the realization of what she'd done hit her. The adrenaline dump was already causing her to feel exhausted.

She moved forward like she had been trained, albeit briefly, weeks earlier. She kept her weapon up and her finger just off the trigger. Glancing down and rotating her grip, she saw she'd used a third of the pistol's charge. She briefly hoped that the person didn't decide to get up for round two, and she panicked, wondering if the perpetrator was alone.

Carla scouted the store quickly. Her target remained slumped in a bloody pile, clearly dead. Cautiously moving closer, she leaned forward and removed the hood to get a look at the face of her would-be killer.

"Oh, shit!"

Breathless, Carla kneels over the body. And as the hood falls away, she recognizes the pale blonde hair. The faded pink jacket.

She scrambles back with a cry. No, no, no. This can't be real. It was not the face of a killer, not even that of a stranger. It was a girl, a face Carla knew. Jenny Harris' lifeless eyes stared up at her. The girl's face was unkempt and smeared with dirt and specks of blood. She no longer looked like the beauty who was the reigning homecoming queen. But it was definitely her, her face twisted in one final expression of shock, anger, and righteous indignation.

But the empty eyes stare at her, accusingly. She's killed her. The pain, the grief, all of it came rushing back but that was then, another time, another life.

Carla blinks away tears, chest heaving with sobs. The harsh truth crashes down on her, as bleak and unforgiving as this dead world.

There's no going back.

Carla was so hypnotized by the sight that she didn't register the sound of footsteps behind her. She jerked as the hand rested lightly on her shoulder. Her partner, Carson surveyed the scene, methodically registering the space for more threats. "Holy shit," was all he could say.

"She was only a kid," muttered Carla, dropping the weapon and stumbling backwards. "I taught her... she'd...she'd have been a senior next year."

Carla tried to control the trembling in her hands as she stared down at them, now stained with blood. She couldn't believe what she had done, and the fact that it was someone she knew, someone she cared about, made it all the more unbearable. A small part of her wished that Jenny would speak up, to confront her with that snarky attitude that used to annoy Carla so much. But deep down, Carla knew that Jenny wasn't prepared for this kind of violence and trauma. As she gently brushed her fingertips against the girl's lifeless lips, Carla couldn't help but feel a mix of guilt and anger towards herself for being part of this horrific reality.

Carson crouched down on the floor next to Carla and pulled his partner close. "There was nothing else you could have done." He pushed Jenny's angry-looking gun a bit farther from the body. "She would have killed you, if given the chance. That's life now, it's survival of the fittest. And for what it's worth, I'm glad that you're the one still here."

He shifted to get between her and the dead girl. "Carla, look at me. You've got people who rely on you. Your sister, your grandmother... me." He hesitated on that last word, as though worried about someone overhearing. "Look, Carla, we'd all go to pieces without you."

She couldn't bring herself to disagree with that statement, knowing how fragile her family was. But no matter how many times she told herself that, she didn't see how she would ever wipe this girl's blood from her hands...or her memory.

"I can't do this..." She rubbed them on her pants. "She...she just wanted water..."

Guilt and anguish churn inside her, a maelstrom of emotion. She killed Jenny in self-defense, but that doesn't ease the remorse gnawing away at her soul. How did the world come to this? They were teacher and student, meant to nurture and guide. Not destroy each other.

With a shuddering breath, Carla forces herself to look at Jenny's pale, lifeless face. She owes her this final moment of witness. Of mourning.

"I'm so sorry," she whispers. Her vision blurs with tears as she reaches out to gently close Jenny's eyes. They will never open again.

Carla bows her head, grief overwhelming her. She doesn't know how long she kneels there in the abandoned store, keening softly beside Jenny's body. The world around her ceases to exist, narrowed down to this one tragic encounter that has come to define her life.

Finally she rises on unsteady legs and staggers outside, gulping in deep breaths of the chill night air. The tears have dried on her face, leaving behind tracks of salt.

She looks up at the sky, stars peeking out from behind tattered clouds. Somewhere in that endless dark, she wants to believe there is still hope. A light to guide her way.

But for now, all she can see is darkness.

Carla lifts her head and walks back out through the ruins of the city, alone.

Chapter Two

Carson resisted holding Carla' hand on the way back home to their subdivision, which pained her because she could have done with his touch and additional support now more than ever.

He comforted her with the same phrase he had said countless times before. "You made the right choice," he told her gently. "It may not seem like that now, but it will in time."

Despite the horror of the day, the pair had made a detour to the food bank to get their 'shopping' done. Now Carla was carrying it home in an old rucksack she herself had swiped from an abandoned sporting goods store. She guarded the meager supplies with her life, as that was what they meant to her family.

The despair in the air was palpable as they walked through the streets. Everywhere you looked, there were people begging and starving, with no sign of help on the horizon. It seemed inconceivable that any part of America could come to this—that any of them would resort to lethal violence over something as basic as a bottle of water.

As the two turned into their street, past the barricades, it felt to Carla as though they were moving into a different world. Children were still playing in the streets; a few adults were out making small talk with one another. It was as though the reality of their situation hadn't reached them yet. It had; they all were facing the same challenges. Cars that no longer worked, power that was off more than it was on, but this area had fared much better than the city.

Few of these people had even ventured out of the relative safety of the cul-de-sac yet. On the one hand, Carla wanted to let them have this moment, this glimpse of what was. If it meant shielding themselves away from the horrors of the world, then she was game for that. But the world was becoming an increasingly dangerous place to live. They were still fooling themselves into believing someone would come and fix it all. The government, or FEMA, or somebody would make it all better. No help ever came, no relief, no trucks with relief supplies...nothing. America, the land of opportunity, suddenly felt a lot like a third-world country. People had even started fleeing south into Mexico,. but the hope that things were better there was nothing she could believe in. She increasingly worried that this was the high-water mark. As bad as it seemed, from here on, it was just going to get worse.

As they drew closer to their houses, Carla found herself growing increasingly hesitant. Coming home was both the best and the worst part of her day in the best of times; best because it reassured her that her grandmother and sister were still okay, and the worst because she knew what she would have to endure upon returning.

"You going to tell them what happened?"

What happened? she thought. As if it was just a result of some natural phenomena. Carson was her friend, but there was no need for him to be so antiseptic. She'd murdered a child. She shook her head.

He nodded, "Okay, well, you know where I am if you need me."

The platitude was wasted on her. She desperately needed him more than ever, but her time today with the handsome man was over. Now he returned to his real family.

Carson waved and walked away, heading up the drive to his residence. Following suit, Carla stepped into her own home and took a deep breath, preparing herself for what lay ahead.

* * *

For six decades, Maria Garcia had been an outcast, struggling to make America her own. No matter how hard she worked, no matter how many of their customs and values she embraced, it seemed that there was always someone else ready to remind her that she was never a 'true' American. Her foreign presence was a constant reminder that no matter how hard she tried, she could never truly belong.

Over the years, that mindset had hardened Carlas's grandmother, who had worked as a housekeeper for much of her life. She'd been determined to ensure her daughter, Santina, got a proper education with a chance for a real career, while at the same time, teaching Santina to always remember where she came from. This 'take-no-shit' mentality had earned her the nickname 'Fiery Maria,' a name she'd come to detest in her later years.

Maria had been harsh with her daughter, maybe too much so. Santina had been a hard-working student, excelling in English and history, the latter of which had influenced her own daughter, Carla, in her own teaching career. But no matter how far she went in school, there was always some way in which Santina fell short in her mother's eyes. Maria had often said, "You give up too soon., If you don't give it your best effort all the time, the bots will replace you like you were a worn-out piece of meat."

Carla had never understood her abuela's near pathological hatred of the mechanical bots, looking down on the easily replaced jobs such as cashiers and warehouse workers, telling Santina that she should never settle for a career that could just as easily be done by a machine.

The woman's intensity meant that Maria was hard to please as a parent. If Santina wasn't doing everything right, she might as well not be doing anything right. At one point, Maria had even said, "You have no Mayan blood, your spirit is dead."

The comment had cut her daughter Santina to her core, and as soon as she had grown old enough to claim her independence, she'd left her mom and never looked back, keeping all contact with her overbearing mother to a bare minimum.

Maria's heart shattered into a million pieces when she found out she was a grandmother through someone else. Santina had refused to even let her know she was expecting until well after Carla's birth. Desperate to make amends, Maria made contact and even offered to help with the baby, and later with both girls. But each time she was rejected. Her daughter's words cut like jagged knives. "I won't let you infect my daughters with your toxic lies," she spat back at Maria, leaving her feeling like a worthless and rejected mother.

The chasm between Maria and her daughter seemed to stretch endlessly, time at a standstill as their bond shattered into irreparable pieces. Then came the fateful night that obliterated any hope of reconciliation. A phone call, the bearer of devastating news - Santina and her husband gone in a heart-wrenching, boating accident. Waves of grief crashed over Maria, drowning her in a sea of loss and regret. She screamed in anguish, clutching her chest as if trying to hold on to her shattered heart. The realization that she would never have the chance to tell her beloved daughter how much she cherished her was a knife twisted deeper into her already broken soul.

But in her two granddaughters, Maria saw the glimmer for possible redemption. Carla and Meredith were nineteen and fifteen, beautiful, smart, and desperately in need of a parental figure. Their mother had been more of a friend to them—Maria worried if she could avoid the mistakes she'd made with Santina. She petitioned and was granted full guardianship of the girls, giving them a home back in San Antonio, and trying her best to support them. She'd managed to take a more delicate hand with the girls, instilling the same drive for independence and financial autonomy as she had with Santina, but never missing an opportunity to tell both how proud she was of them, and saying all the things she wished she had said to Santina when she was alive.

A year or two ago, Maria found herself forgetting things. She had always prided herself on an excellent memory. But she'd been losing track of things more and more, misplacing her SmartComm, walking into stores and completely forgetting what she had gone in for. Simple things at first, but it became more frequent. She had tried to brush it off as getting forgetful in her old age.

Carla had always been the pragmatic one, unlike her grandmother, who was stubborn and independent to a fault. When Carla finally convinced Maria to see a doctor, she knew it wasn't going to be good news. The autodoc could have easily diagnosed Maria's condition, but Carla wanted her grandmother to face the cold reality of human diagnosis. Alzheimer's was cruel in its onset; stealing precious memories and moments from people until they no longer even recognized their own loved ones.

Maria initially refused to accept the diagnosis, and Carla understood. But as time passed and more information came to light, the truth could not be avoided. The disease took hold of Maria quickly, pushing Carla into the unexpected role of primary caregiver.

Carla struggled with conflicting emotions as she watched Maria suffer from the debilitating illness. She couldn't help but feel resentful at being burdened with the responsibility of caring for her loved one, yet immediately felt guilt for having such thoughts. She was torn between feeling anger towards the disease and empathy towards Maria. It was a constant battle within her heart.

Maria sometimes called her by her mother's name and treated Meredith as she did Santina. Despite the history, their grandmother was good to them and worked to make amends for past mistakes. But her hurtful words would still resurface. Carla couldn't abandon Maria now when she needed her most, despite feeling conflicted. And unfortunately, caring for her ailing grandmother was only part of her responsibility. Her sister Meredith also had her own issues tat they all had to deal with.

The last few years had been challenging for Carla, but then the bombs ripped through San Antonio like a Texas-sized twister, leaving rubble and the dead in their wake. Every day she went out in search of anything that would keep her family alive. Hunger and the smell of the dead were constant, and rumors of encounters with even worse elsewhere made her skin crawl.

Every now and then, Maria's dementia-riddled mind transported her back to a pre-collapse world, Carla found herself frequently having to explain to her grandmother how the world had changed for the worse, only to realize her grandmother didn't believe her, assuming it was a cruel prank her grandchildren were playing on her.

Ultimately, it had gotten too exhausting for Carla to explain what had happened over and over. Instead, she tried to keep up the pretense that life was carrying on as normal, which meant herding Maria back into the house whenever she wanted to venture outside. It pained her now to even see her abuela, her grandmother, knowing every time she looked at her, a little piece of her seemed to break away, never to be recovered.

Carla closed the door and walked up to her grandmother tentatively, as though she were approaching a wild animal. "Grandma?" she asked. "You all right?" Maria was gazing absently out of the window; Carla couldn't tell if she even knew she was there.

Without turning away from the window, her grandmother said, "You should speak Spanish. Never forget where you came from, Santina." She turned to look at Carla, blinked, her face awash in confusion, then was back in the present day once again, the fog having temporarily lifted. "Sorry, dear, some days you just look so much like your mother."

"Where's Meredith?"

"She's upstairs, reading some guy's fortune," Maria stated.

"What?" Carla blurted out, instantly heading for her sister's bedroom.

The world might have ended for everyone else, but this had made little difference to her sister. Truthfully, the girl hadn't been living on the same planet with the rest of them for the last few years. It had started back when she was just a young teen. She had been having hallucinations, imagining strange scenarios. Lucid dreams and...even weirder stuff.

But to Meredith, they hadn't been hallucinations. They had been premonitions of a dark future. She began attaching deeper meanings to many of them and even linking them to evil that just seemed to follow some people. The visions weren't the problem...not really. No, it was the depth of Meredith's conviction that they were divine, that she was the true harbinger of tomorrow's secrets.

Before the accident, their parents had decided Meredith should see a psychiatrist to hopefully explain these hallucinations away. They were under no delusions. It was obviously some sort of mental illness, but they had no idea what it was and thus, no clue as to how to deal with it.

The parents had done all they could to shield their daughter from ridicule. It also didn't help that Meredith was strikingly beautiful. She got attention, lots of attention, but her friendships rarely ended well. Truthfully, it was exhausting for the entire family.

Finally, they'd planned a family holiday away on a boat, and had decided, upon their return, that they would take Meredith to see a specialist. One final, happy family excursion before getting down to the business of treatment. But Meredith had claimed that she had a bad feeling...seen a premonition that something bad was going to happen.

Every fiber of her being screamed that this trip was a deadly mistake, and she would do anything to prevent it from happening. But her mother's forceful grip dragged her towards the car, her screams echoing off the walls as she fought against her impending doom. Their father, weary from their constant fighting, ultimately caved and allowed Carla to stay behind and care for Meredith while they embarked on their doomed voyage. In the end, it was the last time either girl would lay eyes on their parents before tragedy struck.

Somehow, the boat's onboard battery bank had caught fire and violently exploded, killing everyone on board. Afterward, Carla recalled the Coast Guard officer could only shake his head in disbelief; the odds of such a tragedy happening were infinitesimally small. In one cruel moment, every soul aboard had perished. A one in a million chance, they said.

Meredith sunk into a deep depression and even Carla had to admit there might be something to her sister's 'gift,' but still, the girl needed help. If not for the visions, then for the depression, guilt, sleeplessness, and delusions. After coming to live with their grandmother, Carla had done what she could to manage Meredith's illness. Now, Carla found herself confronting it alone with none of the medications or understanding of how to keep the crazy at bay.

The illness had ravaged Meredith's chances for an ordinary life. She had lost friends who didn't want to be associated with her anymore, she had lost jobs because of public meltdowns. The only thing she seemed to be doing with her time now was reading the future of anyone who cared to listen to her.

As Carla turned the doorknob and pushed open the door, her eyes fell upon a teenage boy perched on the edge of the bed. He held out his hand, palm up, and Meredith's slender fingers traced its lines delicately. Carla noticed the dark circles rimming her friend's usually bright eyes, and she couldn't help but wonder if Meredith had slept at all the night before. The dim light from the bedside lamp cast shadows over the room, making it seem even more somber and mysterious. A faint scent of lavender lingered in the air, providing a calming presence amidst the tension in the room.

"In your future, I see... a leader-"

"Meredith, what have I told you about having people upstairs?" asked Carla, taking on the role of the parent. She looked at the teenager. "You, beat it."

Not needing to be told twice, the frightened teenager gathered his things and headed out the door.

Carla realized her semi-official uniform and the gun and cuffs probably did scare the shit out of the kid.

"I was reading his future," Meredith said sullenly.

"You have to be careful with strangers," Carla exclaimed. "Who knows what this guy could have been up to? He could have been a thief, or worse." Immediately, she started searching through Meredith's drawers to ensure that nothing had been stolen.

"Why don't you let me read your future?" asked Meredith.

Carla sighed, exasperated. "If I said 'no' to you the first time, why the hell would I say 'yes' the next fifty times?"

"I thought you'd want to know what is coming," said Meredith. "You need to know."

"Nothing is coming, Meredith." She had tried to be gentle in her approach, but years of looking after her sister had taken their toll, and Meredith's inability to grow up was testing Carla's already-limited patience. "It's all in your head."

"That's exactly what Mom and Dad said," Meredith snapped back. Thankfully, she didn't include her normal rejoinder of 'And look what happened to them,' for a change.

Carla couldn't deny how eerie it was that Mom and Dad had died in the boating accident, just as Meredith had predicted. But she worked hard to tag it as extreme coincidence, nothing more.

As though reading Carla's mind, Meredith quickly said, "And I predicted last month, don't forget. I told you the world was ending."

"You say that shit all the time, Meredith."

Honestly, it was true; a week before the airstrike, Meredith had said that the sky would start falling down, and indeed it had. But Carla forced the idea from her mind. It was bad enough having Meredith tumbling down deeper into her fantasy world. She didn't need to get suckered in herself.

As she retreated into her bedroom and shut the door, she couldn't shake off the feeling of being invaded. This was her safe haven, her sanctuary, and she didn't want anyone else to enter it. As she sat on the floor, she noticed her hands trembling uncontrollably. She wondered if they had been shaking like this the whole time or if it was just a recent development. Her nails were caked with dried blood, a reminder of what she had done. She desperately tried to scrub it away with her other hand's nails, but it only made her feel more conflicted and guilty.

She thought again about Jenny, and then to the girl's family, wondering whether she had someone who was relying on her, waiting for her to come home. What if Jenny had been forced into a role of responsibility herself? The tears welled up, and Carla couldn't hold them back. She wasn't as strong as people thought. Honestly, most days she was only barely holding it together.

Carla knew she wouldn't face any immediate charges for what she had done. The police sergeant had stated that she was 'obliged to uphold the law in whatever way she saw fit.' But that didn't stop the overwhelming sense of remorse, the thought that maybe she could have talked Jenny down. That it didn't need to end in bloodshed. Maybe this was the next step. Everyone was moving backwards, now that the constraints of society were lifted, having little reason to abide by the quaint notions of fact or fiction or even just right and wrong.

In a way, she was grateful for the remorse. It meant that she was still human and that she still cared. But what if there would come a day when she would have to pull the trigger again? What if a day would come when she could no longer recognize herself in the mirror? What happened when she no longer felt anything real?

Carla couldn't bear to think about that. She pushed these dark thoughts to the back of her mind. She had to be strong, for her abuela, and for her sister. And at this rate, maybe for the whole of San Antonio.

Chapter Three

She was up early the following day. Carla kissed her grandmother goodbye before heading out. Before she left, Maria held her close.

"I just want you to know, love, I'm so proud of you. I know you put yourself out for this family time and time again, taking care of an old girl like me, and of course, your sister."

Carla appreciated the acknowledgement. It was nice to hear that someone appreciated what she did. "I had a good teacher," she said.

Maria blushed, her wrinkled cheeks turning a soft pink. "Oh, I only wish I could take that credit, dear. But you turned out the way you did thanks to your mother. She was strong-willed, determined to make her own way in the world even from a young age. Back then, when she was just a child, I didn't think that was a good thing. I wanted her to be more obedient, more traditional. Now I know better. Her strength and independence shaped who she was, and in turn shaped who you are. You have her fire in you, that unwillingness to back down from a challenge. I see so much of her in you, and I'm so very proud."

Maria squeezed Carla's hand, unshed tears glistening in her eyes. Though years had passed since her daughter's untimely death, the pain still lingered, raw and aching. But she took comfort in the fact that her spirit lived on in her granddaughters. Her legacy endured.

Carla was glad to see her grandmother was starting off the day clear-headed. It often got worse later in the day, but she didn't want her dwelling on guilt and remorse regarding her mom. Carla kissed her again on the cheek and left for work. She didn't say goodbye to Meredith. She knew anything she could possibly say would be met with resistance. Hopefully, this would be a better day for them... and her.

She walked next door to Carson's house. The early morning sky was painted with pink and orange, the bright colors in sharp contrast to her mood. She wanted to start work while the day was young, and the temperature was marginally bearable.

She and Carson would normally rummage through deserted homes for any usable provisions. Things such as nourishment or pharmaceuticals, they kept for themselves and their loved ones. However, if they discovered anything of worth, they relinquished it to their civil patrol liaison in order to get additional food vouchers. The system was crudely effective on occasion, but truthfully at present, there was not much available even in the reserve stockpiles the municipality possessed. In two weeks, it was the best system they'd come up with to redistribute food and supplies.

Carla walked up to the front porch and looked at the small InterLock terminal on the side of the door. *The P-cells in these things must last forever*, she thought. *Or the power is back on today*. She moved her eye close to the terminal for a retinal scan, which gave a small klaxon sound as it flashed red several times.

It frustrated her but wasn't a surprise. After all the times she had babysat for the kids, she had hoped that by now, Carson's wife would have added her to the access list for the house. Chelsea was an odd bird, though. One that had no interest in sharing anything, including a kind word for a neighbor.

If she only knew...Carla's mouth curved into a brief smile as the InterLock signaled green. Someone inside had deactivated the lock.

The door clicked open, and a young girl of about five stood in the doorway, her face instantly brightening at the sight of Carla. "Mommy, Daddy!" she squealed excitedly. "Carla's here!" at which point she grabbed Carla's hand, taking it in her two smaller ones. "Come and see what I've been doing!"

Carla allowed the little girl to drag her into the kitchen where their NannyBot stood at the table. NannyBots were low-grade robots designed for the sole purpose of monitoring and entertaining children. Carla's family had considered getting one for Meredith when she was younger, but as a small girl, she was highly afraid that the NannyBot would want to kill her. Some of the horror movies back then loved that theme. That, plus later on, their grandmother's innate fear of robotic technology made it a non-starter.

This one was as docile as they came, covered from chest panel to base in an array of cartoon stickers, undoubtedly from one of the little girl's sticker books. Carla saw the bot was in low-power standby mode, its systems actively recharging.

"That's very nice, Rachel," said Carla. "What are you going to do when you run out of space?"

Before Rachel could answer, Chelsea entered the kitchen. "Hello, Carla," she said in the same unpleasant tone you might use when addressing a rodent rooting through your garden.

In an instant, the child's cheery mood ebbed away. "Sweetheart, Mommy has put your favorite cartoons on the holo for you. Why don't you go and watch a few of them while the grown-ups talk?"

"But I want to stay here with Carla!" whined Rachel in a petulant tone that somewhat reminded Carla of Meredith.

"You're my daughter, you do as I say!" Chelsea suddenly snapped in a way that took everyone except possibly the NannyBot by surprise. "We have power today. Go take advantage of it."

Rachel stood there defiantly, hands on hips.

Carla, sensing the tension crackling like a live wire in the air, crouched to Rachel's level. Her voice, a soothing murmur against the backdrop of raised voices, offered a compromise. "How about you listen to your mommy, sweetie? Later, you can spill every little detail about the cartoons to me, okay?" Her eyes held a promise, a small beacon of calm in the gathering storm that was Chelsea Adams.

Rachel smiled, wrapping her arms around Carla, and just for a moment, Carla was scared to return the hug, almost wishing that the little girl was her own. And then Rachel turned and walked away, without even turning to look at her mom.

Carla caught the flash of anger in the other woman's eyes as she looked up. Chelsea was clearly hurt by the lack of affection from her own daughter. Affection that was clearly reserved for her babysitter.

In what Carla now knew to be typical of her neighbor, Chelsea decided to use what little leverage she had. "She's not your daughter, you know," the mother said spitefully. "If you love them so much, why don't you just have kids of your own?"

This question burned Carla more than she wanted to acknowledge. She adored kids, and that was part of what had drawn her into teaching. She'd love to be able to have a family of her own one day. But she had her own priorities to think about with her grandmother and her sister. And even if she didn't have to worry about them, who would want to bring a child into the world now?

But Chelsea knew all of this. She was just rubbing salt into the wound. *No,* Carla thought, *she was just being a bitch.*

Before Carla could offer a response, Carson appeared in the doorway. He read his wife's expression and correctly gauged the temperature in the room. "Carla," he said. "Morning. I'm just getting a few things together, and we can head out."

Chelsea gripped her husband firmly by the shoulder, vice-like. "Why do you have to go?" she moaned. "Why can't you just stay here with me? You know how it is out there."

"Honey," Carson said, "it's a job. One we have to do just to make sure we have all the things we need."

"The government will bring help," insisted Chelsea, her voice shrill and grating. "I don't see why you have to take the risk and do this every day." She cut her eyes at Carla, her pretty features twisting into an ugly scowl, as if to silently add, 'With her, that home-wrecking slut.'

Carla tensed, biting her tongue to hold back the torrent of curses she longed to unleash on the insufferable woman. Chelsea had always been petty and jealous, but her behavior had grown worse since the blackout. The posh housewife clung desperately to her delusions of normalcy while the world crumbled around them. She couldn't accept that her gilded life was over.

"We can't rely on the government, honey, not anymore," Carson said gently. "They have their hands full in the major cities. Out here, we're on our own." He checked his watch, shifting impatiently. "I need to get going if I'm going to make it back before dark."

Chelsea's lower lip quivered. For a moment, Carla thought she might burst into tears. But the blonde simply spun on her heel and stormed from the room, leaving a tense silence in her wake.

"We don't know when they're coming," said Carson. "We could be waiting for a while, and well...we have kids who need food today."

Wanting to offer the man an exit, Carla suggested, "Why doesn't Chelsea come with us? Get a taste of the outside? The NannyBot could keep an eye on the little ones for a while."

As predicted, Chelsea quickly said, "No, no...you're right. Someone's got to stay here and look after the kiddos. The bot's not charged yet, anyway."

Which, to Carla, translated to making her kids' lives miserable. "If you're sure," said Carla, just glad to be getting away from the ghastly woman. And with that, the two patrol officers were out for morning rounds.

Today, they walked down the road. In a past life, they would have ridden on hoverbikes or taken their autocars to work, but with most of the city's technology knocked out of commission, they had to get wherever they needed to go on foot.

As they walked, Carson looked over at Carla from time to time. Finally, he said, "Carla, I wondered if you wanted to talk about yester..."

"If I want therapy, I'll go find a working autodoc, thank you," said Carla, more sharply than she had intended.

Carson accepted the rebuke although it clearly stung. They soon stopped at a deserted house on a corner of two small streets. There were no signs of broken windows or vandalism. But the family had clearly moved on.

"You know," said Carson, a sly grin on his face. "I bet they have a master bedroom."

Carla looked at him differently. She knew she had hurt his feelings. Now maybe she could make it up to him. "Your seduction talk could really do with some work," she teased.

Carson held out an outstretched hand. "Maybe I can take your mind off all your problems for a while."

She smiled; this was what she looked forward to most days. Carla took his hand and allowed him to lead her into the house.

She was aware that there would be consequences for her actions, just as there always were. Days of remorse and embarrassment awaited, as they did after each encounter. Sex between willing grown-ups was no longer the scandal it had been for past generations, not since her grandmother's time, but the old-fashioned values still held sway in the Garcia home, and she was violating a fundamental rule. Yet Damn, it felt so fucking good.

Chapter Four

During the search of the houses, Carson found only a few cans of food and some toys, which he decided to take home for his children. The intimate rendezvous with Carla had not improved his mood either, and she seemed to be replaying the unpleasant events from the previous day in her mind. The rest of the patrol went on without problems, but the two officers stayed absorbed in their own thoughts.

She sat down later in the shade of a weathered oak, its gnarled branches twisting up toward the relentless sun. Resting her back against the rough bark, she tried the comms again, static hissing in her earpiece as she turned the dials. Reaching out, calling over and over, just hoping someone would answer. Someone, anyone out there not in the same sorry state as San Antonio. But all she heard was the empty crackle of dead air.

"There's no one out there," Carson said, walking up worn out from his segment of the patrol.

"You don't know that. They couldn't have hit everyone. This is a big country."

He agreed, that much was accurate. "It is, honey." He stooped and gulped down a considerable amount of water. "If someone possessed the necessary knowledge to target precisely, they could significantly diminish our nation's capacity to respond with considerably fewer projectiles than one might suppose."

"So, you're a military strategist now," she scoffed. He was a bright guy but she just loved giving him hell.

"Hey, don't be mean. I'm just making conversation."

Carson Adams had been a sub-contractor running a crew of mostly Mexican day laborers and the small BuilderBots doing construction jobs all over the Metroplex. He was smart and surprisingly well read, but Carla also knew him to be impulsive and prone to untimely shows of emotion, particularly toward her. He took risks, some that could put them all in danger.

"So, if no one is out there to help us—what?" she asked.

"We have to start thinking long-term," Carson said, his voice low but firm. "We can't keep scavenging like vultures among the ruins forever. Eventually people are going to have to start rebuilding, producing things again from scratch. We need to figure out how to be self-sufficient, grow our own food, generate our own power. The old world is gone but that doesn't mean we can't build a new one from what's left."

She'd been increasingly thinking the same thing, but had no idea how to even begin. Right now, they were in survival mode, and honestly, it was exhausting. Most days, she didn't know if she was going or coming.

The following day, Carla decided to take a break from her routine patrols. She joined forces with Maria to clean up the overgrown backyard instead. It was no surprise that Meredith chose not to participate in this particular task.

She thought there were some better tools in the old shed, but over the years they'd lost the keys to the rusty, old lock. Fortunately, their garden had always been tended to. Texas has a long growing season. They took care of the plants that were barely hanging on and placed them in a small Ecosaver, basically a box that acted as a miniature environment for the seedlings providing soil, water, and heat.

Carla had picked up a number of other seeds and gotten those started as well. Maria insisted on handling much of the gardening, which had always been something she'd loved to do. Carla watched her, understanding that this must be one of the few aspects of her life that she still had control over.

"Never had you pegged as the down-and-dirty type!" a voice rang out.

Carla looked up, smiling at the source of the voice.

It belonged to a man about her age whom she found herself checking out, despite herself. Somehow, he was keeping himself in good shape, even at the end of the world. Joshua had worked as a coach and fitness instructor at the local high school where Carla had taught. Just as Carla's job had shackled her with permanent responsibility, Joshua's had shackled him with a permanent need to push himself physically. Though, as different as night and day, they had become fast friends over the years.

"Figured that was more up your alley," Carla responded, mirroring his broad grin. Joshua had a way of eliciting her more upbeat side—a sense of mirth, an airiness, an acknowledgment that life was meant for enjoyment.

"Where's Meredith?" Joshua asked, scanning the garden. He was one of the only people Carla had actually introduced to her loony sister. He had previously told Carla, "You can't treat her like the madwoman in the attic," to which Carla had claimed that the 'madwoman in the attic' would actually be preferable to what some of the people called her.

"Hi, Maria!" Joshua said, waving. Maria gave him a wave before winking at Carla, who just put it down to one of her grandmother's growing eccentricities.

"I was wondering if I could steal Carla away for a few minutes, maybe take a walk around the block?" suggested Joshua.

"Sure, why not?" said Carla, scrunching up her face and taking off her gardening gloves before turning to Maria. "You going to be all right, Grandma?"

"Certainly, dear," Maria replied. "Enjoy yourself and return when you're ready. I'll remain here until you do." The tone in her voice left an ominous feeling, as if she was daring the universe to challenge her.

Carla left the garden and started walking with Joshua down the street. "With all the free time on your hands, I'm surprised you haven't found the time to get your car fixed," she stated. Joshua's car had broken down months earlier, forcing Carla to pick him up each day for school. She didn't mind the company as they both chatted about school, kids who got on their nerves, and lessons that they would rather be teaching. He'd not seemed eager to actually repair the car, and that hadn't really registered with her until now.

"I'm surprised you haven't found the time to get back to writing," Jordan retorted.

Carla's earlier ambition in life had been to be a writer. She had fallen in love with the book *The Great Gatsby,* making a point to reread it every few months, and hoped that one day, she might contribute something to the world of literature. Now...the world was gone. No one was left to read her stories, unwritten or not.

"I'll do it when I get 'round to it," she muttered.

"You know, that's what I've always liked about you, Carla," said Joshua kindly. "You always try to take on everybody else's problems. But you need to have time for yourself. You're already a great sister, teacher, and writer – if you actually took the time to put the work in," he added in a softer voice. "You don't need to be a martyr, too. You can't save everyone, nor should you try," he finished, letting the words hang in the air.

"You've got something to say, haven't you?" asked Carla, her tone frosty.

Joshua sighed. This wasn't how he had imagined this conversation, but he could see no other way of skirting around it. "Carla... I know about Jenny."

And just like that, Carla's mood clouded over. "Goddamn it, Carson..."

"You shouldn't be angry with him. He was just looking out for you. Just like the rest of us. I remember her..." He trailed off, seemingly unsure if he should be discussing this. "She was very sure of herself, even then. She knew she didn't need teachers or anyone to tell her how the world worked. She'd find her own way regardless."

"Stop it! Just, please stop."

"What?" Joshua asked.

"I killed a kid," said Carla breathlessly. "She could have been so much more..."

"You don't know the full story," said Joshua. "The attack... it changed people. And not for the better. If one of you had to go, I'd much rather it was her than you. You've got too many people relying on you. You are a good person, you've stepped up. Others are...well, they're heading in the other direction."

They rounded the corner, the silence hanging thick between them. "I...you, shouldn't be going out on those patrol rounds with Carson, anyway. You two spend far too much time, together."

Carla rolled her eyes. Joshua was literally the only person who knew about her ongoing affair with their mutual friend. He'd weaseled it out of her months earlier during a planning period at school. And even though he had been sworn to secrecy, she could tell how uncomfortable he was about it. He and Carson were friends, or at least friendly. They played ball together on summer leagues and hung out at some of the family get-togethers. He liked Carson but not the Carson who was banging his friend.

"It's just a bit of fun," Carla said weakly as Joshua confronted her.

"Yeah, I'm sure that excuse is going to go down just fine with his firecracker of a wife," Joshua said sardonically. "Carla, they're a family. It's going to end in heartbreak. Even if you can manage the pretense, is that how you want to live your life? Sneaking into abandoned houses for a quick screw? You need someone who can be there for you. Someone who can take care of you. Someone to make you feel complete — who makes you feel like all of this..." he waved his hand around at the desolate suburb, "...is just background noise."

Joshua burned with passion, aching to be the one for Carla. But, he kept his desire secret, determined that no matter who she chose, he would make sure that she was in a healthy relationship, one that would make her blissfully happy. A smoldering fire lingered deep in his soul, igniting him with the hope of just possibly being that person she would one day want.

Deep down, Carla had known that the affair with Carson wasn't meant to last. It had just been a bit of fun. Some solace that would have allowed them both a distraction from the stresses of their home life. Hell marriage itself was intentionally temporary these days. No couples took out permanent marriage contracts anymore but of course, Carson and Chelsea had.

She'd meant to end the affair for months now but had never been able to find the right timing. Of course, when the world had already ended, there was no such thing as 'the right time.' Then, they found they had lots more time and privacy, so the rendezvous had gotten even more frequent, not less.

"I don't need a man to 'complete' me!"

She saw the hurt in Joshua's eyes. It had been inadvertently cruel but not untrue.

Chapter Five

The tree-lined streets did little to dampen the afternoon heat. The sun had begun its dip toward the west, and yet, it still felt like high noon. Joshua and Carla rounded the block in silence and approached Carson's house, a two-story brick affair with craftsman touches and high, arched windows. Consulting on her love life aside, Joshua didn't feel the need to lecture Carla on anything else. She knew how he felt about her current boyfriend...and she hated that this was what they were spending their time discussing. She liked talking with Joshua. His quiet encouraging of her helped bring out the better parts of herself, showing her who she could be.

Carson was playing with his children in the front garden. He and Carla briefly locked eyes before he continued chasing Rachel who was dressed in a fairy costume.

"Does Carson know you know?" Carla asked softly.

"I hope not," said Joshua. "It's hard enough lecturing you. I'd rather not try my luck with him. And of course, if it does get out, then I'd incur Chelsea's wrath along with you two."

"Chelsea doesn't scare me," said Carla. "She doesn't make

Carson happy. The only reason he married her was because she got pregnant."

"Try telling that to her kids," said Joshua, pointing to the idyllic scene of both children playing with their dad. "You try explaining to kids how you wound up causing their parents to split up."

Now, that did get through to Carla. Chelsea was a user, who had often roped her into babysitting for the kids. *Okay,* that was an unfair thing to say. Carla genuinely loved the children; she didn't need to be coerced into spending more time with them. She went out of her way to do it because she was genuinely fond of the tiny people they were. They were also a welcome respite from the drama often going on in her own home.

She found she could talk easily with them and maybe give them some support that their mother could not. On one occasion, Rachel had walked in on Chelsea's weekly Book Club, prompting the already high-strung Chelsea to lash out at the girl. Rachel had gone running next door to Carla's and asked, "Why doesn't Mommy love me?" And Carla had been at a loss for words because she wasn't even sure if the child was wrong. More often than not, Chelsea treated her children as unwanted props she had been forced to make space for in her life..

"You've got to think about what you want in life, Carla," advised Joshua, who Carla noticed had slipped into the concerned teacher role effortlessly, like a well-worn glove.

He wasn't wrong, she needed to end this thing. But God, the sex was fantastic, and well, there again it kept her from facing her own problems. Still, she couldn't risk it for the kids. She'd been stupid and selfish, plain and simple.

In the distance, they heard gunshots and someone yelling. A month ago, that would have been cause for alarm. Now, it was just a normal day. Carla twisted the fraying hem on her jacket before responding.

"What I want..." she let the response die on her lips. "Josh, I have my sister to think about. And Maria. I... I can't." It was as she said those words, she felt like a bird that had had their wings permanently clipped.

"Carla, you hear that, right?" He pointed back toward the city. "The rioting is happening nonstop, and it's getting closer every day," Joshua said, shaking his head. "Sooner or later, it will reach us out here.

"Yeah, I know, Josh, the world ended. I get that along with the nine thousand other effed up things going wrong right now. You do remember I shot a former student —right?"

He placed a calming hand on her shoulder. "Look, I...I know it's been rough. You need to be ready before it comes to your doorstep. Or hell, find a way to get away from it."

"I'm a cop now, Joshua. I'm not blind to what is going on out there."

"I know, girl, and that's my point. You and Carson are out there just to help feed your families and all...but the shit is real. Have you actually seen them...the rioters, I mean? In action? I have. I drove down there a few days ago to get a look. And I'm telling you, I've never seen anything like it. People in the streets using anything and everything as weapons, turning their anger on the buildings and each other. The last mayor who tried to keep order was strung up. It's social Darwinism at its most primal. Your grandma and Meredith, they'd be like lambs to the slaughter."

"Mayor Chavez?" Carla asked.

"Yeah, it was gruesome."

"Wait a minute," said Carla suddenly. "I thought you said your car wasn't working."

Rather than fixate on his slip-up, Joshua went on. "My point is that you're a capable woman, Carla. In fact, you're the most capable person I've ever known. But I don't need to be a genius to see how you going up against a mob of rioters is likely to pan out. I don't like you being on the civilian patrol."

"The world is the world. Where else would we go? What else can any of us do?" asked Carla, becoming more agitated. The stress of always being the one with the answers was grating on her. "My grandma has lived in that house for decades. She's made it clear that she'd rather die there than leave it. Every day I have to explain the current events to her, and every day, she forgets."

"There might be a place…somewhere safer. I used to know of a place over by the river. We could go check it out," suggested Joshua, keeping his voice low to ensure no one else could hear him. "Would you be interested in coming with me? We have time."

Carla shrugged. She took note of the emphasis on his use of the word 'we.'"

"Maybe. I just need to make sure that my abuela is OK to keep an eye on Meredith for a while longer."

Meredith was in her bedroom doing God knows what, and Maria was still busy in the garden, so they went to the garage where she brought out two old pedal bikes. Joshua observed the smaller of the bikes, one which clearly hadn't seen any action for some time. "I'm going to take a wild stab in the dark and assume that one was Meredith's."

"Yeah, I was the one who put a stop to her going out on it," said Carla. "If she has a meltdown sitting down or walking down the street, that's one thing. But if she gets one of her premonitions while she's out there riding a bike, then… well, hell, all I could think was her darting out into traffic."

Josh was more than familiar with her sister's issues. Every family had their oddball, but he didn't know how Carla could watch out for her all the time, especially now.

They mounted the bikes. It felt odd; Carla was more used to riding hoverbikes, but there was something about the old-fashioned mode of transport that spoke to her, a certainty that she didn't get with technology. Maybe Maria was right, the old ways were better. Seemed like every day a new gizmo was coming out. If you listened to the marketing hype, most seemed so great they might change the course of humanity. But these out-of-date bikes spoke to a simpler, predictable time.

As they rode down the road, they took in the sights around them. BuilderBots, construction robots utilized for automation on building sites, were frozen midway through their task, unable to get up and move forward. Carla noted that soon, they would become relics themselves. In the fields beyond, a tangle of the iconic green John Deere AgroBots looked like they had gotten into a fight. Treads and articulated arms were intertwined in a twisted mess.

They rode in silence for much of the journey before Joshua finally spoke. And when he did, he spoke slowly, as though he were choosing his words very carefully. "Do you think there's a chance anything in Meredith's... visions... could be true?"

Carla looked at him as though he had just grown an extra head. "Did you honestly just ask that? Out loud?"

"I'm just saying, with your parents and the missile strike. It would be extremely naive not to at least consider the possibility."

"It's not possible," said Carla, refusing to indulge the notion.

"If you had said that to me a few decades ago, a lot of the possibles today would be impossible." He gestured to another one of the AgroBots, kneeling over a seed drill still impaled in the ground, it was as still as a statue. "I certainly wouldn't have imagined those hunks of metal taking over from actual farmers. Yet, here we are."

Carla shook her head. "Thank God you've never actually said any of this to her. She'd love that."

"People know about her..."

"Who, Meredith?" Carla asked.

Before Joshua could continue making his case, both were distracted by a glow on the horizon. As they got closer, they could see it was from a fire.

"Oh, shit," muttered Joshua. "They're coming."

Chapter Six

Carla's eyes widened in fear as she heard the distant roar of the mob. Her heart pounded in her chest, and she softly moaned, "No, no, no..." They appeared over the horizon like an unstoppable force, a sea of angry faces coming closer with each passing second.

"What do they want?" Carla asked, suddenly wondering why she hadn't brought her gun.

"Who knows?" Josh said nervously. "Answers, someone to take responsibility. They feel cheated out of the life they had, everything that was rightfully theirs. They're gripped by the mania of not having enough. And they are finally figuring it out that no help is coming. All they can do is take their anger out on anyone and anything that comes into range." And Carla and Joshua were at the far end of that same road.

"We...um...we need to turn back," Joshua said, the nervousness in his voice bordering on full panic.

"You think?" Carla snapped back already reversing course with her bike. "Was that what you wanted to show me?"

Joshua didn't answer. They both pedaled hard. The unusual workout was quickly wearing them out. They left the mob in the distance but soon heard something equally distressing. The sound of smashing glass somewhere down a side street. The patrol cop in her took over as Carla turned down in that direction. Joshua reluctantly followed.

The noise was coming from a nice suburban house. The lights were off, but there was clearly a commotion going on somewhere inside. Carla saw the remnants of a smashed window off to one side of a large porch. Then came the sound of a frantic woman screaming.

She dropped the bike and headed toward the house. Josh caught up and put a hand on her arm. "I don't think you should get involved," he whispered.

"If it was you, wouldn't you want to know that someone had your back?" asked Carla.

Joshua couldn't help but concede the point. "You take on enough causes, Carla. Don't try to save everyone. Please!"

She could do it, just ride away, pretend she was none the wiser. It was far from the first injustice to take place that night, and it certainly wouldn't be the last. No one would ever know that she had just kept on riding.

But she would know. Doing the right thing had always mattered to her. She was no Girl Scout, but damnit, somebody had to stand up for those who couldn't.

"Fuck it," she murmured and marched towards the front door, leaving Joshua with no choice but to follow her.

As they crept toward the door, there was the sound of gunshots from inside. Both Carla and Joshua froze, as though they had been shot themselves.

The door flew open with a deafening bang as a hooded teen stumbled out backward. Then, with an almost animalistic roar, a woman hurled him down the steps of her house with seemingly inhuman strength. The thief crashed limply to the ground at Carla and Joshua's feet. Blood stained his pale skin, rivulets running from two gaping wounds in his chest.

The woman was older, probably in her fifties, and she cocked her gun again and swung the barrel at the two of them. "Were you with him? Are you two looking to steal from me, too? A few more corpses means nothing to me. Worms gotta eat, just like the birds."

Both Carla and Joshua immediately threw up their hands in surrender. "No, we aren't!" shouted Carla.

"We just thought you might need some help!" Joshua added.

The woman chuckled. "Young man, do I look like I need help? I came prepared, even before the end came. This has always been a dog-eat-dog world, even before they threw the rule book out. And I take steps to ensure that no one screws with me. Mandatory gun legislation was the best thing that happened in this state. Anyone who wants to live to see another dawn best be equipped with one, or ten."

They looked down the row of houses along the street. She probably wasn't exaggerating. Carla imagined the number of rioters would be drastically reduced come the morning if they invaded any of the older neighborhoods. These guys were serious about protecting what was theirs. She made a mental note to be more cautious doing her own scavenging from houses in the future.

"And you've got no one to watch out for you?"

"I look out for myself," the woman said harshly. "It's all I can do."

"The government will come," insisted Carla, as much to herself as to the woman. "The government will come to help."

"Ha, remember Reagan's line? 'The nine most terrifying words in the English language are: *I'm from the Government, and I'm here to help.*' Darling, if you really buy into that fairy-tale crap, then I worry you're not long for this world. No one is coming for us. We've been left to fend for ourselves. No president is ever going to set foot in a warzone. And make no mistake, San Antonio is a warzone. And as with any war, the same rules apply; we fight to the last man standing."

"Ma'am," Joshua started, "Reagan also said, 'We can't help everyone, but everyone can help someone.'"

She raised the gun to Joshua's chest.

"Too late for sentiments like that, boy. Now, do you two want to move along? If you're not part of that mob I hear coming, I'd rather not waste my bullets on you." She retreated back into the house while muttering.

Carla and Joshua remounted the bikes. Carla asked, "Who's Reagan?"

Night had fallen and both were having trouble even keeping the bikes on the pavement. "The nights are really dark now," Josh said unnecessarily. With none of the super-bright streetlights working, nor the embedded illumination strips common on most modern smart-roads, the pair had to navigate by the feeble starlight.

Carla felt her stomach heave as she careened towards something large in the road ahead. Unable to check her momentum, she smashed into the shadowy object with a sickening thud. She cursed under her breath as the force of impact threw her off the bike and into the ditch. Pain shot through her entire body like jagged lightning bolts.

Joshua was by her side in seconds. "You all right?" he asked, checking her for broken bones.

"I'll live," said Carla, rubbing her knee, her elbow, and feeling a wrist that was stiffening up already. Two of the places would be deeply bruised, but she didn't feel any blood seeping.

"Ouch!" she suddenly yelled.

Carla was now scrambling away backward. In the darkness Joshua had no clue what was going on.

"What is it?"

"Something bit me, or stung me or something!" she said, struggling to stand.

"Come on," said Joshua, hoisting Carla to her feet and brushing at her clothes. "I don't see anything." He realized how dumb that sounded. It was pitch black now. "I mean, I don't feel anything on you."

"What did I hit?"

He didn't know. "An animal, maybe a dog. I couldn't see in the dark. My place isn't far. We'll take a look at it and get you patched up."

"I've got to get home," insisted Carla. "My family."

"They can survive for a few more hours without you," finished Joshua, before trying another tactic. "How can you take care of them when you can't take care of yourself?"

Carla nodded her head in reluctant agreement. She had allowed herself to get into another situation, one that could have been worse. She had to start making better decisions. "Hey, this was all your idea. By the way, what was it you wanted to show me?" She was hopeful it would be something that might make their survival a little easier but knowing her friends she had doubts.

Josh didn't answer. Whatever plan he'd had earlier had been quickly dismissed. A romantic gesture, a moment of clarity for them both, he wasn't sure. Around Carla his head often felt like it was full of bees. So many things he wanted to say and do but none of it ever seemed to come out right.

Joshua's house, was modest but neat, the living room having been converted into a makeshift gym with weights and a VR simulated jogging machine called a sprinter in the center of the room. He flipped on a portable lantern, then helped Carla onto the sofa and went looking for supplies.

The knee was just bruised but had begun swelling. "Let me see that ant bite."

Carla shifted position so he could see her thigh and back. She laughed despite the pain when he seemed embarrassed about being so close.

"How long have we known each other, Goofy?" she asked jokingly.

"Forever," he answered. He moved the light closer. "Not an ant bite."

"It burns like fire," she said.

"Honestly, that's what it looks like. Just like you'd been burned but in a long thin line."

"What was on the side of the road that would have done that?"

"I don't know, Carla, lots of weird stuff going on now. I think we have to just be extra careful. I'm going to get some burn cream for it, maybe that will help."

He took his time gently cleaning her scrapes and patching up her leg, then he looked up and said, "Something else is bothering you. What is it people say? Sharing is good for the soul?"

Carla shrugged, "I keep thinking about that old woman we saw. The way she spoke. She's given up on the whole idea of humanity, only trying to survive just for the sake of surviving."

"And that scares you? All the crap we've witnessed over the last month, and you're worried about some gun-toting granny?"

"No... not really." She stared off into the darkness before continuing. "I'm worried how far off I am from taking that same mindset."

Joshua took her hands in his and spoke gently, but firmly. "You listen to me now, Carla Garcia. You are one of the best people I have ever met. And life has dealt you a shitty hand. What with your parents, your sister, your grandmother. You've had every reason to just give up, look out for number one. Granted, your taste in men could be a bit better... but you've got a good heart. And I don't think you're in any danger of losing it."

"But..." she began.

"No buts," he interrupted. "You had to do something awful, something not so different from that woman tonight. It sucks balls, but you were placed in a no-win situation, and your actions haven't been heartless. You are still beating yourself up over it."

He patted her leg and had her get comfortable. "Carla, the world is the world. It's going to take people like you for us to even have a chance of making it. Don't forget that—and don't try and change."

Carla smiled. He always knew exactly what to say to make her feel better. His friendship meant the world to her. Carson kept her on edge, alert, thrilled, happy. But with Joshua... he made her feel safe, like it was safe to want things in life, to know that life was something to be enjoyed and to not be fearful of losing it.

Josh kept vigil at the window until he saw the flickering glow of the mob moving away in the distance. That sense of safety and joy sustained her as they played with a deck of cards that he had pulled out. They played into the early hours of the morning until finally, Carla's resilience had worn out, and she fell asleep on his couch.

She awoke with a start the next morning, a blanket draped over her. Her thoughts immediately went to Meredith and Maria, wondering what could have happened to them in the time she had been gone. Throwing off the blanket, not even waiting to see if Joshua was awake, she hobbled outside, grabbed the bike, and began painfully pedaling for home, worried about what awaited her.

Chapter Seven

Carla pedaled fiercely, her injuries screaming against the strain as she pushed further and further away from the consequences of her moment of selfishness. She cursed herself for leaving Meredith and Maria to their own devices, knowing all too well that without her, the family might fall apart, crumbling like a sandcastle in the rising tide. With each pedal stroke, her resolve hardened; she had to get back to them. She just couldn't take chances with the world the way it was now.

Yes, she'd shirked her responsibilities. All for a few hours of peace with her friend. It had been a rough week, and sure, she might have deserved it, but if anything had happened, she'd never forgive herself. Her nervousness increased as she neared her street. Dawn was just breaking as she topped the hill near her home, and her world came crashing down.

"No!"

The house was gone, only a crater left in its place. Smoke was rising from the recent wreckage. Carla fell to her knees in despair, knowing that she had failed both her sister and her grandmother. She didn't even have time to acknowledge the mob behind her before they set upon her...

Carla woke to the sound of screaming. But it wasn't hers. She was sitting upright in her own bed, safe in her own home. She had come home earlier but then fallen right back to sleep. It had been an awful dream. A cruel prank of her subconscious punishing her for those few hours of levity before coming home in the wee hours before dawn.

So why did the screaming still persist?

Carla reached under her pillow and grabbed her gun. She followed the directions of the screams, down the corridor towards...

...Meredith's door.

Outside the door, Carla sighed, no longer feeling the need for alarm. This was becoming a recurring part of their lives, more and more frequently.

She twisted the doorknob, taking care to safety the handgun and slip it into her waistband before entering. Meredith sat up in bed, her pajamas soaked in sweat, her face in her hands as though shielding her eyes would block out whatever monsters were coming to get her. The sight crushed Carla. How did a person deal with anything when their own mind could do this to them?

"Hey, hey, hey," whispered Carla, sitting down on her sister's bed, wrapping her arms around her and trying to pull her into a hug. But Meredith resisted and began screeching again, at which point Carla gripped her younger sister by her shoulders and forced Meredith to meet her gaze. "Meredith, it's me. It's only me. Whatever you think is happening, it isn't! I'm right here. Nothing's going to happen to you."

Sudden recognition seemed to blossom over the girl's face like sunshine, and then came the tears. She cried into Carla's chest and hugged her sister tightly as though she was afraid that if she let go, she might lose her forever. Meredith's face was a mask of horror.

She didn't need to ask Meredith what the nightmares were. Most often, it was the same thing. Mom and Dad going off on that boat and not coming back, and Meredith feeling powerless to stop what was going to happen to them.

"It was my fault," sobbed Meredith. "If I had tried harder to stop them, they'd still be here."

"No," insisted Carla. "There was nothing that you could have done. What happened happened, do you understand?"

"I miss them, Carla," Meredith whispered, much softer. "God, I miss them so much."

"So do I, Meredith," said Carla. "So do I. You know that it's just a dream, it's not real, don't you, Meredith? I know it feels all scary, but it's really not real, nothing more than your brain dredging up fears from your past."

"Yes, it is," protested Meredith. She dried her eyes on the sleeve of her gown. "I think that's why I keep going back to that day. I was supposed to do something different. I was supposed to save them and...and I failed. What's the use of having this gift if I can't change anything?"

Carla held her close. Sometimes that was all you could do for a person.

"I don't just see it happen; I feel it happen. I feel myself..." she gripped her chest tightly. "...coming to terms with what has happened. I'm going to have to pay for failing them...I just know it!"

"Meredith, listen to me. I'm here, Maria is here. We've all paid enough. I'm here. I will always be here to protect you." Her sister shook her head knowingly.

"You don't get it, do you?" Meredith said in a tone so low Carla had to lean in close. "You never have! You're always on the outside looking in!"

"Meredith... you're twenty-four now," said Carla gently. "How long are you going to let these dark thoughts ruin your life?"

In truth, Meredith had tried to block them out at first. She pretended it was just her mind playing tricks on her. But as they grew in intensity and became more frequent, she just couldn't deny them any longer. At seventeen, she realized that these crazy visions weren't going away any time soon. They were a part of her now. She was going to have to live with them for the rest of her life. Strangely, much of the time now, it didn't even feel like her life she was living. She certainly wasn't the one in control. Maybe that's what being crazy always felt like.

Carla looked at the end of the bed and saw a ratty stuffed animal that their dad had gotten Meredith when she was a little girl. Even going into adulthood, Meredith had treasured the toy hippo. Her sister held it out to her. Meredith took the toy and slowly brought it to her chest, hugging it as though it were the lone source of comfort in her life.

"Why do you do it?" asked Carla.

"Do what?"

Carla knew this wasn't a good time for this talk, but she also knew that when Meredith's mind was set on something, there was no deterring it. She may not be able to dispel Meredith's belief in these premonitions, but she could at least try and see her point of view. "Why do you try and tell everyone's future?"

Meredith sniffed and looked up at Carla with wide eyes. "I couldn't save Mom and Dad," she said. "But I can at least try and help other people. Isn't that what we do? We try and help people? You do it all the time."

Carla couldn't help but smile. Even in her own bizarre way, the fact that Meredith was trying to emulate her filled Carla with a sense of pride. She always worried about never doing anything right with Meredith. So, it was nice to know that her efforts weren't going totally unnoticed.

The older sister had often wondered what kind of life Meredith would have without her. She certainly couldn't take care of herself, which meant that Carla would have to find a way to include her in all of her future life. How would that work out? Her dreams of getting married, becoming a writer, maybe even children.

Who was she kidding? Out there were the ruins of San Antonio, they didn't have food to last the week. She feared none of them had any future to look forward to.

But Carla could never let her sister down. She felt the weight of responsibility from being a guardian, but yes, there were times she found herself thinking what life would be like without her sister. They weren't cruel thoughts, but as siblings had done for eternity, sometimes they just wanted to be alone. Truthfully, she needed her sister as much as Meredith needed her. For she hadn't worked out who she would be if she didn't have Meredith in her life. Carla, too, shared the pain, guilt, and loss from that awful day years earlier, she simply dealt with it differently.

She held her sister close and began humming a song that their mother used to sing to help calm her down. Somewhere in the melody, Carla, too, could feel that soothing pull as though her mother was there in spirit, reassuring her that she was doing all right. She, too, understood how real the ghost of their parents could be. Unlike Meredith, though, Carla wasn't haunted by the past as much as she was the present.

Chapter Eight

Carla headed to the food bank early the very next day, unaccompanied. She chose not to wait for Carson, unwilling to confront Chelsea's piercing gaze on her return. Her recent encounter with the unruly rioters had also spurred her determination to acquire as much food and supplies as she could.

Unfortunately, the scene that awaited her at the food bank replaced thoughts of food with confusion and fear. Two large security officers stood vigil outside the entrance. Normally, the place had one security person inside. Only in the early days had there needed to be outside guards as well. "What's going on, guys?"

"Hold on," the guard snapped, the curtness of his words earning a stern glance from his partner.

She was obviously authorized, she had on the shirt and the sidearm. Rather than get into it with these two, Carla pushed on past. As she moved toward the door, both men promptly blocked her path. "Is this some kind of joke?" she asked.

The guards remained still as stone, unwavering. "Due to recent thefts," the less tight-lipped of the two began, "we've had to heighten our security measures."

The phrase was well-rehearsed and probably repeated every few minutes.

"I get that," Carla replied. "I come here each week. This is the food bank for my sector. Why this sudden uptick in security?"

"A casualty was found nearby a few days ago," the amiable guard admitted, after a moment's hesitation. His eyes cut to the nearby storefront.

Carla surmised it must have been Jenny Harris.

He then sternly added, "From now on, only those with valid clearance are allowed beyond this point."

"So, what does everyone else do?" Carla asked. As bad as it was, this place fed hundreds of families.

"Can't answer that," the larger man said curtly.

"I do have my official ID," Carla said. "Would that be sufficient?" She pulled her SmartComm from her pocket, thumbed it over to her badge, its screen flashing her photo along with the designation CIVIL PATROL OFFICER, L2 CLEARANCE.

The guards exchanged a brief, but uncertain glance before relenting. "Alright, proceed. But be quick."

Carla stepped inside as they held the doors open for her. The guards' gazes bore into her back.

The manager was new, a gruff woman, also in uniform, and awaited her just inside. "You're a patrol officer?" she asked, eyeing Carla from head to toe.

"Indeed. For now, at least," Carla responded, growing increasingly impatient.

"And your clearance level?"

"Level 2. What's with all this? I've never had to go through this much crap before."

With a curt nod, the manager instructed, "New rules. Just follow me. I'll show you to the reserved section for patrol officers."

Carla followed her through the maze of empty shelving units. The supply rooms had been rearranged since her last visit.

"You have credits?"

"Yes," Carla answered.

"Understand that all city resources are scarce. We have had to prioritize certain individuals for allocation." Her face impassive, the manager led the way, not sparing a backward glance at Carla, treating her with a dismissive air.

"You mean the mayor's lackeys?" Carla interjected, alluding to the rumors that anyone who pledged loyalty to San Antonio's interim mayor enjoyed special privileges.

The manager responded with a rude sound. "I can neither confirm nor deny the allocation of resources is based on anything but need. Also, you may want to watch how you speak in public."

"This is America, I can say what I want."

The woman spun on her heels. "No...it was America. Now it is whatever they say it is. Our illustrious new mayor is making the rules now. No one else—you get that?"

Carla nodded blankly; things really were getting more desperate for everyone. At the back of the store, the manager inserted a key in the lock and opened a door. She swept the light switch, illuminating the small room.

"You can't be serious," Carla protested, staring at the nearly bare shelves. Other than a few cans of tuna, an expired box of dehydrated fruit, and a few cartons of strange snack chips, there was little else.

"This is what we have," the manager said, unfazed. "Take it or leave it."

"But wait," Carla protested. "I have been serving as a patrol officer. Just days ago, I prevented a theft. Doesn't that merit something?"

"Oh?" The manager's interest piqued momentarily. Carla anticipated recognition, only to be met with, "So you're the one who left that mess for us? Do you know how bad that body smelled?"

"I protected the store's inventory from being stolen," Carla asserted, agitated. "Surely, that counts for something?"

The manager exhaled a resigned sigh. "Show me your credits." Carla held out her hand with her token rings. The manager ran the hand-held scanner over them, then checked the numbers. "Fine. I'll rummage through our special reserves. But remember, this is a one-time exception."

"This one time?" Carla echoed, disbelief tinging her words. "I have a family to feed!"

"Join the crowd!" the manager replied in a tone of defeat. "There's a long line of desperate souls out there. You aren't special, sweetie."

"When do you think we can expect government supplies?"

"The government?" the manager scoffed. "There's no governing left. I told you, Mayor Cleveland is it. Even if there was anyone else higher up, they've abandoned us. There will be no replenishment of stock. You have this chance to get a bit more up because you are doing your part, and ok, maybe you helped deter that thief. But remember, it won't make a difference to me whether you leave with or without supplies. We're all in the same predicament. This is what I have today. Tomorrow, it will be even less."

Carla was speechless. "What are we supposed to do in the future?"

"Are you a religious person?" the manager asked after a thoughtful pause.

"Not particularly."

"Perhaps it's time to start praying," she suggested.

Carla carried the cardboard box back home, having loaded it up with as many items as she could before leaving the food bank for what she presumed would be the last time. She used one hand to try and keep the box steady and the other to hold onto her pistol in case anyone tried to jump her.

She couldn't believe this. Everything she had done. All the struggles she had made, the lines she'd had to cross. And now she wouldn't be able to even feed her family. She knew they'd have to ration the food, try and make it last. It was a question of how long they could do so before they ran out.

Chapter Nine

"You're kidding...right? This is the best you could do?"

Carla had been briefly tempted to take everything and hide it for herself and her family. Carson, on the other hand, had a wife and children, too, and some of those credits she'd used were his. She knew she would be unable to look him in the eyes if any of them went hungry. Carla's remorse after sleeping with a married man was making her overcompensate. Now, despite his wife, she desperately needed to 'do the right thing.'

"Don't get me wrong: I appreciate you doing this," Carson said. "I wish you'd let me go with you, but I get it. Chelsea was always the frugal one, making sure we always at least had the basics, but I don't think she would be so thoughtful toward you."

"Can't say I blame her," Carla remarked.

"You do realize you can't give this to everyone?" Carson stated. "I mean...I really appreciate you doing it for us, but if you're right, and they're almost out...what then?"

Carla despised herself for being in a situation where someone's salvation or famine might depend on her. She knew they were simply delaying the inevitable. Eventually, there would be nothing left for anyone except those favored by the mayor.

"So, you have a plan, don't you?" Carson asked with a smile.

Carla attempted to stay pragmatic in the face of tremendous odds. "Well, there's always the possibility of more salvaging. We expand out in search of more houses to see what we can find."

"Carla, we've already checked through all the houses within a ten-block radius," Carson remarked. "They contain nothing of worth. We'd be wasting our time. And you know how distracting it is to be with you out there, alone and all."

"Then we'd have to move out and broaden our search even more," she answered quickly, anxious to keep the conversation off the topic of 'them.'

"If we do that, we could be walking into a lynching. We've avoided most of the danger by staying close. Out there, we have no idea what houses are empty, which ones are traps. Raiders practically control all the east side already. We show up on any of those guys' turf, it'd be the same as asking them to kill us…or worse."

She decided not to ask about what was worse. "Look, I won't deny that it's a risk, so why not do it in turns every night instead of doing it together? I go scouting one night, and you go scouting the next. That way…" she breathed in deeply, "…if one of us gets hurt or, you know…taken, the other will be safe."

Carson shook his head as he restacked some of the food back into Carla's box. "First and foremost, Carla, we have a greater chance together than apart. Second, if one of us dies—and I have no doubt you'll try to help care for my family just as I would for yours. But how long could that last? I mean, we can barely feed ourselves now.

"Look, I love Chelsea, but let's face it, she's not a good mother. She never has been. I've come to realize she simply wanted a child because all her friends did. She scarcely pays attention to them anymore, leaving all mothering up to the NannyBot."

Carson leaned back and stared out past Carla's shoulder as if staring into a future none of them could see. "With me gone, I don't see her suddenly becoming Mother of the Year or anything. And your family needs you. I mean, I would do my best for them. But I'm not familiar enough with Meredith's sickness to know how to help her. Hell, Joshua is closer to them than I ever will be."

It was a rare moment of truth from a man Carla had known for much of her adult life. Confession may be good for the soul, but his words were in no way comforting.

Carla looked out at the yard where her sister was entertaining both of Carson's kids. It was rare to see her outside, but the scene brought a rare smile to her face.

"What about the mayor?" she asked. Carla would have turned down any option to work for the mayor in the past. But current circumstances might demand more desperate measures. "If we went to work for him..."

"Cleveland?" Carson stated flatly. "You know he set up his new office over in Lehigh. Problems in San Ant were just too much for them apparently."

They both nodded in the direction of the old city center. No one wanted to go down there these days. Even the promise of life-saving supplies was not enough to take them into the heart of the city of the dead.

Carla nodded.

"Believe me, I've considered it," Carson continued. "The mayor, I mean. But that would mean relocating over there. I've also heard he's formed a militia, supposedly to keep the peace. But every day, they go out on recovery missions. I've heard some get pretty messy. And yeah, they may treat you well, feed you and shit, but can you truly say they'd make the same accommodations for our families?"

Carla stayed silent, every idea she had seemed doomed lately. And when the silence was broken once more, it wasn't by Carla or Carson.

"And what are you two doing?"

Chelsea had entered and was inspecting the box of food now

sitting on her kitchen table. "Someone's been shopping," she remarked dryly.

"I just got back from the food bank," Carla revealed. It wasn't exactly a closely guarded secret.

"All by yourself?" Chelsea asked. "I'm shocked. I thought you always had to have your sidekick." She glared at her husband. "You two are like peas in a pod."

"Drop it, Chelsea. I was busy, she did us a solid, okay?" Carson explained. "Carla went grocery shopping for both our families."

"How very generous of her," Chelsea remarked as she leaned in looking over the meager haul a bit closer. Carla detected the strong scent of alcohol coming off the woman.

"Is there something you'd like to say, Chelsea?" Carla, tired of the passive-aggressive jabs, squared off at the blonde.

Meredith walked into the kitchen before Chelsea could respond. Carla, grateful for the distraction, remarked, "Hey, Sis. I went out and found you some of those chips you love." She grabbed a bag of the spicy vegan chips and handed them to Meredith.

Meredith, on the other hand, was not so excited. "You might as well get used to not having them. Having...any of this stuff."

Carla exclaimed, "Meredith!"

"It's true," Meredith answered in a tone devoid of real emotion. "We're wasting so much time clinging to the life we once knew in the hope that we'll get it back one day. But we never will. That time has passed. The sooner we accept this new reality, the sooner we can begin to cope with it."

Chelsea rolled her eyes and gave a snort of derision, but Carson quickly stepped in. He wrapped his arms around Meredith and pulled her close. The other kids watching them could not avoid sensing the tension in the air as they strained to hear every word.

Carla exclaimed angrily, "Meredith! For God's sake, stop scaring everyone!"

"Truth is always scary," Meredith stated solemnly. She then turned around and walked off.

"I'm so sorry about that," Carla apologized to Chelsea. "My sister, she..."

"Just keep that freak away from my kids," Chelsea snarled.

Carla tightened her fist. "That 'freak' has been the one watching your kids while you were off getting drunk, bitch." Regardless of how much stress Meredith gave her, she was not one to take shit from anyone about her and was only a split second away from ramming Chelsea's head through the wall.

Carson, correctly assessed the situation and told Chelsea, "I think you could probably use a nap, honey. Thanks again for the food, Carla."

He escorted Chelsea toward their bedroom, leaving Carla alone in their kitchen with her thoughts. *No good deed goes unpunished.*

Chapter Ten

Days later, Carla and Carson were again both patrolling the familiar streets late at night. In the absence of any other options, they both reasoned that working the high-risk night shifts would allow them to earn even more credits, which was good since word had come down that rations were supposedly being restocked, but also that the value of the credits had been halved yet again. Of course, the new credits meant little if the food bank wasn't restocked. This venture, like many things in this new world, was a gamble with no assurance of a payoff.

Carla briefly pulled her mask down. "It's bad tonight."

"The smell? Yeah...it is," Carson agreed. The overwhelming smell of decay from the millions of dead downtown hung over the ruins like an ash cloud from a volcano. It was ever-present, even weeks after.

"It's not going to get better, is it?"

Carson ignored her question. It was said as more of a statement anyway.

"We're going to have to do something, Carson. We only have food for a few days. Others are desperate already"

They had seen more and more instances of how bad it had become. They'd spray painted numerous red Xs on the homes of suicide victims. None had been for a single person. Whole families ending it all together was the stylish new way to exit this world.

A Klaxon Drone had flown through the streets earlier that day, announcing a new, earlier curfew. This one included an even stricter penalty for violators. With each new statement, the mayor seemed to be projecting more and more control over the survivors. The curfew also seemed to be getting increasingly earlier. "At this point, we'll soon be living inside our homes 24/7," Carson joked.

They passed another home with the dreaded red X marked on the door with the number four underneath.

"Or not living in them," she said morbidly. "Increasingly our homes are becoming our graves."

"I don't know how that would work," Carson said, recalling Chelsea's relentless verbal attacks on him and Carla and Meredith. I truly believe my wife would kill me before the first week was up. And then she'd come after you because..."

"Somehow I made her do it," Carla finished the thought laughing. "That does sound like her doesn't it? Can only imagine one of us dead and the other being falsely arrested for murder. Do they even hold prisoners anymore or have trials?"

"I'd probably be the one who ended up dead," Carson said. "Her nails are sharp as daggers." He paused before continuing. "I do have to say, my wife... she will be watching me even closer now. She'll be stuck at home even more due to the curfew. When I leave the house, it's always 'Where are you going?' or 'How long are you going to be?'"

He pulled his shirt away from his body and fanned himself with it. "I tell you, if the mayor ever needs an interrogator, she'd be excellent for the job."

Carla noticed he was no longer looking at her. She knew where this was headed.

"This means that our hookups will be much more limited."

Maybe Carla should have been more concerned about Chelsea's

growing suspicion. Instead, she was simply relieved. "Perhaps it's for the best," she stated.

His eyes widened, the hurt obvious. "Ok, that's not exactly the reaction I was expecting."

Carla let out a sigh. She expected they'd have this conversation sooner or later, but she'd been mostly ignoring it. But maybe this was the right time to 'lay the cards on the table' as they say.

"Look, Carson, I have a good time with you. I enjoy your company, and I think it's been good for us to have time with each other and get away from all of our obligations at home."

"It has," Carson agreed. "When I'm with you, I feel like I'm doing something worthwhile. I can't even recall the last time Chelsea touched me. But I feel like a million bucks when I'm with you. You'd be a better mother than she is. You are adored by my children. They're growing up in a society where positive role models will be scarce. I'd much rather they behave like you than Chelsea."

"What are you trying to say?" Carla asked. She was flattered by his words, but she wasn't going to let it stop her. "She is still your wife. She's Rachel and Ryan's mom. There has to be a way for you to make things right with all of them. None of that includes me as anything but a friend."

Carson sighed. "It's not that easy. Our marriage is like a candle that flickers in its last signs of life. I wish it weren't so, but is there just enough warmth left to keep it going? We're essentially running on empty. To be honest, I wish you had entered my life sooner."

"Look, Carson, we had a great time. But we both understood that was all there was to it. It was never intended to last."

"Just for a little fun? Do you really believe that's all you are to me?" he asked. "Just a little something on the side? Carla, I adore you!"

"Do you love me? Do you truly believe we have a chance? You have a wife and children. And what we're doing is wrong, in every way possible, it is wrong."

"Even if it's wrong, that doesn't mean it's not real." His words stabbed a dagger of truth deep into her own heart.

"If I did say it…if I told you I loved you, would it make a difference?"

"I'm not looking to hear the words, Carson. I want you to focus on your family…that's all."

Carson paused in the street by the burned wreckage of a Mercedes aircar and stared at her. "What's up with the sudden moral compass?" he asked, shining his flashlight in her direction. "As I recall, you were as excited about it as I was. I didn't notice you protesting as you were removing my pants and about to jump my bones."

Carla reddened, embarrassed by the memory. "I was mistaken. We were careless when we did it. We were under the impression that we had all the time in the world. We felt we were unbeatable. You are desirable, Carson, always have been, but then came the attack. I'm sorry…I …"

He nodded, understanding that things had changed, but he wasn't ready to let go of one of the best things in his life. "We could try, Carla. I'm not saying it would be easy, but we'd be a team."

She felt his emotional pivot propelling her from side chick to potential top billing. "And how are you going to explain that to your kids?" Carla asked. "I love them, but I can't replace their mother."

"You spend enough time doing that for your sister!" Carson said, immediately regretting his words. Carla's pain echoed silently across the darkened streets.

She was quietly furious, unwilling to show that he'd scored an emotional hit. She forced herself to calm. "We need to take stock of what we have in our lives. And what we require. Your kids still need me, and I'll be there for them in whatever way I can. But I'm only their babysitter. I can't be anything else."

"And my needs?" Carson pleaded.

"Are not my problem," she snapped back.

Carson opened his mouth to say something, but he knew Carla

had already heard everything he had to say. Nothing was going to change this outcome. Carla was unyielding when she set her mind to something.

"I still think you're making a big mistake," he grumbled as he walked away, leaving her alone in the dark.

Carla despised the fact that she had had to drive a stake into the heart of their relationship. But she knew she was doing the right thing, regardless of the pain.

Chapter Eleven

She'd made the correct decision. Carla kept telling herself this while she patrolled the streets alone.

Carson no longer went out on patrol after that night. They'd only spoken briefly a few times in his front yard. She knew he was hurt, but he claimed to be working on his marriage. He wanted to be more involved in his children's lives while also seeing what could be done to repair the damage with Chelsea.

Unfortunately, Carson's timing couldn't have been worse. The food banks were now closed more than they were open. Also, due to the growing scarcity, fewer and fewer patrol officers were showing up for assignments each day. No one wanted to work for free, most also preferred to protect what they had rather than risk losing them to the mobs of rioters.

Carla considered doing the same thing. However, staying at home meant doing nothing and being constantly exposed to the ravings of her sister and the sad decline in her abuela.

Carla's latest problems began as she was doing her regular rounds in her local neighborhood, trying to ensure that at least the people on her street had what they needed to get through the day. Reluctantly, she forced herself to ask Chelsea if there was anything they needed, partly to bury the guilt over her affair with the woman's husband.

It was obvious that Carson wasn't around, and Chelsea seemed unnaturally calm. As they talked briefly in the driveway Meredith opened her bedroom window and shouted down at them.

"IT'S COMING...THE END DAYS ARE UPON US! I'VE SEEN THE WICKED, THE MONSTERS WITHIN US. YOU ALL HAVE NOTHING AHEAD BUT ROT AND RUIN!"

Chelsea growled an obscenity, then yelled her own insults as Carla dashed back to her house, wrestling Meredith to the ground, and closing the window. Meredith had struggled and shouted, fighting hard to get free, to finish her diatribe against humanity. She managed to get a sedative down Meredith's throat and sat up with her until sleep mercifully took her.

The episode also set Maria off. Once again, she had suffered a total memory lapse. This one took her back to a time before the world ground to a halt. She wanted to go out front, to tend to her flowers and visit the neighbors. Carla tried in vain to prevent her. Each time she went out front was the same. "You don't want to go out there," Carla shouted, desperate to shield her from the ugly truth. The reality of the world as it was not the world in Maria's memory.

But her grandmother was surprisingly strong, despite her frailty. And she shoved Carla out of the way and opened the front door...

It was a gradual build-up as she stepped outside, taking in the unfamiliarity, looking at the few houses that were still standing, seeing the city she loved in the hazy distance, now more a massive rubble pile than a shining metropolis. She saw some of the homeless wandering the streets, clothes like rags, haunted eyes, and the awful, relentless smell of death. Gunshots rang out in the distance, just another of the regular sounds of San Antonio.

Maria dropped slowly to her knees. With no memory of what had occurred, each time she did this, she experienced the loss of the world for the first time. Maria's mournful wail for a world that ended was heartbreaking. She broke down into long, pitiful sobs. Carla tried to get her back inside, knowing this would last most of the day and likely not be the last time her grandmother suffered this same trauma.

"Bless you, my Santina."

Carla needed to get out of the house. Most days, she was able to bear the difficulties and carry out her tasks. That's what she kept telling herself while she patrolled the streets. Carla told herself she did it to make sure she could feed her family, but in reality, she was just happy for the space.

Today she knew she had to do something more for the people she loved. She needed to find medicines that would help Meredith and Maria deal with their difficulties. The two main hospitals downtown were both destroyed. Several others were farther out, but she doubted any were still functioning. She didn't think it wise to try a trip that far away with her family in the shape they were in.

There was another place she could try, a familiar spot for Carla. It felt like coming home in some ways. In other ways, it made her incredibly nervous.

Carla stared at her former high school, which she'd considered her second home. Outside, nothing had changed; the traces of degradation had not yet taken hold. But she was aware that the school's interior would have changed dramatically. She knew that the classrooms had been converted into patient wards. And the school had suddenly become the closest thing her part of San Antonio had to a hospital.

She walked up to the entrance to the makeshift clinic and pushed the door. All sense of familiarity vanished as a horrible stench hit her, making her gag and retch. Carla had grown accustomed to the odor of decomposing flesh in the weeks since the strike, but this was something else...something even worse.

A woman wearing a bloodied apron appeared from a nearby doorway. She wore a yellow armband, identifying her as one of the medical volunteers.

"Can I help you?" she asked flatly. The voice sounded equally of exhaustion and frustration.

Carla was suddenly ashamed and uncertain if she should even be here. This woman was dealing with life and death and the pressure of that was etched across her face. The thought of her grandmother facing the recurring downfall of the world around her day after day steeled her resolve. "I hope so," she said, digging into her pocket for a scrap of paper. "I was wondering if you had any of these drugs available?"

The nurse glanced quickly at the list. "That depends; do you happen to have any experience in the medical field?" she asked, looking up.

"Not much, I was a teacher...here, in fact." She waved around the old hall. "I do know basic first aid," Carla answered hurriedly, before adding, "and I can do basic stitching."

If the nurse's frown was any indication, this was more than what she had expected. "Close enough." She removed a pair of rubber gloves from a box and placed them in Carla's hands. "Put these on and follow me."

"Wait, what?" Carla stammered, unsure of what was happening.

Carla attempted to keep up with the woman as she began to briskly walk away. "We're not in the business of free healthcare, honey. You can work for those drugs if you want them. We're horribly understaffed. As a result, we could use your help. If that doesn't appeal to you...well, you know where the door is."

Carla recognized that this was a take-it-or-leave-it proposition. She couldn't afford to return empty-handed. Meredith and Maria had to get these drugs just to try and stay functional in this dysfunctional world. She told the woman yes, she would help.

"Excellent," remarked the nurse. "I'm Betty. And what do I call you?"

"Carla—I'm Carla Garcia." Her words stumbling out awkwardly.

"Pretty name," Betty murmured hurriedly before leading Carla to a room she knew well as one of her previous classrooms. Carla felt a sense of comfort as she prepared to return to familiar land ...only to be confronted with a terrible new reality. The workstations were crammed together against a wall, so makeshift beds occupied the space. Apparently, when the nurses ran out of beds, they used exercise mats from Joshua's gym class. Carla had to take cautious steps across the human minefield of injured, sick, and dead.

Patients were packed into the treatment room, nearly lying on top of each other. Most seemed to be in various states of consciousness; some were comatose—Carla wondered whether some were already dead, and no one had noticed. Others writhed in pain.

"Come help me!" Carla jumped to attention and moved closer to Betty, where a patient was resting on his side.

"What the hell happened to all of these people?" Carla asked, motioning around the room.

"Some were animal attacks, others are gunshot wounds," Betty responded casually, as if such incidents were routine... which they technically now were.

"I'm guessing this guy was an animal attack," Betty explained as she looked down at her patient. On his body, there were four severe cuts. All deep wounds. "I'm going to need you to stitch him up."

"I've never stitched a person. Even if I can, will it even help? Those wounds look bad." They were red, and the edges were puffed outward.

"Infection," Betty said as she cleaned the wound with a dark antiseptic solution. "Maybe a toxin...who knows? We don't have enough antibiotics to go around so we have to do what we can." She pointed to the suture kit already on a tray nearby.

"If it doesn't work, don't let it bother you. We just do the best we can. People are always dying here. It's the way the world is these days. We help where we can, that's all."

Chapter Twelve

Carla pulled her long hair back into a ponytail and began stitching the wounds. It was an awkward process with the ancient medical equipment, her lack of competence, and being unnerved by the nurse's non-existent bedside manner. Because there was nothing but localized anesthesia available, the patient was awake and in pain throughout the procedure.

"Didn't actual stitches go out with 2D television?" the young man groaned.

He wasn't wrong, bio-adhesives could not only seal the wound instantly, they also provided a nanobiotic boost and stimulated rapid regrowth. Unfortunately, this clinic had none of that.

Carla was sweating as she pierced the man's flesh time after time. She engaged him in conversation as much to distract her from what she was doing as him.

"How did you get these?"

The man tried to turn and look back at her but just groaned. Finally, he answered, "My unit, we came under attack. We were supposed to be retrieving some bigwig at Lackland."

"Wait, you're military?" Carla asked. She pulled up the piles of shredded clothes from the floor and studied the patches.

"Yes, Alliance Army regular," he said weakly.

"Who attacked you?"

"It wasn't a who..." He went unresponsive and Carla was afraid he had died.

She tied off the last stitch, cleaned the wound, applied a dressing, and rolled him over to his other side to get a good look at him. Mid-twenties, good shape, and most of all, still breathing.

"You did well," Betty said, glancing over her shoulder.

"Why isn't he in a field hospital? He's Army."

"No idea, girl. Someone just dropped him off like a lot of the others. I don't ask any questions anymore. Just treat them, move to the next and hope for the best".

The two women struggled to move him off the table, taking care not to rip out the sutures. Carla gathered the bloodied blankets and prepared to discard them.

"No!" Betty yelled loudly, scaring Carla. "What on earth do you think you're doing?"

"Replacing the bed linen."

Betty shook her head and pulled Carla's blankets from her grasp and began remaking the surgical table with them. "What?" she asked. "Do you believe we have a linen fairy making regular deliveries? We must make do with what we have around here."

Carla couldn't disagree with her reasoning, but the image of the next patient being placed on a bed of blood-soaked blankets made her sick.

She spent the next few hours rushing through her duties, giving each patient the care they needed offset by what little she could actually provide. The stream of people she saw all began to blur together, but she was most haunted by a small child, thin and malnourished. She guessed he was around seven or eight-years old, making him almost the same age as Rachel, her neighbor's child. The boy's skin hung off his body like it belonged to someone else. And Carla thought of her sister's warning and wondered if this was what awaited all the other children in San Antonio—a future of starvation and despair.

Betty approached Carla and placed a hand on her shoulder. "Why don't you just take five?" she said gently. They were the first words of compassion Carla had heard come out of the woman's mouth all day.

"No, I want to keep going," Carla said unconvincingly. In truth, she wanted to give up, to be anywhere else. This place was worse than anything else she'd had to do. Still, the handful of nurses, volunteers, and doctors were doing this day after day. It made her feel small, useless, and unworthy.

"Trust me," Betty said. "If the constant flow of sick and injured doesn't kick your butt, the smell will."

Carla nodded quietly, already overwhelmed by what she had seen so far. She did excuse herself and went outside into the schoolyards, happy even for the not-so-fresh air. She inhaled as though coming up for oxygen after nearly drowning.

She'd met a few of the others helping in there. They were all pleasant but also showed signs of stress. Carla wondered how long Betty had been there, what kept her going. The woman might have been compassionate at some point, but now that facade had been eroded down to hard bedrock. She didn't seem to care, acted like it was just a job...but that couldn't be true. This wasn't a job you did just for an extra ration credit, and no one was getting a paycheck anymore.

A part of Carla wanted desperately to walk away, get away from the horrors back in there. Forget the meds, and just go back home. But that would mean facing her sister and grandmother again and seeing repeats of earlier episodes with them until...She couldn't even see what the end of the cycle might be. The last few hours had changed her, or at least her perspective, she could only do so much. But like Betty, she had to be able to at least do that.

There were people inside who could use her help. Carla felt she should be thankful that no one had died yet as a result of incompetence. After several minutes of collecting her wits, she stood. She couldn't just leave, that wasn't how she was wired. She needed to 'make a difference' as Maria would say. Today it was in that trauma ward. Carla knew one day soon it could easily be her or someone she loved lying on those bloody linens and makeshift tables in need of saving or at least in need of a friendly face and a caring touch as they passed.

Betty rushed past waving her to quickly follow. A huge military truck parked at the front door of the school, and several soldiers leapt out.

They unloaded a lot of stretchers all bearing more and more wounded patients from the truck. Carla helped the other volunteers sort the injured by severity. "Third room on the left," Betty yelled as she pointed at a litter passing by. The troops nodded and the line of stretchers disappeared down the darkened hall.

"What the hell happened to them?" Carla asked as her light illuminated some of the grotesque wounds.

"Who knows? One of the soldiers said, 'Food run gone bad.'"

"You would think animal attacks or something." Betty shrugged as she lifted a bloodied linen, peered underneath, then motioned for it to join several others already placed against a wall. "When the food started to run out, some people began looking for calories wherever they could. I used to be a dog person, you notice they are nearly all gone now? Of course, this is cattle country and yeah...some tried with larger animals. And, as you can guess, nature has a way of retaliating. I'll leave the rest to your imagination. These look like something else though."

The thought made Carla nauseated, outraged that humans had already resorted to such barbaric measures to survive. But soon, similar actions might be totally normal. She began to hope she wouldn't be around to see that day.

Betty lay a hand gently on Carla's shoulder. "These patients aren't going to make it very long. However, one of us has to stay with them...you know. Nobody should die alone."

Carla got it, but she didn't much want to be the one. She and another volunteer held a vigil over the dead and dying as the truck drove away and the doors to the school closed.

The other helper, a girl about her same age, pointed at the man she was sitting with. "Wow, what were these guys shot with?"

"What do you mean?"

"One of the others said they were attempting to get food from Lehigh when they were attacked," the girl said sadly. "Should have realized that would be a suicide mission."

The words made Carla shudder. She made eye contact with the girl and shook her head, as if to say, 'Don't ask too many questions.'

"So, these aren't soldiers coming from a battle?" Carla asked.

"Militia maybe, soldiers that have gone AWOL and just got hungry. Who knows?"

The woman Carla was kneeling over suddenly seized her hand in an unyielding grip. She had a large puncture wound in her abdomen. Dark blood continued to seep out and soak her clothes. She struggled to draw in breath but was obviously trying to speak. Carla leaned in closer.

"Where?" she began, sputtering and wheezing, as if every breath she drew hurt her and brought her closer to death. But she was determined to say something. "Where are my children?"

Carla wanted to reassure her. To reassure her that they were safe. But she couldn't bear the thought of lying to this dying woman. Instead, she could only stammer, "I- I don't know. I'm sorry."

The woman grimaced and began writhing on the stretcher. The other girl looked up and shook her head. The woman grasped her once more with surprising strength and Carla struggled to think of anything helpful to say.

But the woman knew what she wanted. Her hoarse voice rasped out exactly what she wanted. "I failed them all. Kill me. I can't go on like this, none of us can."

Carla recoiled, as if stung by wasp. This woman was no different than her or the countless others who were just trying to feed their families. The woman was in horrendous pain, the body moving so much Carla had to lay on her to keep her on the stretcher. Still, she couldn't find it in her to take this woman's life. She was here to help people, not kill them.

Obviously hearing the woman's words, Betty came out of the classroom and put her hand on Carla's shoulder. "Leave this with me," she murmured, her tone warm and cold at the same time. "I've changed my mind. You don't have to be here for this."

Carla understood what was about to happen and was totally repulsed by the idea.

Betty sensed the shift in her new apprentice and offered a sad smile. "It's called mercy, Carla. We give them what they need."

Betty held out a small bag, which Carla accepted. In it must be the two medications.

"Thank you, Betty." She looked down at the dying mother once more, then pulled Betty in for a hug. The older woman stiffened at the touch but slowly relaxed to the embrace. "Thank God we have you."

"Hopefully, we'll see you again...if you can handle it, of course. You did well today."

Carla walked away from the building feeling the almost imperceptible weight of the bag in her hand. She mentally weighed the pills she had worked all day for against the piece of her soul she knew she'd lost forever. She did not expect to ever go back.

Chapter Thirteen

Somewhere in that long walk home, Carla realized the most terrifying aspect of today was not witnessing the horrors. It was realizing without any doubt similar fates awaited them all. She'd spent so much of her adult life as a caregiver but today trumped them all. Tonight, she needed someone to comfort her, to take her in their arms, and tell her everything was going to be okay.

She stared longingly at Carson's house, jealous of him and his wife, his family. Yet he was willing to throw away the very thing she needed. She didn't understand men, or love or anything about the world anymore.

Nobody was out on the streets, no children were playing, and no civil patrols. Despite the chaos elsewhere in the city, tonight her street was calm. She found Maria in her favorite chair, telling Joshua stories from her youth. It didn't matter whether she was telling him for the first or twelfth time. Joshua was always a good listener.

"Nice to see you, Carla," Joshua remarked as he stood up quickly.

"Come in, dear," Maria said motioning Carla into the living room. "I was just telling your young man about everything you do at school. I hope you stayed out of mischief today."

Carla knew that at that moment to Maria, she was a teenage girl with her entire life ahead of her, free of worries, or tragedy. Tonight, she wished she could see herself through Maria's eyes... but she couldn't.

Everything was too much for her. And there was no stopping it this time. She ducked into the kitchen instead, not wanting to appear weak in front of others. She slumped into a chair and sobbed gently into her hands, afraid that they would see this side of her. She was being stupid and weak, but she couldn't help it.

Joshua peeked his head in first, then eased in the small room slowly. He could read the room as well as anyone and debated whether to console his friend or leave her alone. He simply couldn't bear the thought of leaving her like this in such a situation, so he strolled over to the table and gently pulled out the chair next to hers.

"I can't do this, Joshua," Carla cried. "I was hoping to, but I can't." I simply cannot. My abuela doesn't recognize me. And my sister..." She burst into tears, unable to fathom Meredith as anything approaching a functional adult.

Joshua looped an arm around Carla, and pulled her close, allowing her to cry, gently rocking her back and forth, a sensation that Carla was unfamiliar with but liked. After several minutes, he whispered, "Why don't you tell me about what happened?"

She shook her head, but realized she still held the paper bag in her hands. She placed it on the table, dried her eyes and slowly began to tell him about their classrooms that had been transformed into trauma wards, the blood-sodden blankets, and the beds built from his exercise mats.

When the mats were mentioned, Joshua stiffened, then remarked, "Well, at least they're in use."

She nodded.

"There's more?"

"There was a woman who was dying. She asked me about her children. I could give her no peace. Then she asked us to..." She couldn't continue.

"Did you?" Joshua asked, obviously understanding.

"I couldn't. The head nurse said she would. I just took the meds and left."

Josh opened one of the bottles. "Only ten pills. The other appears about the same."

"They don't have much of anything," she responded.

"Well, we should get them to Maria and Meredith, a few nights of peace for you maybe. Look, Carla, I though the civil patrol was crazy, but working at the clinic, I don't know how you're doing it."

"But I can't fix anything!" Carla sighed, her hopelessness overpowering her. "Nothing I do really matters."

"Everything you do matters! Who you are matters, Carla Garcia. No one can fix the world right now, we just have to survive it. You are moving forward, even if you fall, you fall forward."

"Why are you always so nice to me?" she questioned very quietly.

Joshua had so many things he wanted to say to her at that moment. He wanted to declare that he fell in love with her the first time he met her. He wanted to tell her that he'd lied about his car breaking down in order to share the commute to school with her each day. He wanted to say that it didn't matter that the world had gone crazy as she was the only part of his world that mattered; he was happy.

This wasn't about him and his dreams though. His emotional needs were trivial compared to his friend's mental health.

"Because you are so good to everyone around you," he replied. "All the people who live around here benefit from having you in their lives."

Carla smiled at the sentiment, "Don't know if Chelsea sees it that way."

"Probably not," Joshua concurred. "But you do way more for those kids than she does, and they're not even yours."

Carla nodded, slightly relieved by his rationalization. Joshua indicated the pill bottles she was nudging around the table. "It's a good thing you got those. I believe Meredith is getting worse."

Carla cocked her brow. "You might as well be telling me that the water is wet."

"Yeah, well, I had to drag her back inside. She was out on the street trying to give a doomsday sermon. She was wild, I mean, I have a feeling she would have scratched my eyes out if I were anyone else."

"Given half the chance, she probably would," Carla said, all too familiar with her sister's increasing outbursts.

"She needs a doctor."

"She needs an exorcist," Carla answered. The laughter faded quickly. "We're all she has."

"But Carla, we have to be practical. We don't have the resources to treat her disorder."

Carla gazed down at the pill bottle, hoping for the best. "Maybe we do, at least for a few days."

Chapter Fourteen

Meredith sat on her bedroom floor, randomly spreading, and stacking the cards. There was a lot of static in her thoughts today, a lot of things jostling for place, distorting her sense of self and making it difficult to focus. She increasingly found it difficult to separate what was real and what was yet to come.

Usually, the cards would bring her peace, or night dreams would offer clarity. It was not always something she could form into words, much like trying to describe a color to a blind person. Their frame of reference was just incapable of fully grasping the meaning. She'd tried to explain this to Carla many times. Carla believed in facts, the here and now. She needed to be able to hold it in her hands before acknowledging that something was real. Now, Meredith was beginning to realize there was an opposing side to her gift. One of darkness and hate. Somehow, she had not been infected by that, but others she knew had been. Their gift was something else entirely.

A knock came, as Meredith had expected.

"May I come in?" Carla asked, a little cautiously. And Meredith sighed recognizing the hesitation in her voice when she had something to say she knew Meredith wouldn't want to hear.

Meredith half-jokingly asked, "Are you here to let me read your future?" She fanned the cards once more across her bed.

Carla's attempt at a smile contorted into a frown, as predicted. "Meredith, we need to talk about something."

"It's always about what you want to talk about," Meredith grumbled, and Carla wondered if she realized how much she sounded like a toddler. "Unless you want me to read your future, we don't have anything else to discuss."

Carla frowned. This was already going sideways, and she hadn't even made it to the difficult part. She didn't like the fact that Meredith held all the cards in the conversation, both symbolically and literally.

Still, she needed them to have this talk. And if it meant giving in to her sister's indulgences for a few moments, that wasn't asking too much.

"OK," Carla murmured, sitting on the bed beside Meredith and attempting to show interest. "Read me my future."

Meredith grinned victoriously as she shuffled the cards in her hands, seemingly at random. Carla tried to imagine the situation from Meredith's point of view. She tried to imagine the cards 'calling' to her... Carla couldn't begin to understand the delusional state one must be in to buy into all this crap.

Meredith flipped over one of the cards, which showed a guy and a woman entangled. "I see... romance in your future."

Carla already knew these were not normal playing cards, not strictly tarot cards either, but a bit of a mix her sister had put together. "Right," she responded cooly, attempting and failing to seem impressed.

Even though she and Carson had been quite careful in their hook-ups, it wasn't unreasonable to guess that Meredith had spied on them. Or perhaps she was thinking about her and Joshua. After all, he was the one male figure in her life who remained somewhat constant. Or maybe that was just something her sister assumed any healthy female around her age would want to hear.

Meredith flipped over a second card, this time a triangle hazard-looking symbol. "I see... danger approaching."

Carla was snickering, trying to remain serious. "Have you looked outside lately, Meredith?" We're in danger all the time."

Meredith turned over the third and last card, ignoring her sister. It depicted skull and crossbones, like an old pirate flag. Meredith leaned back and quickly placed the card face down.

"What was that one?"

"Nothing." Meredith said firmly.

"It was bad, wasn't it?"

Meredith bit the inside of her cheek, a nervous habit since she was little. She nodded.

She flipped the card back up. "It's... death. Death approaching you."

"Finally, something that makes sense. Shit, Sis, there is death everywhere. I had my hands in death all day long. It doesn't need to approach. I'm going out and finding it."

Carla didn't want to make fun of her sister. She was indulging her for a reason, but all she had been through and her sister's unwillingness to face what was really going on was just too much.

"OK, that's it," Carla remarked, cutting Meredith off. "I'm sorry, Meredith, I'm sorry, but this shit is nothing more than some fantasy reality you've cooked up. Real people are dying out there. I saw a child dying of starvation today. Here, in San Antonio, children are dying because they can't get enough to eat."

"They aren't just fantasies!" Meredith objected softly. "These visions are actually happening!"

"It's time to grow up!" Carla said, her tone growing harsh and demanding. "This clairvoyant nonsense may have seemed fun as a child. But you're an adult now. I can't continue to be responsible for you like way back then."

Meredith stammered, her eyes welling up with tears, "But I'm doing this for you! I'm doing this so that I don't lose you like I lost Mom and Dad!"

The words were like a verbal slap. "I lost them too, you know!" Carla said, her bitterness of being forced into the parenting role rising to the surface. "I had the same crappy luck as you. But you don't see me projecting my thoughts onto everyone around me!"

Carla took the bottle from her pocket and shook out a single blue tablet. "I want you to start taking these."

Meredith picked up the pill and held it up for closer inspection. She turned it several ways examining it as if it were poison. "No," she stated flatly. "If I take those, I won't be able to see my visions. I won't know what's coming."

"This isn't up for debate, Meredith," Carla said. Her tone growing increasingly demanding.

Meredith, on the other hand, refused to budge. She wasn't taking the medication.

Carla had been through too much today just to get the meds. She leaned closer, grasped her sister's chin, and attempted to shove the pill into her sister's mouth. "Carla... you're hurting me!" Meredith screamed in between tears.

"It's for your own good," Carla said emphatically as she pushed her sister's cheeks together forcing the lips to part.

But just as she was about to open Meredith's mouth, Carla felt a stinging slap across the face, She flew off the bed onto her back; blue pills spilled all over the carpet.

The sudden violent outburst from her sister stunned her. Carla only wanted to keep her sister safe. Meredith also looked shocked. Neither girl spoke for several minutes. Meredith sobbed quietly, Carla rubbed her face.

"All right," Carla grumbled as she returned the pills to the bottle. "Would you like to live in your fantasy world? That is perfectly OK. But how nice will it be when you are starving or a mob shows up wanting to tear you apart?"

Despite the intimidation, Meredith was unmoved. "I know you don't believe me, Carla. You never have. But there will come a day. You'll see the world for what it is, and you'll beg me to forgive you.

Not today, and most likely not tomorrow. But it'll happen you'll see how right I was."

Chapter Fifteen

The following day, Carla felt trapped and knew she had to get out of the house. They needed food, but that was an uncertain daily chore. She wasn't sure she could face going back to the makeshift hospital. So instead, she headed back to the local civil patrol station.

She was surprised to see four guards outside the old police station. She knew the interior of the building was likely scorching hot already. Summer in central Texas. Still, with all the looting going on, it seemed odd to see the guards all grouped together.

"Can I help you?" the cop she didn't recognize asked dismissively. He was a large man with dark skin and accusing eyes. He stared down at her as if she were a bug.

"I'm Patrol Officer Garcia, Level 2 Clearance," Carla said, hoping that the cops would recognize her despite her lack of real authority.

"So, you're one of the last ones standing," the guard said with a dry laugh. "What exactly do you want, a medal?"

She guessed that because of the cuts in food credits, few, if any, of the civilian patrols had even been showing up.

She plastered on a fake smile, "No, I need to do something to get more food for my family. I was wondering about maybe a new assignment." Carla continued, "I wanted to ask about going over to Lehigh," speaking in one rapid breath before losing her nerve. "I understand there's some problem over there. I was wondering if I might go over there and look it over, maybe plan a supply run for the food bank?"

The guards exchanged glances that revealed nothing. They burst out laughing. When Carla did not join in, the large, black man who apparently was in charge said, "You're serious, aren't you?" Why would anyone want to go down that rabbit hole? Did you hear what happened to the last group that tried to negotiate with those people?"

"Look, I've got people in my neighborhood who are starving, people with families and children," she said, attempting to elicit sympathy from the man. "I owe it to them to try if there's a chance, I can get things sorted out for them."

"Join the fucking club, honey." The guard then attempted a different method. "Hey, I admire your enthusiasm, Miss...umm, Garcia," he said, remembering her name. "But going over there is damn sure not recommended." He looked at one of the other men who nodded in confirmation.

"Might as well just go off yourself. Guaranteed to get raped at the very least. Sorry to be so blunt but those are the facts."

"But isn't that where the government is based now?" she asked. "Someone over there has to be thinking about the survivors. Where is the mayor?"

One of the other officers spoke up. He was wiry, with a sweat-stained shirt unbuttoned too far down his chest. "The real mayor? He's over there."

Carla followed his gaze to the large building. "Apex Tower? But it's..."

"Yeah, we know. Everyone died. The EMP blast took out all the elevators, door controls locked, and the entire building went into lock-down. Even the few who made it into the lobby couldn't break down the Armorglass windows to get out. Those luxury apartments became their overpriced prison."

"And their tomb," said the other man.

"The assistant mayor became the acting mayor and had emergency services abandon any rescue attempts at Apex. Since his boss was stuck up on one of the higher floors, it was a simple way to advance his own career.

"So, this new mayor, guy named Cleveland, took office a few weeks ago over in Lehigh as you know. I suppose we all work for him now. Even if he is in absentia. I don't know much about the dude. He had us put your patrol groups together. Sent us supplies to keep it running, he imposed resource restrictions everywhere. Put the brakes on the looting fast, which was pretty damn smart, if you ask me."

The black man, whose name badge read Hightower, pulled her away from the others and over into a shady patch on the south side of the building.

"Look, miss, I'm not trying to get in your business, but anyone who has attempted to go into Lehigh has been turned away or simply disappeared. It's an armed camp over there."

He continued, "I admire what you're attempting. But if you do this, you'll be on your own, we can't come bail you out if you get into trouble. You yourself know we have enough of that right here."

"I understand," Carla said weakly, feeling as if this was just one more challenge in her life... one more thing that she'd have to tackle on her own.

* * *

Carla made her way back to her bike which was becoming her main mode of transport. She hadn't totally made up her mind when she'd left the house earlier, but now, she was committed. She stopped by one of the caches of supplies she and Carson had made. It wasn't much, a stretch of ancient looking self-storage units. They'd managed to find one with a key hanging in the lock.

It was a fast stop, and the space only held basic supplies; no food, just bottles of water, which she placed into a knapsack and then got back on her bike. She hadn't gone more than a block when she heard the sound of someone panting to catch up. She spun around.

"What exactly are you doing?" Carla asked.

Carson held up a hand and took a pull from a water bottle before answering.

"I went by the station to turn my stuff in. They said some crazy chick had just left on her way to go see the new mayor. I figured that had to be you. Thought you could use some backup."

Carla was still a bit pissed at their prior conversation and coldly replied, "Thanks, but I think I've got this." She began pushing the bike down the street, only pausing when Carson ran in front of her.

"I understand you're still upset. I can't say I blame you. But you're venturing into unknown area by even trying to meet with this guy."

"Oh, whatever, he's a politician."

Carson shook his head, "I mean it, Carla. This isn't going to be what you expect. Cleveland is cold as they come. Most likely you won't get within five miles of him. Let me go with you just to...you know, provide some cover."

"How touching," Carla remarked wryly. "All you need is shining armor and a gallant steed."

"I know him...the mayor," Carson said, surprising Carla. "Back in the day, before he was in office and a hotshot politician, I did some construction work for him... at least until he decided to replace us all with some stolen BuilderBots."

"And you think that is enough of a connection to get you in front of him?"

He shook his head. "No, but I have a better feel for him than you do. I'm telling you this is dangerous. You have a better chance of coming back if I go with you," Carson reasoned. "And you need to come back if nothing else but for your family's sake."

"What about your family? You're taking an unnecessary risk, does your family not matter?" Carla asked.

"Yes, they matter, but I think I know what you're trying, and if it works, it could help all of us."

Carla couldn't exactly argue with his logic. "All right," she replied. "I think we saw a spare bike in one of those units a while back, go find it and make certain that you can keep up. And I'm not going to wait for you."

Minutes later, they were heading toward the unknown of Lehigh. Neither said anything for the first mile, but Carla felt the need to fill in the silence. While the chasm between them was growing, they'd been so close just days before. "Look," she began. "I apologize for being so abrupt, you know cutting you off and all. I never wanted to hurt you. Guess I just I had no idea that it...we meant so much to you. I mean after all, it was only meant to be a little fun. A—"

"A fun distraction, right?" Carson asked, taking Carla's words from her mouth. "Yeah, you'd be correct on most of that, but let's be real, Carla. We both know that the only reason I married my wife is because she was expecting Rachel. And I adore that tiny girl with my whole heart. But I've spent so many hours imagining what my life would be like if I hadn't met Chelsea. If..."

The rest of the thought died on his lips, but she thought she knew what he was thinking.

Carson continued, "I know you want me to focus on my family, and that's smart, it's just, Chelsea is growing increasingly distant. Not just from me but from the kids, too. I mean, she was never a great mom, but she used to try. Everything now just seems to be a reminder of the life she lost. I think in her mind, I've grown to represent everything that's wrong with the world."

"I hate hearing that, Carson." And she did. Carla sensed he was being totally honest, but in her mind it was a bit too late for redemption for either of them.

"I know you don't love me; I get that. What I miss, though, is the fact that I felt like I mattered to you. I'm a better person when I am with you."

"Well, I'm sorry if I led you astray," Carla remarked, her remorse growing with each mile. Now she was regretting even bringing the subject up again.

"Hey, it takes two to tango," Carson pointed out. "We like to say that we started volunteering out of a sense of obligation to keep the world turning. But seriously, I believe we both did it because we didn't want to think about what awaited us at home."

And there it was again, that tiny truth, that sense of kinship that had drawn her to Carson in the first place. He wasn't wrong. They were both running away from something as much as they'd been running to each other.

"We can never go back to being lovers," she stated emphatically.

"I know," he murmured, smiling hopefully. "But can we at least be friends?"

Chapter Sixteen

The roads were packed with people, most walking in single lines, the closest Carla had seen to mass order since the strike. The sheer volume of people let her know she wasn't the only one thinking Lehigh held the answers of a better tomorrow.

A few miles outside of the small town they found themselves waiting in that same long line at a guarded barricade. Many of the people passed through with a nod. Those seemed to be regulars; they all shambled and held on to all manner of possessions.

Carson and Carla made it to the front of the line about an hour later. They were met by a man dressed in riot gear, as if waiting for the daily mayhem to erupt. "Yeah, what's your business in Lehigh? He directed his question at Carla, while making notes on a datatab and yelling orders at someone behind him.

"We'd like to speak with the mayor," Carla said in as strong a voice as she could manage.

"The mayor isn't taking any appointments for a while," the guard said, motioning for the next in line to move forward. He then looked at Carla and Carson and added, "Look, we've already screwed ourselves by taking in too many refugees. We can't afford to take in anyone else. All the rest of this lot will go to Vineland."

"We're not refugees," Carla said, denying the assumed accusation. "We just need to speak with the mayor, in an official capacity," she said again, the only thing she could think of.

Carson also chimed in. "I worked with Mayor Cleveland before, you know...before he was mayor and all," he explained, a big PR grin on his face.

He was given a sidelong glance by the guard. "Mayor Cleveland has employed a number of people in a variety of positions. I doubt he'll recall you directly."

Carson nodded reluctantly. The man had already started questioning the next man in line. Whatever other arguments Carla had to make were abandoned.

She walked back toward the line of homeless heading toward the wooded fields of Vineland. The stench of the mass of unwashed bodies was overwhelming. "Screw this," she said as she rode her bike around the barricade, much to the guard's surprise. Carson soon followed suit.

Several of the guards tried to catch them, all were screaming insults, and one shot tore up the road beside them, but they cleared the next rise and were quickly out of sight.

"Let's hope we don't see him again," Carson said with a nervous laugh.

"We do still have to go back by them," Carla said, but recalled that the outbound foot traffic seemed to be mostly ignored by those manning the blockade.

The small-town square looked mostly like she'd remembered it, maybe a bit more beat down, fewer cars around, but a surprising number of stores seemed open. People walked the streets and other than a few security people, she saw no one else that was armed. That was rare these days.

"You ready for this?" Carson asked.

She nodded and pushed her bike up the steps of City Hall and into the foyer. Neither trusted the bikes would be there when they returned, especially if they left them outside.

They didn't have to look far to find Mayor Cleveland's office. But what they saw as they opened the doors astonished them. The space was filled with everything imaginable, correction, everything that was in short supply everywhere else.

The entire space felt like a time capsule. A candlelit conference table, mahogany furniture, and scarlet carpets. In a richly paneled boardroom off to one side, a portly man was digging into a large, delicious-looking steak. Carla felt her stomach growling at the mere thought of it.

Mayor Cleveland raised his eyes at the two intruders. In between munching, he asked, "What are y'all doing in here? Kincaid!" he yelled to someone.

Carson attempted to portray a kind employee. "Mister Mayor," he introduced himself, "it's great to see you again. I collaborated with you on..."

Carla, on the other hand, was way past polite behavior. "An entire town is starving out there," she replied, her voice soft as ever but her rage apparent. "Children will go to bed hungry, again tonight. And then there's you, sitting there all high and mighty at the end of the world, sipping your wine and devouring a steak for lunch."

The mayor rose slowly to his feet. "It's a very good steak, though." He smiled. "It would be a shame to let it go to waste just because someone else's kids didn't eat. How does my eating or not affect the rest of the world?"

"You're taking advantage of the people," she yelled. She knew this was going off the rails, but damn, the scene had flipped every breaker in her system.

"Security!" he yelled. "Where is Kincaid?"

"Carson, the door," Carla said, her gaze fixed on the mayor and his meal.

Carson slammed the door shut and bolted it.

She hoped to see a hint of fear on the mayor's face. But he kept his cool as he eased himself back down in his chair. The man had probably spent a lifetime swimming in shark-infested seas of politics and business.

"It appears you have me as a captive audience, miss," he replied, dabbing his mouth with a delicate napkin and tossing it on the table. "So, why don't you tell me exactly what you really want?"

"Maybe you can shed some light on a few things," Carla suggested. "Like why you've stopped the flow of supplies to the food banks in the city."

"Ah, you're from the city. I see, yes. Well, resources are scarce," Cleveland replied, sounding perfectly fair and justified. "We're going to have to rely on rations to get by."

"You seem to be doing pretty well," Carla commented, referring to the man's meal.

In response to the insult, Cleveland nodded, "I am the beating heart of this city." Without me, the entire system crumbles. That was one of the problems with the last mayor!"

"Funny you should mention him," Carla said, becoming engrossed in this verbal chess game. "What happened to Chavez?"

Cleveland appeared momentarily put off by the question, but quickly recovered. "Our previous leader was tragically lost on Last Day."

Carla knew she could make different references to the previous mayor's demise, but she remembered she was here for a reason.

"Why are your people turning away and even attacking refugees from the city?" she demanded.

"I'm guessing these people were..." Cleveland looked Carla up and down, before making a tactless answer, "Non-Americans?"

"Excuse me?" Carla couldn't believe what she had just heard.

"You come over here with a sense of entitlement, leaching away at our resources."

"I was born and raised here!" Carla exclaimed with such zeal that Cleveland wondered whether he had possibly pushed her too far.

"I helped treat some of those people your men attacked. They weren't rioters intent on destroying everything. They only wanted to feed their families!"

"That's not my problem," Cleveland responded, taking a forkful of steak and stuffing it into the open maw of his mouth. Carla wondered whether this was a display of power.

"You're supposed to be mayor! That must be within your capabilities!"

"I can only provide so much! However, I do not provide favors to foreigners who come uninvited and interrupt by day. Who do you think you are to come in here and make demands on me? You are trespassing on an important American landmark. How many rights do you really have?"

Carla said, "You think we'll be the last people to show up on your doorstep?" When news comes out that you're stockpiling all the goods for yourself, an entire crowd will descend on your home!"

She hoped that by threatening Cleveland, he would comply. Instead, he returned his focus to his meal, taking a hearty drink from the wineglass. "That would be a monumental mistake on their part."

Before Carla could ask him what he meant, the doors sprang open, and a tall, well-dressed man entered surrounded by security. The guards poured into the room.

"Mister Kincaid, please escort these two off the premises," Cleveland muttered, finally tearing his gaze away from them. "You're lucky, young lady I don't also charge you for the damage to the doors."

Carla recognized Kincaid as the man who used to top off the credits each week. She turned back to Cleveland, not about to give up without a fight. But as she looked at the heavily armed men, she wondered how far they'd go, what they'd probably already done in Cleveland's name, and she knew they'd have no problem killing her or Carson and dismissing it as collateral damage.

She raised her arms and reluctantly allowed the soldiers to lead them out of the room.

Chapter Seventeen

"What in the hell were you thinking back there?" Carson was furious with Carla. Both were anxious to get back to the relative safety of their own neighborhood.

"I, I know...I just couldn't let it go. I mean, the shit he was saying!" Carla said, trying to defend herself. "I wanted him to know we were serious! We have to stand up to bullies like Cleveland."

"With what, our non-existent army?" Carson asked, "Carla, this isn't your high school. Bullies don't get sent to the principal's office, they instead make the rules now. Most of the people alive around us have no fight left in them. We are all malnourished, and some are just children. Like my children!" he exclaimed. "Are you going to lead Rachel and Ryan into war, with the mayor?"

She was ashamed of herself, not for her anger or the idle threats she'd made. She had been so offended by the pig of a man. She just wanted him silenced. In doing so, she'd likely lost their only hope of getting anything out of Lehigh.

"We both know Cleveland is not above dispatching his goon squad to deal with people who irritate him! What are we going to do if he decides to bring this fight to our doorstep?"

"He doesn't know who we are. I never gave him a name."

"Grow up, Carla. You are wearing a CP uniform shirt. You let him know you worked at the clinic, too. He'll know exactly who both of us are by the time the sun sets."

Carla prayed that would not be the case. She desperately hoped none of that mattered. She knew now, she would have to live with the possibility of recriminations hanging over her head. As if she didn't have enough other shit to deal with already.

She would be grateful to be back home, surrounded by the safety of friends, family, and familiar surroundings.

* * *

"You filthy, lying sacks of shit!"

Carla ducked fast to avoid something coming at her face. It nearly knocked her off her bike. She turned to face her attacker, already seeing another object coming toward her. She caught this one as it went by. A white baseball.

Chelsea stood in the middle of the road, tears streaming down her mascara-streaked face, while both her kids stood on either side of her. Both kids' expressions were stark terror, unsure of what was going on, but their mother's anger let them know something bad was happening.

"Oh, you fucking bitch!" Chelsea yelled, charging at Carla as she hurriedly dropped off her bike and rolled into the sparse lawn. "I ought to fucking kill you both!"

"Chelsea!" Carson yelled, sprinting over to place his body between Chelsea and Carla. "For God's sake, what's wrong with you? Don't do this, especially not in front of the kids! You're scaring them."

"Why not!" his wife yelled, attempting to shove by him like a caged lion. Her sole focus was getting to Carla. "Don't they deserve to know that you ran off again with that whore! Again!" Chelsea pointed an accusatory finger toward her. Carla always knew this day was coming, but she was exhausted and had zero fucks to give for it today.

Chelsea was unconcerned if Carla fought back or not. "Why?" she yelled, her voice suddenly sounding pleading. "In this Godforsaken dumpster fire of a world, I mean, shit, you could have anyone you wanted! Why did you feel the need to fuck this guy...my guy...their dad?"

Carla turned to Carson. "Handle this." She began walking away from the scene and toward her own front door. The sound of running feet racing up behind her was no surprise. Carla had been on edge all day, prepared for attacks. This one from the neighborhood bully barely registered. She gauged the distance, then quickly leaned far to her left, only leaving one leg outstretched, which Chelsea promptly hit running full speed, launching herself face first down into the dirt.

Carla was apologetic and sincerely regretted the pain she'd caused Carson's family, but she didn't deserve the girl's wrath for anything they'd done today. Chelsea was a shallow, petty woman, mostly unworthy of her husband and children. Still, Carla felt pity for her as she saw her now, sobbing and bleeding in her husband's arms.

He ushered Chelsea and the kids inside, leaving Carla standing on the edge of her yard. She could see the silhouette of other people watching from their own homes. People she'd been trying to help, now they all were judging her.

"Are you all right?" Joshua said, coming out of the house. He could see she was exhausted, both emotionally and physically.

Carla shrugged; it had been another very long day.

"I take it she knows..."

"Seems to, yes. Chelsea believes Carson and I were doing something today or planning to run off together or something. I don't know."

Joshua grimaced slightly. "It's not too much of a stretch. You are seeing him, right?"

Carla locked her gaze on him. "Is this the part where you say, I told you so?"

"I'm not looking to judge," Joshua explained calmly. "I'm your friend, Carla, always."

"Well, if it's any comfort, we're not seeing each other anymore," Carla said. "We ended it a few days ago. It was a mutual decision."

"Good," Joshua murmured, a little too quickly. "I'm glad you guys came to your senses."

"I wouldn't say that," Carla responded, thinking back on her pissing off the mayor. "I believe I just found someone even worse to make an enemy."

"Well, then, why don't you come back to the garden and tell me about it," Joshua said, motioning for her to follow.

Chapter Eighteen

The two walked behind the house to Maria's garden, where she was busy working something into or out of the ground. Carla saw Maria's precision and care as she worked, which she hadn't seen in a long time and assumed she'd never see again.

"I heard that people with Alzheimer's can sometimes improve when placed in familiar situations," Joshua said quietly to her. "Seems to be similar to muscle memory."

Carla nodded. "Good thinking," she said as she quietly moved closer to Maria, "So, what are you up to, Grandma?"

"Trying to figure out what these damn thistle things are. They are everywhere!" She pinched something between her fingers and flicked it off into the weeds outside the tilled soil.

"Joshua has been helping me plant some vegetables. We have squash, okra, some beans, mainly hot weather stuff. It's a little late but better than waiting around any longer."

Carla realized she had misjudged her grandmother. Carla had had that same determination and iron will for so long that she had almost forgotten where it came from.

"How long will it take to grow them?" Carla asked, wanting to believe Maria's renewed clarity and optimism but needing a reality check.

"Well, if your boy there can be trusted, maybe just a month or so."

Joshua chuckled, "They are some of the new radical hybrid seeds. Supposedly drought tolerant and very fast-growing. Basically, mutant crops."

She didn't much care for his phrasing, but Carla could readily see the benefits of growing food in the garden for themselves and maybe the neighbors. At the very least, it might help them cope with food bank shortcomings. Mostly, she was glad that apparently Maria had ignored the ugly scene next door.

"So, where's Meredith?" Carla asked, bending down to help pull some of the weeds and creeping vines from the row Maria was planting.

Joshua shrugged. "I did ask her to help. But she seemed preoccupied with those damn cards."

"Of course," Carla stated flatly. She and Meredith hadn't spoken since their disagreement in the bedroom.

"What about you, dear?" Maria asked. "How was your day?"

It was unbelievably refreshing to hear Maria sounding like her old self. Obviously, the medicines Betty had given her had helped.

Still, Carla despised admitting her carelessness and poor judgment today. But if Mayor Cleveland planned to follow through on his plans, both Maria and Joshua should know. Carla told them about the meeting with the Mayor.

She braced for the coming backlash from her grandmother. She already knew how dumb she'd been and that she'd likely put them all in danger.

Maria, on the other hand, beamed. "I'm so proud of you, Carla."

"You are?" Carla asked, unsure if Maria was mentally processing what she had said or not.

"I am," Maria stated emphatically. "When I first came to this country as a young girl, I learned a lot of things, but the most important lesson of all is that you have to fight for what is right and for what is yours. Anyone who makes this place home should be willing to fight to help make it better, even when it's uncomfortable. You are strong, and you are wise, Carla Garcia. If your parents were here now, they'd say the same thing."

Carla could feel the tears welling up and made no effort to suppress them. Instead, she sobbed into Joshua's arms and let him hold her, allowing those long-repressed feelings to sweep over her. She hugged Maria as well, then looked up to see Meredith staring at them from the bedroom window. Her face was a mask of hurt and something even darker.

Chapter Nineteen

One of the patrol officers summoned Carla to the police station early the next day. Her first thought was Chelsea had sworn out a complaint, but even she knew they didn't concern themselves with stupid shit like domestic squabbles anymore. Hell, no one even cared about murder anymore.

That left one possibility: Cleveland. She reasoned that if the mayor wanted her locked up, he would have done it in Lehigh. Carla decided quickly that if that was what was about to happen, she would make it loud and ugly. She didn't know if the police would stand with him or maybe support her. She was almost one of them. But she had no choice but to try.

The large black man named Hightower from the previous day met her at the door. He looked her over approvingly. A lone toothpick held loosely in the corner of his mouth. "Well, damn! You're still alive," he said. The man seemed genuinely surprised, "You defied the odds, girl. And you must have made quite an impression on Mayor Cleveland."

Carla was only slightly surprised at the sound of the man's name. Obviously, she'd been right as for the reason of the summons. Now she braced herself to hear what punishment he had in mind for her outburst.

"Yeah, wanted to speak with you about that," Officer Hightower said.

"Look, I know I said some things," she began defensively.

"It must've worked...seems like he is quite taken with you," Hightower chuckled and motioned to the other man who had escorted her to the station. "Bring it in." The other man nodded and disappeared.

"I'm sorry," Carla said, perplexed. "I'm not entirely sure what's going on."

"The mayor himself and his entourage came by the station a few hours ago asking about you." He motioned back to the other man to come on in. "He wanted you to have this."

It was a box of food; she could see all manner of dried goods as well as fresh fruit and eggs. Carla wasn't sure she'd ever seen so much in one place in months. She was so hungry, her mouth began salivating at the sight.

She noticed a cream-colored envelope on top of the box. She grabbed it and opened it.

Ms. Garcia,

First and foremost, I apologize for my behavior yesterday. The pressures of leading a city have taken their toll on me. Still, that is no explanation for my impolite behavior toward you and your friend.

I was pleased by your willingness to work on behalf of your people. That kind of dedication is rare, and I'm sure they look up to you. I'd get a lot further in life if I had more folks like you on my side.

Which leads me to my next point. My team is always looking for new talent to help me out. I believe you would be an excellent addition to our ensemble. In exchange for your services, I'm confident we can form a trade agreement through which your neighborhood will receive regular supplies.

If you think my offer is appealing, please come to the office tomorrow to discuss it further. Use the enclosed pass to enter, our guards will stand down when they see it.

I feel we may all benefit greatly from this cooperation. I'm hoping to hear from you shortly.

Yours sincerely, Jeremiah Cleveland, Mayor

"I must confess, I am quite jealous," the top guard said grudgingly. "There aren't many people who can win points with the mayor like that. I would seriously consider accepting his offer. Shit, girl, you'd be crazy not to."

Carla reached in and handed Hightower an apple and several packs of some beef jerky that was lying atop the rest. The man made a move to decline but then gratefully took it. He looked at the shiny apple, lost for a moment. "What we are all willing to do for food now is scary. Be careful...whatever it is he is offering. The cost may be more than you're are willing to pay."

"He has tons of supplies." Carla said.

The man shook his head, then took a bite of the apple. The look of pleasure washed over him as some of the juice trickled down his chin. "Food is power, Carla. You may dislike the man, but don't ever underestimate him."

She had no plans to but was immediately curious as to what Carson's take on this might be. He'd been there too. Would any of this make sense to him? "I really need to talk to my partner about this," she said.

"Good luck," Hightower said. "He turned the rest of his stuff in yesterday. Guess patrolling isn't for him."

Carla wasn't surprised and remembered he'd said he was quitting, and that was before the fight last night. She thought he was still coping with the aftermath of Chelsea's meltdown; no telling what else he might have to do to appease her. Whatever his plan was, it probably meant staying as far away from Carla as possible. Hard to do when they were neighbors.

The note made no mention of Carson, so it was safe to presume that the offer was limited to her and her alone. That meant once again putting herself out there for her friends and family. But she couldn't deny she had a responsibility to them all.

"OK," she replied. "Tell him I'll see him tomorrow."

"Will do," Hightower answered, finishing off the apple. "Good luck miss...and thanks!"

She walked back to her street, using a rolling cart she found to haul the case of food. She kept going over the note in her head. Hightower was right, food was power, and accepting this gift had just given Cleveland leverage over her. How much was the question?

Chapter Twenty

Carla realized she couldn't handle all this alone. She needed to tell someone about Cleveland's proposal.

Naturally, Carson was her first thought; she had no doubt he would have helped her make sense of it. But the mayor's proposition was intended solely for her. Should she risk the mayor's fury by sharing it with him? Plus, she had to let Carson have his space. He had to deal with his own problems right now. He didn't need more from her.

Her thoughts then wandered to Joshua. She felt she could tell him anything. After all, he had been supportive of her affair with Carson, even if he had not approved of it. Carla told herself she couldn't inform Joshua of the proposal because she wanted... no needed to keep him safe. And if she told him, he'd make her turn it down. And she didn't think she wanted to do that. She really needed to discuss it with someone. Someone who could serve as a confidant. Someone who would go unnoticed by the mayor.

She looked up to see Meredith peering out her bedroom window, as if in response to her thoughts. Carla did wonder why Meredith was continually glancing out the window, searching for something.

She climbed the stairs as she entered the house. The two hadn't spoken since the event with the pills, so she couldn't gauge her sister's feelings for her. She entered the room carrying the fruit basket and yelled, "Heads up," before hurling a peach at Meredith.

Meredith dodged out of the way as the peach landed next to her on her pillow. "Surprising," Carla commented. "Despite your foresight, you did not see that coming."

"It doesn't work like that," Meredith grumbled as she picked up the peach and began to eat it. The look of joy spreading across her face nearly made up Carla's mind for her. "Where did you get the fruit from?" she asked in between bites.

"That's what I wanted to talk about," Carla said as she walked up to the bed and sat at the foot of it, keeping a safe distance from her sister. "The mayor has made me an offer." He has urged me to come and work for him, and in exchange—we get more food."

"Is this one of those 'sell your soul to the devil' kinds of deals?" Meredith asked, finishing the peach off with surprising speed. She licked down her arm where the sweet nectar had oozed out.

"I don't know," Carla said. "However, I need to be able to talk to someone about it, or I'll go insane. So, you've got to promise me you're not going to tell anyone about this, okay?"

Meredith was silent for a brief period. "Why should I keep it quiet?" she finally asked.

"Excuse me?" Carla asked, surprised.

"I wanted you to believe me about your future, but you wouldn't," Meredith explained. "You all thought I was the crazy sister who no one should listen to. So why should I keep this secret for you?"

Carla regained her steely determination and stated, "Because I have cared for you day in and day out since Mom and Dad died. I didn't always get you, but I tried to be there for you since you were my sister and my obligation. I was the one who stood by you when you lost your job. When Grandma started losing it, I was the one who stepped up to attempt to keep everything running. And now it appears that I will be the one who must sell her soul just to put bread on the table. I don't expect you to be grateful to me, Meredith. However, it wouldn't hurt to acknowledge it occasionally. I don't believe it's too much to ask for a small favor from you, do you?"

The older sister didn't like using guilt to manipulate her sister, but she hoped there was room for a spark of appreciation somewhere down in the maze of Meredith's mind.

"OK," Meredith finally responded, much to Carla's relief. "I'll keep your secret, only if you keep mine."

"What kind of a secret is that?" Carla asked cautiously. "You don't have a guy hidden under your bed, do you?" Meredith had taken to sneaking her adoring guests into her room to read their fortunes, and Carla was inclined to check the room herself just to be sure.

"Oh, no," Meredith responded, her smile frightening Carla despite the assurance it should have conveyed. Meredith rose from her bed and extended her hand to Carla. "Come along with me, and I'll show you."

Carla couldn't help but notice the switch in roles. She was always the one who tried to persuade her sister to trust her. She had no choice but to take her sister's hand and follow Meredith downstairs and out back to the shed by the garden. Carla was terrified the entire time of what Meredith was taking her to see. Her heart raced as they neared the small building. *What has my crazy sister done now?*

"I always come down here for a little privacy," Meredith explained as she took out a key and opened the lock. "That... and some other things..."

Meredith yanked the doors open before Carla could realize what she was saying. Inside were shelves full of canned food, crackers, dry goods, and bottled water; every type of sustenance they would require to survive. Meredith entered the shed and opened a mini freezer, revealing a variety of meats, fruits, and veggies. There was extremely little space to move about. Meredith had turned the shed into her personal food pantry. Carla wondered if she had ever plundered a delivery service when she had gone away by herself.

"How..." Carla started to ask, unable to fathom the scene in front of her and wondering whether she had begun hallucinating. "How long have you been storing this stuff for?"

"A while now," Meredith replied. "Long enough to see us through the end of the world. We could live off of this for months while the rest of the world went hungry and died. You provide for the family, but I have prepared us for the end of the world.

"Carla, I really have seen the future. I've seen hordes of robots rise up against us. I've seen vines engulfing the landscape and killing everything in their path." Carla almost wanted to believe her when she stated the words with such conviction.

"I know we haven't always seen eye to eye," Meredith said, holding Carla's hands as if urging her to pray with her. "But I love you, Carla, and I promise you that I will never let anything bad happen to you."

Carla desperately wanted to believe Meredith for the first time since her illness began.

Chapter Twenty-One

"Well, if I'm hallucinating. I really hope it doesn't stop."

Joshua was peering into the shed, open-mouthed, at the contents.

Despite Meredith's wishes to keep it private, Carla felt she couldn't keep this to herself. This was too big a secret for her.

But if she told anyone else about the shed, human vultures would fall on it like a downed carcass. She would have approached Carson, but then she'd have to worry about it reaching Chelsea. As a result, Joshua was the only one she could rely on.

And she was relieved to have someone to share the burden with as Joshua stared into the shed, speechless. "This is some serious long-term planning, even for Meredith," he added.

"I guess I shouldn't be too surprised," Carla said. "She spends most of her time thinking about the future; it only makes sense that she would be planning for it."

Joshua looked at the shed, obviously attempting to figure out if he was hallucinating. "How in the world did she do it all? No offense to your sister, but it's difficult to see her going into town."

"While I was still working, Meredith was the one doing the grocery orders," Carla explained. "It was one of the only things I felt like I could trust her with." Knowing how handicapped Meredith had become as a result of her illness, she felt a sense of regret for that final bit.

"It must have taken her months to accumulate all of this stuff," Joshua remarked. "This is what's going to save us all." He looked at Carla. "How come you're telling me this?"

"I felt... as if I needed to confess."

"I'm pretty sure there's still a priest out there who could fill that role," Joshua remarked.

Carla stated, "I needed to share this with someone... because I feel guilty. Everyone in this town is starving, and the children are turning into skin and bones. And now we have a mini-mart in the shed." She averted her gaze from the food, as if she couldn't look at it without feeling guilty. "How am I supposed to look people in the eyes, knowing what we've got back here?"

Joshua rested his hand on her shoulder. "You're always thinking about other people rather than yourself. It's one of the many things I lo...like about you," he replied, hoping Carla didn't notice the slip. "However, don't overwork yourself. Carla, it's turning into a dog-eat-dog world. First and foremost, we must look after ourselves. I apologize if that comes across as cynical." When Joshua noticed Carla was still skeptical, he asked, "Do you think they would do the same for you if it was the other way around? Because Chelsea certainly wouldn't, and most of the others wouldn't either."

"But I have a responsibility to help these people," Carla stated emphatically.

"Why? Why should it be your responsibility? You agreed to take on those obligations. You were willing to take the initiative and step forward. That's the issue with leaders. People can spend so much time waiting for someone else to help them that they never think about how to save themselves. People in charge have the ability to make us all complacent...dependent." Joshua saw that his friend wasn't as convinced. "Are there other ways to help the community other than feeding them?"

"Like... like what?" Carla asked. "What exactly do you have in mind, Saint Joshua?"

"We can protect the children and train adults to defend themselves. I'm not sure, Carla," Joshua admitted honestly. "However, I know this. Your sister took a big risk in telling you about this stash. She may never speak to you again if she learns that you've told me. Meredith is unquestionably the type to retreat back into her own world, that protective shell she surrounds herself with. Believe me, that's what hurts the most when it comes to family. When they quit talking to you, not when they lash out."

Carla couldn't disagree. She remembered how many times Meredith had shut down and stopped talking to her. That hurt her more than anything Meredith could have said. "Keep the peace for now," Joshua advised. "That's all you've got. We'll figure out another way to serve our people...something that doesn't involve martyrdom."

She liked the sentiment but wondered if she would have to compromise herself in any case because of the possible arrangement with the mayor. She just couldn't bring herself to tell Joshua. She was worried that he would never look at her the same way again.

Carla and Joshua were looking at the shed and failed to notice Chelsea staring at them through slits in the privacy fence.

Chelsea had a deep-seated hatred of her neighbor, an almost inhuman dislike for Carla since they'd first met. Now she had even more reason to hate her. The woman was not just screwing her husband, they were hoarding food. Carla must have been stealing it for weeks. Her kids were going hungry, while the Garcias had more than anyone.

She recalled the birth of her daughter Rachel. Carson happily held his infant daughter in his arms. When he handed her back to Chelsea, though, she sensed a distinct disconnect from the infant; as though there was a barrier between her and the child. Her husband said it was postpartum, the famed baby blues, which would pass in a day or two. Instead, it had continued for months. Carson had finally convinced her to get out of the house, and that was when the book club got going. More like a group of women, mostly mothers, drinking wine and complaining about their husbands more than anything literary, but it had helped.

But that was when Carla started babysitting the kids. She brought out a sense of playfulness and delight in Rachel that Chelsea couldn't. She had tried to compensate for this by engaging in play sessions of her own, but it never seemed to click with the youngsters. It was far too late. As a result, Chelsea had always suspected Carla of stealing her daughter's love. That love should have been hers.

And she had long suspected Carson and Carla of having an affair, but she wanted to pretend she was mistaken. Carson would never betray her so easily. But she couldn't keep her eyes from seeing reality any longer.

This woman was taking her children, her husband, and possibly their life. And Chelsea vowed to make her pay.

Chapter Twenty-Two

Mayor Cleveland was standing on the opposite side of the room, giving Carla a disgusted look.

"I'm so glad you could make it," the mayor remarked cheerfully, his voice not as hostile as it had been the previous time.

Carla had gone over her options numerous times, evaluating the benefits and drawbacks of donating her soul vs. assisting the townspeople. It was either the risk of incriminating herself or the certainty of the townspeople going hungry.

Carla reasoned that she should at least hear him out. Learn what he expected of her. "Well, it wasn't like I had much of a choice."

The mayor took a step forward. "May I offer you something to drink? We have some extremely fine wine down in the basement that I can have brought up."

"No, thank you," Carla respectfully said. "I'm a bit of a lightweight, and I prefer to keep my wits about me when I'm on the clock."

The mayor nodded thoughtfully, as though unsure whether that was a veiled insult, before finally responding, "Smart woman. Please take a seat then?" He motioned to an empty seat at the far end of the dining table. Carla hesitantly approached it and sat down.

The mayor took his place in his chair and pulled it a bit too close to her own. He leaned in to speak, "I wanted to apologize for my earlier... crassness. It was never my desire to dishonor your history. And I truly apologize for that. This job can get the best of me at times. And I vent my rage on other individuals. It's not a quality I'm especially proud of, but it's one I'm working on."

Carla wondered how long he had spent practicing those words, each syllable meticulously chosen. He was now in sales mode, employing the same demeanor that had worked him well in his prior political career.

"But hopefully, you can look past your first impressions of me, and then hopefully, we can help each other," he continued.

Carla didn't reveal anything since she didn't want to let her guard down for this man.

"I did a fair bit of research on you, Carla Garcia." Carla blinked as her entire name was mentioned. "Don't appear surprised. If you delve deep enough, you can find material. I also had my men dig." She noticed him leafing through a file that was kept together with paper clips. "Given your background, you've certainly come a long way from teaching history." He raised his eyes to her. "You are now in the enviable position of being able to make it."

"How did you come by that information?" Carla asked, curious whether someone she knew had revealed more about her to anyone, especially this creepy guy. Did he know that she'd killed a girl or that her family was a bit insane? Did he know about her encounters with Carson? Thoughts raced through her head like fireworks.

"My methods are my own," the mayor stated flatly, and Carla had the feeling she wouldn't get any more from him.

The mayor went on. "There is nothing in this town that's beyond my grasp. I can have anything I want within a few hours. But when I'm feeling generous, I see no reason why other individuals in my orbit shouldn't be able to also reap the advantages."

Carla saw where this was going and hoped the mayor didn't notice her wriggling nervously in her chair.

"I understand that San Antonio is running low on food supplies, so in exchange for your assistance, I will be willing to set up a more robust distribution route. Let's say, hmmm once a week, ensuring that everyone in your neighborhood is healthy and fed."

Carla disliked asking the question, but she knew it had to be answered, if only for her own peace of mind. "And what kind of services do you anticipate from me?"

To her surprise, he didn't respond right away, instead shifting his copious weight in his seat. "Well, I can't give you any specifics, because this isn't your typical job description. However, I will make every effort to identify positions that match your 'unique' qualifications. Because I understand you were a teacher, there is a charter school where you can work some shifts.

"Of course, given that you will be spending a significant amount of time in Lehigh, it only makes sense that you have appropriate lodging; I will be provide you an apartment in exchange for your services."

The man's eyes kept roaming over her body; it gave her the creeps, but she was here to see what he had to say. Though the man's words should have comforted Carla, she had to consider who was making the offer and that she would have to leave her family behind to accept it.

"I recognize that this is a big decision to make," the mayor added, sensing her discomfort. But I guarantee you that working for me will provide you with all you need to satisfy both my requirements and the needs of the town of Lehigh."

Carla reasoned that the demands of the community and the mayor were likely the same thing in the self-serving man's head.

"And if you're still worried about your family," the mayor continued, his sales pitch unwavering, "there is a fully-stocked clinic equipped to treat your sister and grandmother's ailments."

Carla remained silent despite the benefits given. The mayor was using her own family as a bargaining chip.

"And I'll say that, while we've had our fair share of problems in

Lehigh, we've never had to worry about looting. For us, going hungry is not an option."

Carla could not disagree; she'd seen the abundance this place offered.

The mayor reclined back in his chair, having said what he wanted and now waiting for Carla to do the mental math that told her this was the best option. "You are not required to respond immediately. Take some time for yourself to reflect on it. But I can tell you that this is the best offer you are going to get. I'll do my best to make sure the resources will be waiting for you when you say yes."

Carla somehow made it out of the mayor's office feeling as if she was going to be sick. Her head was spinning, her palms were sweating and everything seemed to have shifted ninety degrees from normal. Outside, she sank onto the stairs, overwhelmed by the possibilities of what she was offered.

"Hey, are you all right?" a familiar voice asked. Carla's ears perked.

"Carson?"

He stood there looking disheveled, with large bags under his eyes and a scruffy beard. She could see sweat stains on his shirt.

"What exactly are you doing here?" she asked, not getting the usual vibe from the man.

"I'm doing a few extra shifts for the mayor," Carson confessed, before hastily adding, "My kids need the food. And it isn't all that horrible."

Carla, on the other hand, knew Carson well enough to know when he was being dishonest.

Chapter Twenty-Three

"How is your love life going?"

The suddenness of the question surprised Carla. She'd been home attempting housework, dusting the bookcases while Maria slept in her chair. The oppressive heat of the day was finally beginning to ease.

She'd almost leapt out of her skin when the older woman spoke. Carla turned back and answered. "I don't have time to think about a love life, Grandma."

"Certainly not with a married man, that's for sure," Maria grumbled.

Carla felt herself becoming numb. "What exactly did you just say?"

"I know about you and Carson. I'm old, dear, not blind," Maria remarked when Carla was too stunned to answer. "I can see his expression when he stares at you. And the way you've regarded him."

"Why didn't you say anything?" Carla asked, lowering herself to her grandmother's eye level. Maria, she would have assumed, would chew her out at the first opportunity.

"Because he brought you joy. And you needed that in your life.

Don't tell anyone, I used to fool around a lot when I was your age," Maria reflected, before adding matter-of-factly, "but child...he's already taken. He has his own family. If you continue, in the end, everyone suffers."

Carla felt a sour pit of embarrassment form in her gut. She would have loved Maria to just yell and scream at her, but her grandmother's silent acceptance inflicted far more hurt and shame.

"You should be with Joshua," Maria replied cheerfully.

"Joshua?"

"He's a far better fit for you. A good man is not only there when everything is fine. He's also there for you through thick and thin. And, despite everything that has happened with the world...and your sister, Joshua has always been there for you. He's persisted. That is the type of man you want in your life."

Carla was glad for this brief moment of clarity but quickly dismissed Maria's attempt to play matchmaker. "Abuela, we're just friends. We have a great friendship, in fact, and I don't want to ruin it." That was the truth, despite her occasional thoughts about something more.

"You will want to be quick," Maria responded, refusing to let go of the situation. "A man like that will be snapped up eventually. But if he is as good as he seems, you should make sure that the lucky girl is you."

Her grandmother was old-school. She didn't think a woman's life was complete without a man. Carla had a very different opinion of them. "We are good friends," Carla said again. "But I don't see us being anything more."

"Who is your good friend?" Maria asked, her face clouding over and her mind again blank.

"Josh and I..." Carla began before she saw Maria's incomprehension, the last few minutes robbed from them, never to be recovered.

Carla's heart sank, knowing she should be accustomed to these 'blank moments,' as she referred to the woman's spells of forgetfulness. But it still gave her the same gut-wrenching feeling it did when Maria was first diagnosed with Alzheimer's.

She patted the older woman's shoulder and made her way out of the room. The personal torment she felt at having no one to share this with was terrible. In the grand scheme of things, though, Maria's not remembering right now might just be a blessing. Still, this new world was no place for someone in her condition. Maybe it was unfair to even hope she would make it, but Maria was half of all the family she had left.

Carla couldn't do it alone for much longer. She required help from the one other person who had a responsibility for Maria but so far had been unable or unwilling to own it.

She didn't bother to knock on Meredith's door. She simply entered. Meredith sat in bed. Carla had come to the conclusion that there was no easy way out, so she might as well say it. "Meredith, we need to talk," she stated severely, her tone reminiscent of her days as a teacher.

"What exactly do you want to talk about?"

Carla was still trying to frame the conversation in her own head. "It's all about Grandma," she began. "She's getting worse. I'm doing everything I can to help, but it's killing me. And...and it looks like I'll be spending more time away from home. So, I need to know you'll be able to step up and take care of her while I'm away."

"Right," Meredith stated flatly before returning to her collection of colored stones spread out atop the bed.

"Did you not hear what I just said?" Carla asked. Her sister's apparent indifference was getting on her last nerve.

"I did," Meredith said, without looking up. "And she won't last long anyway."

"Excuse me?"

"This new world is putting us to the test," Meredith began. "Separating the wheat from the chaff, attempting to determine who can survive in the new world and who will perish. Grandma, on the other hand, is not built for the world out there."

The room was stiflingly hot, sweat rolled down Carla's face and back. "How can you say something like that?" she yelled.

"It's not a judgment, it's just a fact of life," Meredith said. "People like Grandma will die out if they haven't already, and they will only drag the rest of us down along the way."

"Meredith...we're talking about our grandmother!"

"I'm not thinking about preferences. I'm thinking realistically. And if we wanted to get into preferences," she said softly, "it's clear that she loves you more than she does me."

Carla was appalled at what she was hearing. She'd always known Meredith operated on a different mental level than her, but she'd hoped she'd have a place in her heart for others, especially the woman who had taken them in and cared for them since their parents died.

She wanted to lash out at Meredith and condemn her sister's vicious comments. But she couldn't come up with anything that would pierce through Meredith's twisted logic. Honestly, it wasn't so distant from what she herself had been thinking minutes earlier. She had just not been so cruel as to speak it.

Instead, Carla stood up and left the room, puzzled as to how she was meant to manage her sister when everything around them was going insane. It seemed like a losing battle. Still, she had some tough decisions to make.

Chapter Twenty-Four

To the untrained eye, nothing much seemed to have changed. The buildings were all in the same places, and the streets were all laid out the same way. There was, nevertheless, an implicit sense of danger. Carla felt as if the early evening darkness was reaching out to grasp her. She was getting spooky vibes, like something Meredith might dream up.

She increasingly felt the loss of Carson's company ever since she began patrolling alone, knowing that individuals would be less inclined to assault a group of people, or even a pair. A lone person, on the other hand, especially a girl, was an easy target.

The mayor had imposed the curfew, and Carla diligently patrolled the streets to make sure everyone was where they needed to be. The sound of breaking glass set her mind racing. She moved quietly but quickly in the direction of the sound, despite the fact that her survival instincts told her to run the opposite way.

The source of the noise was an old convenience store that had formerly been owned by a family she remembered fondly but had long since been abandoned.

Except for tonight's visitors.

Carla dashed up to the charging stations, her fingers resting lightly on her service weapon.

She counted three people coming out of the building, each holding baseball bats, evidently having been unsuccessful in their search.

Carla could make out the youthful features even in the darkness, and her heart sank at the realization they were just kids, maybe early teens. She stood and held the gun up for them to see.

"You can't be out here. We have a curfew."

The kids barely seemed to notice her or just no longer cared.

"Get out of here and don't come back," she said, attempting to sound braver than she really was.

"Or what?" asked the teen in the middle as he moved closer. Carla surprised herself by standing firm.

"I'll do what I have to do to keep the law. I'll put you in the ground if I have to," Carla declared. "It certainly wouldn't be the first time." She found herself remembering Jenny Harris and wondering if she had it in her to kill another child.

She slowly lowered her gun toward the boys. "This is your final chance. Move on before it gets ugly."

"You were Ms. Garcia, weren't you? You taught my sister."

Was she Ms. Garcia? That was an apt statement. She wasn't that person anymore.

"I'm not that person, and I am not here to make friends. Final chance, boys." Her steely tone seemed to finally convince the trio that she meant business. They weren't going to take that chance. They moved off quickly, no doubt in search of less risky pursuits.

Carla lowered the pistol as soon as they were out of sight, gasping for air as if she were being kept underwater. She had no doubt that if the occasion had called for it, she would have pulled the trigger. But that was not what frightened her. What worried her was the thought of becoming accustomed to it. The recurring sense of regret and shame over Jenny's death had to fade over time. She had to replace it with a stone-cold necessity to accomplish whatever needed doing.

Her sister's survival of the fittest mentality was bearing fruit. Now she knew she no longer knew who the woman in the mirror was.

She wished Carson, or heck, even Joshua, was here to help keep her company, to tell her everything would be fine, and to give her something positive to focus on. The world was a sad place. San Antonio was nothing but ruins, and the future seemed just as dismal.

Carla reflected on her grandmother's comments about how she and Joshua may be a nice fit under the appropriate conditions. He had been the one constant in both her old and new lives, the one person she could rely on to be there for her. He rarely told her what she wanted to hear, but he always told her what she needed to hear.

Maria might have been correct. They'd be a good match for each other. But they already had a wonderful friendship, and she didn't want to jeopardize it. She simply didn't think of him romantically or sexually. He was just Josh. Why on earth was she even dwelling on this? The world was coming apart at the seams. Food was scarce, fresh water disappearing fast. Thieves and rioters everywhere, and in the last few days, rumors of even more dangerous things out in the countryside. Her love life was the least of her concerns—or should have been.

Carla's thoughts were interrupted as she neared a long-abandoned church. She had been religious as a child, but after a string of losses, including the death of her parents, her grandmother's mental acuity, her sister's mental decline, and now the end of the world, Carla found it difficult to believe in the existence of a just and forgiving God.

The flickering glow of candlelight drew her toward the ornate building, and she was shocked to see the church was apparently once again in use. This was Texas, and many called it the last stronghold of Christianity, but something here didn't feel right. Her hand was again on her holstered weapon as she approached the church, entering quietly through the open doors.

Nothing Carla could have imagined could have prepared her for what she saw. A mass of devotees sat in the pews, listening with rapt attention to the lone speaker down front. She could read the expressions; these people were in awe of the person. It was her sister, Meredith, who stood at the altar. Carla initially assumed Meredith was making a scene and having another of her episodes. But as she listened, she realized her sister was giving a bizarre sermon. A talk that she'd herself heard bits of over the last few weeks.

"God is selecting those who will see us through the end times," Meredith explained. "And this isn't the first time he's done it. Consider the enormous flood that swept away everything for forty days and forty nights. Those who were left behind were then granted a second chance, just as we were.

"God's plan included that attack. He's gazing down on us right now, judging who among us deserves to live and—who deserves to die."

Carla felt as if she were watching mass hypnosis at work as the audience gasped.

"Monsters will be coming from the East! This is the stuff of nightmares! But I've had even worse nightmares than that. We must be ready!"

Carla couldn't decide which was scarier, Meredith's maniacal sermon, or the fact that the gatherers seemed to be hanging on every word of it.

Chapter Twenty-Five

Carla's first thought was to run down to the altar, pull Meredith out of the church, and take her home. She knew she'd have to deal with the crowd after seeing how they were affected by Meredith's words.

Instead, Carla calmly approached her sister after everyone else had left the church. She didn't say anything, but Meredith's expression took her by surprise. There was a sense of confidence that Carla hadn't seen in years...maybe ever. Her face radiated joy and something deeper.

"Carla?" Meredith asked, seemingly unsurprised to see her sister there. "I'm glad you got to see the service," she said smiling.

"What the hell was all that?" Carla asked, motioning to the altar.

"I was showing people the way," Meredith continued, her eyes dreamy, and Carla wondered if she was actually here in the present or deep in one of her visions.

"Meredith," Carla patiently said. "These visions do not exist. It's one thing to go through them on your own. It's another thing entirely to lure other people into your dream world."

"It's not a dream, no fantasy!" Meredith responded abruptly. "If anything, it's a nightmare, but a real one. It will come to pass. Don't you believe the people have a right to know what is going to happen?"

Carla moved Meredith to the side so no one could hear her. "These people are already pumped up. They have no other news, no entertainment...no hope. They'll believe almost anything." Carla said, "Let's go home," realizing that having this conversation on the church's doorstep would be inappropriate. "With the curfew, we're already pushing our luck."

* * *

"What in the world were you thinking?" Carla asked later once they were back in the relative safety of their house. Meredith started for her room, but her sister pointed for her to sit. They both sat heavily on the old sofa.

"I was thinking that people needed warning," Meredith said, evidently bored with the subject, but Carla was adamant about continuing. "They want answers, and no one but me seems willing to provide any."

"First and foremost, Meredith, you left Grandma alone," Carla chastised. "What if she'd been in an accident while we were both out? But, set that aside for a moment, you're playing with fire. You have no idea what impact this will have on the community. And by the way, we are under a mandatory curfew, one I am legally bound to enforce. You have no idea how volatile and dangerous crowds can be right now. You pervert their religion, and you will regret it."

"Oh, you're suddenly the mind reader?" Meredith grinned.

"I've seen what people can do when they get riled up," Carla explained. "You could be causing havoc by convincing them of your lies."

She suddenly regretted her choice of words when Meredith exclaimed, "It's not lying! It has happened to me! I'm doing this to protect you all! What would you prefer I do? Remain silent? That I simply allowed everyone to walk into a mass grave? Because no one would listen to me about the attacks, everyone that's still here survived by chance. I was the only one who prepared for it."

"For the last time, Meredith, you didn't predict the missile strike!" Carla yelled before dropping her voice so as not to wake Maria. "It's purely coincidental. A strange coincidence, but nonetheless, a coincidence."

"You know what I think?" Meredith said. Her tone was dripping with disdain. "You're envious. You're used to being the golden child, and when suddenly I'm the one who gets some attention, you're wishing it was you."

Carla grumbled, wishing she could shake Meredith out of this craziness. And she probably would have if it hadn't been for the sudden sound of another voice.

"Is everything all right?" asked Joshua as he walked down the stairs.

"How long have you been here?" Carla was perplexed, temporarily forgetting her manic sister.

"I was walking by and saw her leaving the house earlier," Joshua added, pointing to Meredith, who was surprised. "I couldn't convince her to stay, so I came in to keep an eye on your grandmother." Carla started for the stairs when Joshua put a hand up. "Don't be concerned; she's fine." She's just going to bed early. I believe she needed it."

"Well, she's not the only one," Carla remarked, turning to face her sister. "Meredith, please go to bed. We'll finish this conversation in the morning."

"Stop talking to me like I'm a child!" Meredith grumbled.

"I will when you stop acting like one."

Meredith opened her mouth to speak, but Joshua interrupted her, saying, "Why don't you go up and rest, Meredith? You've had a long day."

Joshua's calming voice seemed to reach the young woman, who nodded and left without saying anything more.

"You do realize that will only encourage her?" Carla stated, still enraged. "Do you believe any of this crazy shit she's peddling to people?"

"Carla, *she* has a mental illness," Joshua stated calmly. "I believe in it no more than you do. But what is a fact is 'she' believes it. And nothing you or I can say will ever change it. We must recognize this without belittling it. Who's to say she doesn't have some insight as to what's going on? I mean, have you heard some of the stories out there? Crazy shit, Carla...crazy!"

Carla huffed, "Easy for you to say!" Carla yelled. "You're not here all the time to see her meltdowns. You didn't see that church full of crazies hanging on her every word."

"I'm around here enough to get a pretty clear picture," Joshua explained. "I'm not saying I have all the answers, because I don't. All we can do is provide her with a sense of calm in the midst of all this chaos."

Carla's rage slowly subsided. "I'm sorry; here I am ranting at you when all you've done is help my family."

"Don't worry about it," Joshua said. "It's understandable that we're all feeling a little worn down."

Carla fell onto the sofa, her body spent. "I nearly killed some kids today who were trying to rob an old convenience store." She pulled a pillow up to her face and screamed into it.

"You were doing your job, Carla."

"No," she said, shaking her head. "It's more than that. It...it simply felt right at the time. I didn't give a damn about what I was about to do, just like with Jenny. I feel like I'm losing myself. Every time I leave the house, I wonder who I will be when I return. And what I'll even return to: Grandma or Meredith dead—or something else. We all live under the same roof, yet I've never felt further apart from either of them."

"You're doing the best you can," Joshua remarked, wanting to help but unsure how. He knew his prosaic answers weren't helping, but maybe he just needed to listen.

"I'm thinking about taking up Mayor Cleveland's offer."

Joshua sat down next to her on the sofa. "You do realize what that means, don't you?"

"Everyone's changing, Joshua," Carla observed. "Perhaps I, too, need to adapt. Grandma and Meredith will receive the medication they require, and folks will be fed."

"For now," Joshua murmured, grasping Carla's hand in his. "I believe you need a good night's sleep. If you're going to make that decision, you have to be clear headed."

Carla let him lead her up the stairs.

Chapter Twenty-Six

Joshua slept on the sofa that night, worried his friend might need him. Maybe he was hoping she would. He didn't dwell on it, just liked being around her and doing something useful.

He'd ventured out to the shed for supplies and made breakfast for all of them the next morning, using the last of the bread, bacon, and half a dozen eggs. He chose not to eat, instead concentrating on having enough breakfast for the Garcias.

Carla awoke, smelling the aroma of a cooked meal and enjoying a few seconds of bliss before the memories of the previous day came flooding back.

She finally forced herself up and slipped on her jeans and tee-shirt. Coming down, she was surprised to see Joshua hard at work in the kitchen. He'd nearly seamlessly inserted himself into the family...her family. She wasn't upset; in fact, she'd been the one asking for help—she'd just imagined someone else. Carla briefly imagined a situation in which he lived as part of the family.

"How did you sleep?" Joshua asked, handing her a huge plate that sadly emphasized the smallish portions.

"I can always sleep better," Carla commented as she sat at the kitchen table. Joshua walked over to the sink and poured himself a glass of water. Carla stood there watching the water flow, wondering how many glasses she could get out of the cistern before it ran out.

She looked at him as soon as the tap stopped running and said, "I'm seriously thinking of taking him up on his offer."

Joshua smirked. "Who is he?; The mayor? Carla, your sister has already taken care of the food. For the time being, you won't have to worry about going hungry."

"I know...but it will happen eventually," Carla said. "And, while we may have everything we need now, we can't say the same for the rest of the town." She waited until Meredith had cleared her plate and exited the room before continuing. "And, as much as I adore Meredith, I don't trust her not to do something rash with the supplies. Maybe that's what she's promising her fans."

"I think you should have a little more faith in your sister," Joshua advised.

"That's precisely the problem," Carla pointed out. "Everybody seems to. All the nut-jobs think she is a saint or something. You didn't see what I did last night, Joshua. They were hanging on every word she said. How do you know she won't start handing out food or, God forbid, do something crazy with it?"

"She is the reason you have it, she's not as bad as you think." He dried his hands on a towel and sat down at the table.

"Look, Carla, this is getting to you." He'd always been aware of Carla's stress from caring for Meredith, but the strain was now more visible than ever. He let out a sigh. "If you're going back there, at least let me go with you."

She shook her head. "I couldn't, Joshua. I couldn't," Carla began. "What if something bad happens to you or one of them?" She pointed back upstairs.

"Don't worry," Joshua answered, clearly knowing the answer to everything. "There is a woman named Alice who worked in a nursing home. She is reasonably capable. You would have to pay her in food, but believe me, she is great."

* * *

Later that morning, Joshua approached Alice. He informed her of Carla and Meredith's requirements, and Alice accepted the offer in exchange for several packs of water and some refrigerated meat. Carla could only hope that she didn't ask too many questions about where the food came from.

Joshua and Carla took in the mayhem around them as they rode their bikes along the road. One of the BuilderBots that had once kept sentry on the construction site had vanished. "Kids must have taken the Bots for parts," Joshua hypothesized.

Carla always felt like she was going to Lehigh for the last time when she made the trip. It wasn't all that far, just not an area she'd ever spent much time in.

"Hey, you guys, wait up!" someone behind them called out. Carla and Joshua came to a standstill and turned around to find Carson attempting to catch up to them on his bike, which was hampered by a wobbly rear tire and a huge rucksack on his back.

Carla wasn't surprised to see him because Carson worked so many shifts in Lehigh that he might have lived there. But she felt forced to inquire. "Where are you heading?"

"I'm heading back to work, but I've got a shitload of stuff to take with me," Carson said, motioning to the bag on his back.

"And you couldn't pick a different time of day to travel?" Joshua asked, as if Carson's presence had been preplanned to meet up with Carla.

Carson laughed. "You make it appear as though I have a choice. Chelsea has evicted me from the house. She says she doesn't want anything to do with me. So, Lehigh is my only option."

"You wouldn't have needed to stop in Lehigh in the first place if you hadn't been fooling around," Joshua added. Carla heard the anger in his voice, something that she'd never heard before, but obviously, he reserved it just for Carson.

"Jesus," Carson whispered. "So you know, too. What kind of bug crawled up your ass?"

"If you're looking for someone to blame, go look in the mirror," Joshua yelled.

"Why aren't you stopping her?" Carson asked, motioning to Carla. "She's going to do the mayor's bidding, isn't she?"

"She's doing what she feels she must. I support my friends even when I disagree with them."

"We were friends, Josh. Besides, it takes two to tango, you know," Carson stated flatly.

Carla's cheeks flushed brightly. "I don't want to get dragged into this, you guys. I'm about to make a decision that will make or destroy my family, and the last thing I need is you two competing in dick-measuring. If you can't go two minutes without starting on each other, I'll just go to Lehigh on my own. Does that work for you?"

"Sorry," both of them mumbled.

Both men remained silent until Joshua spoke. "If you're coming with us, we might as well ride on. I don't want to be here when the looters get out."

They rode on in silence, Carla trying to conceal her surprise at the sudden change in Joshua's easygoing demeanor.

Chapter Twenty-Seven

Carla, Carson and Joshua rode on for another half an hour before stopping to rest. Carla pulled Joshua to one side to 'have a word' the way she used to do with one of her students. Carson was busy going through his backpack, making sure he had everything he needed. "Would you mind telling me what in the hell that was all about?"

"I'm not sure what you mean," Joshua said innocently.

"Oh, come off it, Joshua," Carla said emphatically. "I know you're smarter than that. I've never seen you lash out at anyone before. Not even the kids in class who drive you insane. So, what exactly just occurred here?"

Joshua let out a sigh. "I'm not a big fan of cheaters."

Carla took the comment like a slap in the face. "You realize you're lumping me into that category, don't you?"

"I didn't mean it like that," Joshua amended quickly. "Sorry if I offended you."

She waved her hand dismissively. "So, what was the point of it all? As I recall, you two used to be good friends, so what happened?"

Joshua was clearly uneasy saying more. He kept glancing over, making sure Carson couldn't overhear. "He didn't make it work with

Chelsea," Joshua said. "Rather than try to fix things, he simply jumped into someone else's bed."

"You've got to put that behind you," Carla advised. "I'm not proud of what happened...what we did. Believe me, if I could go back and undo it, I would. We're no longer together, but he is still my friend. And it appears that this job and our affair is...costing him more than he can handle right now. He made a mistake, and yeah, now he's paying for it. He doesn't need us to tell him anything he doesn't already know. So, maybe restrain yourself just a little?"

Joshua shrugged and let out a sigh. "Fine. You know I can't say 'no' to you. I'll try and put up with him for you."

Carla touched his shoulder. "Thank you so much, Joshua." She began turning away, then stopped. "Seriously, I'm not sure what I'd do without you."

Joshua wanted more than a touch from her, but he kept his words silent. "Shall we get started? I'm a fighter, but I don't want to put my skills to the test out here in the badlands."

They headed out again once Carson finished his bag check and did a bit of rim straightening on the bike's rear wheel. They passed through the small town of Vineland on their journey. It had never amounted to much, with its closest claim to fame being the location of a massive new P-cell plant. They hadn't completed it in time; it was just an empty shell. Now they saw that Vineland was quickly becoming a smelly, over-crowded refugee camp, luring the desperate out of San Antonio. The occupants were fleeing one bad situation only to find themselves in something even worse. Carla was always alarmed by the sheer magnitude of scents that assaulted her; a mix of wood smoke, sewage, body odor, and decay.

When they were closer, they noticed that small crowds had collected on either side of the roadway, paying far too much attention to the three people on bikes.

"I wouldn't worry about them," Carson explained. "I frequently pass through here. These folks aren't dangerous." Carla wanted to believe it. However, as they went through the neighborhood, she had to admit that the number of observers was increasing rapidly. She began to imagine a future in which her own family might wind up in a camp like this, desperate, hungry, and with no real possessions.

Thick, oily smoke began clouding the path ahead. As the trio rounded a curve, the source came into view. There was a bonfire ahead, in the middle of the road, and a group of desperate-looking people were gathered around it.

There was no other way out of the area. To get through, the three would have to go right by the fire.

Up closer, they noticed guys with rifles patrolling the area, like a little army armed to the teeth. *Could these be the mayor's men?* Carla thought.

Carla and her companions tried not to stare at the men. She wouldn't even make eye contact as they moved around the fiery barricade. Too late, she realized they were being funneled into a gauntlet of gunmen. Dozens of them formed a straight line, blocking their passage.

"What is your business in Vineland?" one of the largest of them asked, his face hidden by a balaclava. There was no indication of rank or uniform, or any indication he was attached to anything official.

"We have no business with you," Carla answered, attempting to appear authoritative. "We're just passing through here to get to Lehigh."

"Nope, can't allow that, sorry," the leader stated. "Only specific personnel are allowed to pass through here, now. So sorry."

"We've got official business with the mayor," Carla insisted, believing she might as well use her newfound position of authority. "I have an official pass."

The leader studied them over and over. "I don't believe you do. Not all of you. at least. Get off your bikes."

"What? You can't be serious," Carson objected.

The commander raised his hand, and his troops advanced, aiming their weapons at the three. "Your getting off, or we'll knock you off. It's all up to you. But we'd rather not waste our time or our even more valuable ammo."

Carla considered her alternatives. They had them surrounded. There would be no way out. "Are you working with the mayor?" She was now convinced this makeshift group of highwaymen were independents.

"That's not your concern," the man said. The road crew lowered their weapons slightly and came closer to Carla's group, jerking the bicycles suddenly to one side, throwing each of them onto the road.

"Hey, what the fuck are you doing?" Carla yelled.

"You're in luck. The goods you carry for your lives. That appears to be a fair trade," the leader replied casually. He motioned for more of his men to get busy.

Two of the smelly men approached Carson and attempted to wrestle the knapsack off his back. "Hey, my whole life is in there!" he said.

Carla, unable to stop herself, grabbed the soldier holding the knapsack. "Give that back!" she yelled. The response was a quick blow from a rifle butt right in the face. She went down hard, blood streamed from her nose, and her lip was split.

"Carla!" Carson gave up his bag and Joshua rushed to her side, shouting in unison.

"What kind of people are you?" Joshua asked in disbelief.

"The kind that survives," the leader answered, as though the answer were self-evident. "You're not welcome in here, friends. You can go back the way you came, but yeah, we're keeping your stuff. And if you like the bitches' martyr attitude," he drew a knife from his sheath, the silver blade gleaming in the light, "we'll gladly make examples of all of you."

Carson and Joshua attempted to stop Carla from trying to get up. It was no use, her fiery Mexican blood was roiling now. She struggled to stand on her own, but once she was up, the world spun around her.

"Here, let me take her," Carson said emphatically. "I'm the stronger one."

"Really? You're pulling that card now?" Joshua objected, but quickly realized it would be better if he had his hands free. There was a good chance they would still have to fight their way out of this mess. "Take her. Guard her with your life, dude," Joshua whispered before turning back to the guards. He was more determined to keep himself between danger and his friends.

Carla struggled but failed to stay upright. She was awake enough to feel Carson lift her into his arms. Then everything went dark. It seemed that even with the mayor's blessings, getting help for her town was not going to be easy.

Chapter Twenty-Eight

Carla had no idea how long she had been out. However, when she awoke, She was still in Carson's arms. And she was well aware that he did not tire easily. She looked up at the moon and wondered how many hours had gone by. Joshua appeared close by, blurry, but unmistakably him. "How are you feeling?" he asked.

Carla had a searing headache and a huge bump where the man had hit her. "It's as if someone tried to crush my skull."

"They might well have," Carson muttered, his grasp on Carla's body still tight. "Animals, the whole fucking lot of 'em."

Then, the prior events came rushing back, and she twisted out of Carson's grasp, almost forcing him to drop her. "They took all of our stuff," she exclaimed. "They took everything."

"Yeah, tell me something I don't know," he groaned. "Everything I owned was in that bag."

"Oh, yeah," Carla said, forgetting that she and Josh still had a home to go back to.

"Can't you just go back to your wife and apologize or whatever?" Joshua proposed.

"Yeah... I've already tried that," Carson confessed. "And right now, I'm not sure whether I'd rather face those thugs back there or my wife."

"So, why did you cheat? I mean, dude, Chelsea is cute. I mean, y'all make a cute couple."

Carla, who was still suffering from a severe headache, berated Joshua. "Are we going to do this right now?"

"It's a long way back to San Antonio on foot," Joshua teased. "We might as well find a way to pass the time. Abusing Carson works for me."

"Jesus dude, why does it even matter to you?" Carson asked bitterly. "Relationships break down all of the time. Few marriages even take out a long-term contract these days."

"That's true, but you still don't rush into another one before the current one is over. That's just wrong. You couldn't have at least tried to make it work?" Joshua said.

"Don't you believe I tried? I tried everything I could to make her happy. But nothing I ever do is enough. I even suggested couple's counseling. But she was insistent that she didn't want a shrink to dig into all her issues. Man, I have no real defense here. I'm an ass, and I know it's worse for you because, well..it's Carla. But she was there for me when I needed her the most."

"Yeah, Carla?" Joshua's comment came off as a shared indictment of both of them. "You're a handsome guy; you could have dated anyone on that street. Why _did_ you choose Carla?"

"Um, excuse me," Carla muttered, forcing Carson to come to a halt as she struggled to stand on her own two feet. "You know, I can speak for myself. I'm not a prize steer at the auction. I was just as much to blame as he was."

"Exactly!" replied Carson, pleased with himself. "And Carla was readily available," Carson added, causing Joshua to grimace. "OK, so hooking up with Carla wasn't the best idea. But guess what? At the very least, I recognized what I desired and pursued it! I mean, if I were you, I'd have spent most of my life pussyfooting around before ever asking her out!"

"What exactly are you talking about?" Joshua asked, his voice seeming very low.

"Oh, come on." Carson smiled. "Everyone knows you have a thing for her. Always have. Anyone with eyes and a brain would know immediately."

"I don't know what he's talking about," Joshua remarked hesitantly. "I believe they gave him a hit on the head as well."

"Guys!" Carla exclaimed, striving to keep walking in a mostly straight line. "Does this appear to be the setting for a fucking love triangle? We've got more important concerns here. Like, what the hell was going on in Vineland? Last week, it was a refugee camp! Now it's armed highwaymen."

Joshua nodded, but realized Carla was suffering more than she was letting on. He moved up close and gingerly put an arm around her waist to help support her.

Carson saw the gesture and smiled. He'd been right about Joshua. Still, that stab of jealousy did arc through his body, seeing the two of them.

"At a guess, I would say our more primal instincts are kicking in," Joshua said, suddenly eager to move on from the previous topic. "People no longer have to be concerned about the police. All they can think about is survival and protecting what is theirs. It makes them erratic and violent. They'll probably attack anyone."

"Do you think they were the mayor's soldiers?" Carson asked, closing the gap behind them.

"I'd like to believe he would look out for his people a little better than that, but I can't think of anyone else who could of organize it," Joshua conceded.

"But Carla and I had official business in Lehigh, we're working with Cleveland," Carson said.

Joshua offered, "Could just be lousy communication. The mayor damn sure isn't coming out here to the front lines to write hall passes. My guess is the man is just barely hanging onto power, and if no help comes, he won't last long. One thing I've learned in life is that you should never underestimate what people in power will do to keep their positions."

"I'm not worried about that," Carson added. "I'm not sure what we're supposed to do when the rest of San Antonio is heading in the same direction as Vineland."

Carla grimaced. Not merely because of the suffering. Carson, on the other hand, had been voicing his concerns for some time. Vineland did represent San Antonio's future. Dog-eat-dog, survival of the fittest. Carla was going to need had to step up her game and decide if she was going to continue being a victim or learn to survive.

"Could someone please tell me what good this doom and gloom is doing for us?" Joshua wondered. "We're too far from home, and we'll be lucky to get back before daybreak. We only have the clothing on our backs."

Carla blinked as he spoke, and looking up, she felt water hitting her face. Thick drops of a hard summer rain began.

"Oh, great!" Carson exclaimed.

"Why don't we try to find someplace to stay?" Joshua asked, still attempting vainly to stay positive.

"Sure, take your pick," Carson grumbled, motioning to the empty buildings around them. They were in an area near the old interstate. Random stores and a few strip malls from a half century earlier. This place had been on the decline long before the war came to town.

"We can stay for a few hours until the rain stops," Joshua said.

The three of them made their way to an old department store. Some of the clothes were still on the racks, as the looters had not yet raided them.

Once inside, the trio constructed a bed out of numerous winter clothes. Carla subsequently collapsed on them. She did like the kind attention she was receiving from the two, knowing that she was not alone in the world. Carla allowed herself to drift off to sleep, giving herself a break from worrying about the future.

Chapter Twenty-Nine

They spent the night in the store rather than risk being caught outside at night in the continuing downpour. "Hey, guys, where is all this headed?" Carla asked groggily when she awoke later.

They'd made a small fire inside the store, the creation of which was its own miracle. The warmth was unnecessary, but the light helped push the shadows back...at least for a while.

They talked for a while, none having any real answers. Carla noticed that Carson was unusually quiet on the subject.

"What's up? Nothing to add?" Carla asked, finally feeling a little better.

"Nothing I should talk about," he said softly as he looked deeply into the fire. "Just stuff I've been hearing, you know. Scary shit. Makes me scared for my kids."

"What kinds of things?" Joshua asked.

Carson shrugged. "Just...stuff. Things that don't make sense to anybody. Guys down at city hall were just repeating shit. Weird sounds in the forest, glimpses of strange creatures. They heard the Army ran into some problems doing something down at the starbase. I'm telling you guys, the world has gone crazy."

"Yeah, I've heard some of that too. " Joshua said. "Some also say that purplish pollen or dust floating around is making people crazy. "

Carla rubbed the raised line on her back, remembering how that other bike ride ended. "We're at war, right? Someone dropped bombs on us, I imagine we did the same to them. Couldn't some of that be like, you know... bio-warfare or something?"

"Those are outlawed, "Carson said quietly. "But hell, anythings possible."

"Makes sense," Joshua said, yawning and lying back on the hard polycrete floor. "Doesn't sound like an invasion force, though. Weird sounds in the forest is nothing new. I'm going to sleep. Wake me up if you see any killer rabbits."

Carla lay there between her two best friends. Her head was still aching but it was more manageable. She felt Carson reaching for her hand. Joshuas's soft snore offered his on reassurance that everything would be okay.

"You alright?" Carson whispered.

She knew the tone of his voice. He wanted her, he wanted to hold her and kiss her and just be close. There was a silent pleading in each word for more. A thousand more words were left unspoken. Truthfully shh wanted nothing more than to hold him close as well but she was seeing him different now. Carson Adams was broken in ways that couldn't be fixed. She had been an emotional bandage for the man and now that she'd ripped it off, she couldn't allow him back in her bed or her heart.

"Good night," she whispered. "Thank you for pulling me out of that mess." She rolled over and pretended to sleep long before it actually took her.

The following morning, they got back on the road. The heat was back, along with the insects and humidity. Carla was still a bit woozy but couldn't stop glancing toward the forest. Something her sister had mentioned kept rattling around inside her banged-up skull. Before heading home, they took a detour to stop by the clinic. "We need to get that head looked at," Joshua explained. "We need to find out if you're concussed or just messed up in the head." She flipped him off.

Carla almost walked on past, not wanting anyone to notice her, but Carson and Joshua were adamant; her well-being was the one thing they both agreed on. So, Carla agreed to go to the clinic if only to keep the peace with both of them.

Betty went out the front as they made their way up the entryway, evidently expecting more patients to arrive for the day. Carla could see the frustration on her face, which turned to concern as she recognized Carla. "Oh, my Lord, honey!" she blurted out as she rushed closer to examine Carla's injuries. "What in the hell happened to you?"

"Armed thugs," Carson said.

Joshua removed Carla's arm from over his shoulder and let her walk on her own with Betty leading the way. "Let's get you all fixed up."

Betty took Carla to the treatment wing, which was surprisingly quiet. "Where have the rest of the staff gone?" Carla asked, half-expecting a rush of personnel to pass her by.

"There aren't many of us left," Betty said, sighing heavily. "I mean...the patients keep coming. More every day. And we're no longer even trying to send them anywhere else. The bigger hospitals are all closed, and now most of the emergency treatment centers are gone. When it slows down, we sometimes go out and search the community for those who have been injured or need medical help. We can't feed them, but we can still do some good."

"So, you're going out on a scouting mission?" Carla asked.

"Basically," Betty replied. "We bring them back here and try to make them feel at ease."

"And there's only you. No one else?" Carla prayed Betty wasn't alone in this desolate structure.

"We have one or two volunteers," Betty stated. "However, all of it, the injuries and the other things, just get too much for some people.

There are only so many people who will die on your watch before you decide it's not worth it."

Carla felt guilty for not returning to the hospital after her shift that day because she couldn't face the reality of what was happening. "So, why do you keep doing it?"

"People talk about things we need, things we can't live without, like food, houses," Betty stated. "But we will always need nurses." She took a deep breath. "However, enough about me. Let's see what we can do to get you fixed up."

"That wasn't too bad," Betty said a short time later. "Not like some of the stuff we've seen lately. Ghastly injuries that... well, I have no idea how they got 'em. Lots of them don't make it. But you, sweet girl, you'll be right as rain. Let me go get those two handsome men to help get you somewhere safe."

* * *

When they returned home, Carla said her goodbyes to Carson and Joshua and went inside, closing the door behind her and cutting herself off from the rest of the world.

She entered the living area to find Maria flipping through photographs.

"What exactly are you doing, Grandma?" Carla asked.

"I'm just looking for some old photos I had of your mother when she was your age." The images were strewn across the coffee table, with no sense of order, just a tangle of recollections, similar to Maria's mental state. "Not many people took photos back then, we'd all gotten used to just using our phones, but your grandad was old school. I'm glad he was, now."

Maria looked up, noticing Carla's bandaged head. "Dear God, Carla, what has happened to you, love?"

"Oh, it's nothing," Carla said dismissively. "I simply tripped and fell. I didn't pay attention to where I was heading." She was afraid to tell Maria the truth about what had occurred. They already had plenty to worry about.

"Your mom was always a little bit of a tumbler," Maria observed. In quiet tones, she added. "I must admit, I'm delighted you returned when you did. Meredith is in a bad way. I tried to comfort her, but she never listens to me, I couldn't get through to her. Perhaps you'll have a better chance."

Carla sighed. "What about Alice? Was she a help?"

Her grandmother just looked confused.

Carla shook her head. Time to take on the role of a responsible adult once more. "All right," she replied. "However, I'm not sure how much good it will do." She climbed the stairs, bracing herself for another round of psychological warfare with her sister.

She was about to enter the room when she came to a halt to listen for any disturbance from the other side. Meredith could be heard babbling incoherently. Carla couldn't understand what she was saying. She could tell, though, she was fully immersed in whatever hallucination was plaguing her today.

Carla gasped as she opened the door, realizing her bandaged head was nothing compared to Meredith's condition.

She sat slumped down on the bench, her eyes wild and frantic, darting back and forth, up and down, as if attempting to capture every detail she could see. Her hair was unruly and dirty, and Carla could see granules of dirt in it when she looked closely. Carla found herself comparing the sight to that of a wild beast digging in the earth, which might not have been too far off the mark.

"What has happened to you, Meredith?"

Meredith glanced at her, and her face broke into a look of frantic excitement. "Carla! Thank God you're here! I had another vision!" She got out of bed, dragging Carla over to sit down. "You need to hear me out on this one, Carla. Ok?"

"Meredith, please calm down. You're letting your imagination run wild, and you're scaring me."

"This is NOT my imagination!" Meredith exclaimed angrily. "I had a vision. It showed me everything."

"Everything?" Carla asked nervously.

"It's all coming, everything that will happen next. Dear sister, you're in the spotlight."

"Me?" Carla said it again. Even though she had never believed in Meredith's visions, the strange synchronicity frightened her. And learning that she had been the subject of Meredith's latest prophecy was, to say the least, unsettling.

"You are in terrible peril. Someone will try to kill you!"

Carla laughed. "I believe someone has already..." She started pointing to her bandaged head. When she started going through it; the militia, the threats to her life, Chelsea, the chance of saying 'no' to the mayor...

It couldn't be a coincidence or maybe it could Honestly she didn't want to believe her sisters 'vision' that in itself didn't make them wrong though..

But it was too late to hide this since Meredith picked up on it and ran with it. "Do you believe it, too? Someone has already attempted to attack you. You won't be that lucky the next time."

"Meredith, you're scaring me!" Carla finally said.

Meredith clasped Carla's hands in her own. "I'm terrified. I'm afraid I'll lose my sister. You are one of the few bright spots in my life. I can't let you go."

It surprised Carla when Meredith started crying. The visions were getting too much even for her.

Carla reached over and hugged her sister, relishing their first embrace in a long time. But she couldn't help but think that this might be one of the few remaining times they'd be this close. Meredith's problems were getting too much and it was guaranteed to keep driving them apart.

Chapter Thirty

Carla was happy for the chance to spend time with Meredith. Most days, her sister seemed to be moving further and further away from her and from reality. So, knowing Meredith was still in there somewhere and holding onto a sliver of who she was, was a big comfort. The prophetic warnings from Meredith were still unsettling. Nothing she really needed in her life right now. Hell, everything was scary out there, why not add the threat of death?

Early the next morning, a knock at the front door roused Carla from a restless sleep. Joshua and Carson were standing at the door, both huddled over several old bikes. "Well, look at you two all chummy again. Where did you get those?" Carla asked.

"It's amazing what you can find with just a little repurposing," Carson said.

"You mean stealing," Carla said, a grin breaking through her bruised face. She pointed to a smaller bike that Josh was holding. "Is that the one for me?" she asked.

"I thought you might want to break it in," Joshua said. "If you're feeling up to it, I mean."

Carla appreciated the effort her friends were making to help her and in trying to get along. She also liked the notion of going on a bike trip that didn't include looking out for road gangs or ending up in the hospital again. The bike ride part of their previous trip had been fun, almost like they were all kids again. "I'd like that," she replied. "Meredith!" she called as she entered the house. "I'm going for a bike ride. Please keep an eye on Maria while I'm away."

Carla heard the smooth click of the gears and suspected Joshua had given her the bike in the best condition. She used to adore riding one as a teenager, getting a sense of independence, feeling the wind rush by, and a sense of freedom she couldn't find anywhere else. After moving here with their grandmother and, in time, getting a license and car, she'd forgotten how much fun bikes were. But, since the attack, bikes had been the easiest way to get around for most people.

"Thanks, guys, this one fits me and works great." She glanced to her right, toward Carson. "Did you find somewhere to sleep last night?" she asked, embarrassed that she hadn't offered to let him stay at her house, even though that might have created its own problems.

"Not really. I did go house hunting this morning," Carson explained. "I discovered an abandoned house." And because I own nothing anymore, I just moved right in. Goober over there helped me find it."

"Really?" Carla was surprised. Just yesterday, the two were at odds, looking for any opportunity to be at each other's throats. They may not exactly be the best of friends, but they were different now. Carla wondered if the brush with those thugs in Vineland had helped change them for the better.

"Have you been able to see the kids?"

Carson shook his head, "No. she won't allow me to get close to them. I know. I could force myself in there to see them. She's not going to call a divorce lawyer, but I don't want to make more of a scene. That would just confuse them even worse. But I will not quit being their father."

"That shit's not fair," Joshua said surprisingly. "Regardless of what happened between you two, you were a good father. I mean you're a dick and all but still, pretty good at the whole dad thing."

"Umm...thanks, I think, and yeah, I think I'm a good dad," Carson insisted. "I adore those children. They need my help more than ever. And I'm not going to let Chelsea use them to hurt me for long."

Carla was well aware that no one could convince Chelsea once she'd made up her mind. She could be as stubborn as she was conniving. But she still felt sympathy for the woman for whom she'd caused so much pain. "Do you think they ate? Chelsea and the kids... I mean," Carla asked, the mental picture of Carson's family going hungry while she had a completely stocked shed at home came to mind. Out of the corner of her eye, she saw Joshua giving her a look as if to remind her not to bring up the matter again. Carson had been kept in the dark about Meredith's doomsday stash, in part because they didn't want Chelsea to find out.

"I don't know," Carson admitted. "I've left what little I can get my hands on at the front door. My rations have increased as a result of my work for the mayor. But I can only give them so much before I go hungry myself. My options are limited now that the food bank has closed. That's why I decided to go full-time with a job from the mayor. To try to gather some additional food to feed my family. And perhaps Chelsea will be able to move on from what happened. I know that's simply wishful thinking on my part. Chelsea has always been the sort to harbor grudges. She never gets over it, she just gets even."

"Wait, the food bank closed? When?"

"Officially today, but in reality, they were out of stock most of this week. Haven't you been to get your box?" Joshua asked.

"Umm...no, I forgot, and I was busy with other stuff." The truth was she didn't need it as much now, but she'd still planned on getting it just to add to the reserves.

"Yep, food is officially gone. Only supplies left require the official approval of the mayor. Now what are the people going to do?" Carson looked out across the ruined city and just shook his head. "What are any of us going to do?"

To Carla, the mayor's offer of restoring the food supply looked like the only option at this point. *How in the hell could she even get over there to make it happen though?*

Chapter Thirty-One

Sounds coming from the lower floor woke Carla. She crawled out of bed and reached for the baseball bat she kept underneath her bed.

She crept down the steps, gripping the bat with two firm hands, wondering why she hadn't grabbed her service weapon, then remembered she'd lost that when the thugs on the road took it. Her first thought was Meredith might be having another of her episodes, in which case neither the bat nor a gun would be the ideal choice.

The sound came again, and now she knew it was coming from the living room. Carla raised the bat, ready to take out all her frustration on whoever it was. It wasn't an intruder. Nor was it Meredith.

Her grandmother, Maria, was staggering around the living room in her nightgown, bumping into furniture, mumbling incoherently, and seeming on the verge of falling.

The bat fell from her hands and clanged off the floor as Carla rushed to the older woman.

The sounds startled Maria, who spun around. Even in the dim light, Carla could make out the confusion on the woman's face. No matter how many times Carla endured these episodes, it always broke her heart to see her abuela look at her and see a stranger.

"Who are you?" Maria asked.

"Grandma, I'm Carla. Your granddaughter," Carla begged, hoping her words might pierce the fog shrouding the older woman's mind.

But Maria's gaze was drawn to the falling bat, and she began to back away from her. "Get away from me," she said, losing her footing as she stumbled against the old mantelpiece.

Carla ran forward to catch her, but Maria fought her with surprising strength. "Get off of me!" Maria screamed as she shoved her granddaughter away.

Carla caught herself before falling, turned, and picked up a framed photograph of herself, Meredith, and Maria standing together when Carla was in her mid-teens. "That's me, Grandma!" Carla said in a reassuring voice while pointing at herself.

Maria studied the photo, running her finger over the picture of Carla. "Santina," she said softly, before looking up at Carla. "If you're not doing it right, you might as well not be doing it at all."

Carla remembered how her mother had told her when Maria had spoken those exact words to her and how she would make sure that Carla would never have to feel that same way. Even if Carla was not the actual target, it still hurt to hear those words.

Joshua came down the stairs, apparently also startled by the noise. They had asked him to stay over for a few nights to help Carla out. As usual, he seemed to know the words to make Maria feel better. Carla couldn't help but be envious of how easy it came to him, that loving quality that made Maria more open. But she was always going to be confused with that 'daughter' who never added up. Maybe this was just Maria reliving the pain she'd inflicted on her own child. That could drive anyone nuts.

"Mrs. Garcia," Joshua began, standing back and reaching out his hand to Maria. "Everything will be OK. It's just an awful night for you." Maria slowly softened and grabbed his hand in hers, eventually letting him guide her back to bed. Carla was left alone and shaken. She wanted to cry, to scream...just release all of her emotional baggage, but she couldn't. The tears refused to fall, and honestly, she knew as bad as it was here, they were way better off than most.

She stayed silent as Joshua walked back down the stairs, straight past her, and into the kitchen. She didn't pay attention to the sound of a kettle boiling or hot water being poured. Carla reconnected with the outside world only when Joshua stood over her with a mug of hot cocoa.

"Here," Joshua offered.

Carla accepted the mug and took a timid sip, the chocolate had a bit of cinnamon in it just like her mom used to make. "Thanks," she replied, glancing at Joshua, who seemed to be increasingly taking on the role of her savior.

"It's nothing," Joshua stated before taking a seat next to her. Neither spoke for a minute, just enjoying the silence. Finally, the man sighed heavily and said, "You guys can't go on like this, Carla."

She sipped tentatively at the now-cooling cocoa. "I know we can't," Carla said, peering inside the cup as if searching for answers. "At times like this, I feel like I should get a NannyBot just for her. Do you think any of 'em still work?" She'd seen some standing silently in the abandoned houses, but those things were keyed to their owners' families. It's not like you could just take one.

"That wouldn't be such a bad idea," Joshua said. "She's growing progressively worse. You can't go on putting out fires for the rest of your life, or hers." He winced slightly at the final two words, knowing what they meant.

"I know that. I guess you know your friend Alice never came back."

He nodded silently. "I'm sorry, but something happened to her. I went to her house, and it was empty. People just disappear now."

Carla sighed in sad understanding as she took another sip and finally began to relax. "You know, we shouldn't be wasting precious resources like this." She pointed at the cup and smiled. "We should only use them in an emergency."

Joshua gave a kind smile in return. "To be honest, Carla, after the week you've had, I think you deserve it."

"How did I not see this?" Carla sighed. "Of course, I missed it. I've been out there putting out fires and getting bashed in the brains for my effort. Meanwhile, my sister is building her own cult, and my grandmother's living thirty years in the past."

"You're too hard on yourself," Joshua said. "Face it Carla, these are awful times for everyone, and your situation is, well...rough. "To be honest, I'm surprised you've managed to keep it together for as long as you have." He picked up the framed picture, which had wound up on the floor. "Who is Santina? I heard your grandmother mention her."

Carla looked off, her face clouding. "She was my mother. She and Grandma didn't get along very well. I think I must look a lot like her."

Joshua pulled the photo closer and nodded. "Sorry, but makes sense."

"I think I need to be around here more," Carla stated after she downed the rest of the drink. "I need to be here to stop all this shit from happening again."

"Carla, you were right in the house when this happened," Joshua stated flatly. She looked at him accusingly. "That came out wrong," he corrected. "What I meant was that her Alzheimer's will continue to act up whether or not you are around. Neither you nor anyone else has any say in it. At the very least, you can focus on finding the stuff you all need to survive. And you're probably one of the only people in the area who can actually provide it."

Carla breathed out and set the now-empty mug on the coffee table. Her bare feet rubbed up the man's leg. "I don't know how I would have survived these last few weeks without you."

They both stared at each other, and for a brief moment, it was as if they were meeting for the first time. Carla had a fleeting glimpse of herself acting on that spark.

She drew back, she knew what she needed, but Joshua deserved more than to just fulfill one sad woman's temporary needs. He wanted her as well. Wanted to wake up every day next to her, but she didn't know if they'd even live to see many more sunrises. She was torn, and he was desperate. It was no way to build a relationship. She lay her head back and closed her eyes. Maybe tomorrow it would make sense.

.

Chapter Thirty-Two

Carla left for work that morning; she'd asked Joshua to stay with Maria and Meredith. The last few times she had gone out on patrol, she felt a growing sense of selfishness. People wouldn't obey the curfew for long, and if the food supplies were indeed gone, it was all going to explode. Survival would be a powerful motivator. Truthfully, she'd had a sense of doom since the very first day; seeing those massive skyscrapers crashing down convinced her that life as she knew it was over. This morning, her thoughts kept returning to her sister's dire warning about her fate.

Carla felt better with Joshua around. She'd never really acknowledged how much she relied on him until recently. He made her feel safe. Maybe even happy. She wasn't sure whether that was love or even if it could be, but she did believe in Joshua. That was enough for now. None of them knew if they had a tomorrow.

Mentally, she had an idea of what resources they had, what she needed to find, and how
long all of it might last. They still had running water, the cistern was getting refilled every few days, but she wondered when the mayor might shut that off as well. Truthfully, the outlook wasn't good,

even with Meredith's stash; that might take a few weeks, maybe a month. Three people, four counting Josh, consumed a lot. Even if they rationed it, how long would it last? That was assuming no one else discovered they still had food, which seemed like wishful thinking. Besides, what were they going to do once it was all gone?

The thoughts were depressing, and she didn't want to dwell on them. The Garcia family wasn't special; every house she passed was dealing with similar challenges, some much more urgent than hers.

A lot of cars were abandoned on the road, and many more were crashed at each intersection. The Smart Road used to control the self-driving vehicles, but after the EMP blast, those that were burned by the batteries exploding stayed imprisoned on the road, everything frozen in time. Would this be the lasting legacy of San Antonio and of human civilization? Miles and miles of ruins and wreckage?

"How are you feeling today?"

The sound of another person startled Carla. Her route had brought her close to the clinic. The nurse, Betty, looked as though she was leaving instead of just arriving for her shift.

"I've had better days, but not as bad as it was," Carla said, recalling the severe headache of the prior night. She stopped on the road, looking off toward the city, before making a bit of a decision. "I was wondering if there was anything I could do to help. To help here, I mean." Carla knew Betty was battling the flood of patients mostly by herself, believing that even if she couldn't fix what was broken, she could at least try. Carla knew that would be a better contribution to society than what she was doing.

"There is," Betty said, pulling on the white jacket she was holding with a large red cross emblazoned on the back. "I was about to leave to see if there were any more patients I could help or convince to get to the clinic. I've turned into an ambulance on legs since the military stopped bringing them to our door."

"Of course," Carla replied, delighted to be of assistance.

"First, let me take a look at that head wound." Betty guided Carla to a treatment cubicle.

She examined Carla's head wounds, looking beneath the bandages. "Hell of a bump," she observed. "However, you must be made of some tough shit to walk away from that kind of hit."

"I've always been hard-headed," Carla said, offering a feeble smile. After she was checked out, Betty offered a backpack of supplies for Carla to carry, and she shouldered the pack, tightening the straps firmly.

"How's your family doing?" Betty asked during the trip, recalling what had drawn Carla into her sights in the first place.

Carla wanted to repeat the typical response, 'They're OK,' but she was tired of lying. She wanted everyone to understand what she was going through. "My grandmother is deteriorating. Last night, I walked down to find her... Well, she had a bad night."

"I really feel for her and you," Betty replied softly. "My mother died of dementia. This was before, of course. She got the best possible care, yet it did little to help. The last few times I saw her, she didn't know me, and she was so angry. She was trapped and stuck in her own mind. And every time I think back, you know, try and remember better times, I find myself remembering only that episode with her. Feeling hurt, frustrated, and not knowing that I was there. I saw her like a light about to go out. That day, I wished that it would. I know that sounds awful, but I was so tired of watching her suffer."

Betty dabbed at her eyes. "Sorry, that was probably not what you wanted to hear. Just know that this disease is a thief. It robs them of their dignity, their memories, and their very identity. No matter what you try to do for her, it is not going to change the outcome."

Carla nodded somberly, her own eyes tearing up now.

"Is there anything your grandma can do to keep herself busy?" Betty asked.

"She used to cook, but no longer, of course. She still has her gardening." Maria was a dedicated gardener who liked to do everything by hand. She had declined to get one of the little residential GardenBots. She insisted on doing it herself.

"If you want, I can always drop by and check on her," Betty offered graciously.

"I'd hate to ask, Betty. You do so much as it is, but yes, if you could find a moment, that would be great."

"With the way things are going, we need to stick together," Betty answered, "And then there are all these rumors about what's to come."

"Oh?" Carla was unsure what the woman was getting at.

"I've heard about the witch. You know, the prophecy woman," Betty said. "A few patients have come in here discussing the end times and what supposedly is coming next. It sounds horrible. If it's true, I don't want to live long enough to find out."

Carla considered telling Betty that this was coming from her sister but decided to save it for later. She didn't want the woman to back out of her offer to check on Maria.

They found three patients within the first hour. All lying in the streets, each had been brutally beaten. There were no bullet wounds on any of them, which calmed Carla briefly until Betty coldly observed, "They probably didn't want to waste the bullets." One was too far gone to help, but the others responded and promised to come down to the clinic later.

It was nearly dark when Carla turned back toward home. She would likely lose the day's rations for helping at the clinic, not that it seemed to matter, but she felt better about herself at least. Killing the girl and realizing how far her moral compass had slipped was taking a toll. Days like today helped restore at least a piece of that.

Turning into her own neighborhood, Carla heard a sound up ahead. She bent low and moved from car to car toward the sound, expecting to encounter looters, but nothing could have prepared her for what she saw.

Carson's wife, Chelsea, was searching through garbage cans, grabbing objects out of them. They appeared to be half-rotten bits of food at first glance. She smelled each, then took a tentative bite before placing some of them into a bag. Others she threw on the ground behind her.

It was a pitiful sight. Carla knew Chelsea was a proud woman. Someone who would rather suffer in silence than acknowledge having a problem. She had assumed that Carson's food would balance things out. However, given that they had two children to feed, they most likely burned through whatever he dropped off rather quickly. Since he'd been robbed the other day, he may not have had anything for them this week.

Carla felt bad for the stockpile of food she was sitting on while this mother rummaged through the trash. A part of her wanted to offer Chelsea help, even though she felt sure the woman would refuse it. Her legs seemed to make up her mind; she shifted weight to a more comfortable position, but she stumbled and fell. Chelsea must have heard enough to realize she was no longer alone.

Instead of coming over to investigate, Chelsea grabbed the bag and ran off into the darkness.

Carla was relieved by her exit but was now even more concerned for the kids. Chelsea was getting desperate, and Carla suspected the woman probably blamed her for everything. Chelsea wouldn't accept any help from her at all, no matter how bad things were. Deep down, Carla felt a real showdown between them was coming.

Chapter Thirty-Three

When she got home, Carla checked on Maria. Joshua assured her that everything was okay and that there had been no other episodes. Meredith hadn't left her room for most of the day but was out back now with Maria. Carla should have felt relieved, but the cumulative effect of everything was really getting to her. Her sister's insane messages were getting out, apparently now all around San Antonio, and Carla knew the rumors of an even more terrifying future would spread like wildfire.

She also worried about the kids next door and Chelsea's scavenging. It wouldn't be long before the woman realized Carla's family was doing better than they were. "You think she's hell to have as a wife?" Carson once told her. "Just imagine how she would be as an adversary."

"Josh, we have to get some food for those kids."

He knew who she was talking about. "That's your call, Carla. Yours and Meredith's, I guess. Tell me what to do and I will, but you know Chelsea will ask questions.

She nodded; it was true. She'd probably toss it out before letting her kids eat any 'Carcia' food. "It will have to be anonymous; she might think its Carson dropping it off. I'll ask Meredith, but plan on taking a box over later tonight. Just knock on the door and run or something."

"Oh, like I am nine. Nice. No problem though. Honestly, Meredith and I had already put a box together a day ago...She seemed to know someone was going to need it."

"That figures."

A knock at the front door set Carla's heart racing. Then she considered that looters and murderers rarely knock. She eased the door open a crack, then wider as she saw who it was. "Hey, Betty, you found the place."

The older woman nodded, but her expression let Carla know something wasn't right.

"What's wrong?"

"I'm going to close the clinic," she said with a firm resolve. Betty's eyes were red. She'd obviously been crying.

"Come in," Carla said, and Betty went in and sat down heavily. The weariness from this brave woman broke Carla's heart. She had given so much, and now it seemed her whole purpose may be disappearing.

"Why?" Carla asked. "Why do you feel the need to close the clinic? Just the lack of supplies?" Carla knew everything had been dwindling.

"It's not just that," Betty stated emphatically. "I've known for a long time that we were fighting an uphill battle. It was under-equipped and under-staffed. But it appears that no one higher up is interested in helping us any longer. Everyone is out for himself.

"But what really hit home was losing the two patients from this morning," she said. "You know, the two we brought back in. They should have been fine with normal care and some nanobiotics, but I was out. Not even any regular antibiotics."

Carla remembered them. They had struggled even getting them

to come in for treatment. Both had severe lacerations and looked bad, but Betty thought the odds of recovery were good.

"Perhaps I could have helped them if they had been in a proper hospital. They would have had autodocs to give them the required treatments." Betty buried her face in her hands, thousands of miles away from the tough woman Carla had gotten to know. "Everyone has a different limit for how much stress they can handle. I guess I've finally found mine. Maybe I felt I could keep the clinic running on just prayers and bandages. Believe me, I would. But it won't be so."

"What will happen to all the patients who are still there?" Carla asked, recalling the rows of sick and injured in most of the rooms.

"I'll have to send them all home. It's all I can do," Betty shrugged in defeat. "They came to us praying for help, I went out asking many of them to come get treatment. Now I'll be sending many of them back out there to fend for themselves. This is the most difficult thing I've ever had to do." She sat back and looked up at the ceiling. The pain etched on her face. "I believe we're all approaching the point where we must make the hard choices."

Carla was well aware of 'hard choices.'

"As long as I can still do some good, I intend to try," Betty remarked bitterly. "I'm sorry. I didn't come here to whine about my problems. I promised you I would check on your grandmother. I may not be able to help everyone today, but maybe I can help one."

"Thank you," Carla said almost reverently.

"It's a nasty thing to have to go through," Betty said. "Watching people waste away when you can't help them. Then you find yourself just wanting it to be over and done with so you can be free of your pain. But having somebody there to lift you up makes the pain a lot more bearable."

"She should be right through here," Carla replied gratefully as she led Betty out to the garden.

"From what you've told me, she seems like a formidable woman, your grandma," Betty said. "Seeing someone who was once so strong become so diminished can make it seem even worse."

"She is...*was* a strong woman," Carla said. "She was a fighter; She took care of my sister and me since we were teenagers. Both of our parents were killed in a boating accident."

"Shit," Betty grumbled. "How old were you?"

"I was seventeen, and my sister, Meredith, was fifteen."

"That's a tough age to lose your parents," Betty said. "Where is your sister now?"

"She's probably in the garden with my grandma," Carla explained, adding quickly, "I should warn you, she's also not quite right. In the head, I mean."

Betty gave a pleasant smile. "I trained as a mental health first responder, honey. Everyone is a little disturbed these days. Trust me, nothing bothers me any longer."

They entered the garden, where Maria and Meredith were both puttering around with the plants, recently dug holes lining one section of the garden. Carla's gaze was drawn to the shed at the far side of the garden, where Meredith's cache was stored, and she was happy to see the door was closed and locked. She didn't want that secret to get out.

"Hello," Betty replied nicely, drawing Maria and Meredith's attention. "My name is Betty. I work at the hospital."

Meredith automatically eyed the woman, skeptically. "Are you a psychiatrist?"

Carla remembered a fiasco when she literally tried to haul Meredith in to see a psychiatrist to discuss some of her issues. Carla grimaced as she recalled Meredith's repeated efforts to bite her. Carla eventually gave up and let Meredith stay in her room.

"Not really," Betty said. "I work mainly as a triage nurse. I'm here to help, maybe give your grandmother a once over. I'm friends with your sister."

"My sister?" Meredith repeated. "You can't believe anything she says. She's a liar."

Betty looked over at Carla, who shrugged as if to say, 'I told you so.'

"Your sister is simply watching out for you, Meredith. You're fortunate to have people who genuinely care about you. I was raised as an only child and would have appreciated having an older sibling to look out for me. Sure would have kept me out of some of the trouble I got into."

"If she truly cared about me, she wouldn't dismiss my visions," Meredith said. Her tone was matter of fact, no doubt that her premonitions were true.

"Visions?"

Carla felt as if someone had lit a fuse when Betty asked. She noticed Betty putting two and two together. "You were the one speaking at the church the other night?"

"That's right," Meredith said triumphantly, relishing the attention that came with her newfound celebrity.

Betty, to her credit, did not back down. Instead, she moved forward, stooping down to Meredith's eye level. "Do you think you could tell me when they started? These premonitions?"

Carla saw how she used her words firmly and with no hint of sarcasm, as if she truly believed in them. Maybe that was Carla's mistake, always dismissing the visions as fantasy, letting Meredith know she didn't believe in any of the nonsense. Perhaps Betty's approach was exactly what Meredith needed. It was good to know that someone was taking her illness seriously.

"They first started before I lost my mom and dad," Meredith explained. "I knew they were going to die on that boat. Even so, I didn't do enough to keep them safe. I've been carrying that guilt with me every day since it happened." She turned to Carla, as if she wanted her to know what she was going through. Carla had often complained to Meredith that she never accepted responsibility, and the words had pained Meredith, making her feel like she had failed at a crucial time. She was curious as to what it meant for Meredith to carry that guilt with her.

"How about your most recent visions?" Betty asked; her words seemed carefully chosen so as to not put the woman on the defensive.

Carla was again impressed with her friend's professionalism and tact with an unusual situation.

"I've seen the sky falling," Meredith added. "I've seen all kinds of horrors shower down, people scurrying for cover. But there is no place to go. Nothing will keep us safe."

Carla listened intently to Betty, wondering if she would believe any of this. "I see," she said. "That must be terrifying for you. To have thoughts bother you all the time. I'm sure you'd prefer it if they all went away."

"You know, I have felt like that before," Meredith replied. "Sometimes I try to tell myself that it's a gift, and that I owe it to other people to share it, to help them prepare. But, to be honest, I miss the silence."

"What about the silence?" Betty asked.

"In my head," Meredith explained, almost sobbing. "Every one of those visions, you know. It can get quite noisy up here." She tapped her brow. "I can't even remember what it was like to have total peace and quiet."

"I'm so sorry," Betty said, expressing genuine sympathy. "I promise I'll do anything I can to help you."

She rose up and turned to face Carla. Meredith couldn't hear them as they walked back into the house. "She requires antipsychotics and sleep aids, neither of which I have," she told Carla.

"Where could we get any?"

"A pharmacy I suppose, or a hospital if any of them are still stocked. I can't get even the basic meds, so I doubt you could find anything that specific. Try looking through the houses you visit, I can get a list of names to look for."

"So, what should we do in the meantime?" Carla asked.

"Set clear boundaries for her. Normally, I would dismiss any discussion of her theories. But if you don't talk to her about them, she can shut down and you'll never hear from her again. She's already demonstrated a modest proclivity for manipulation, withholding information in order to get knowledge. And it appears to run in the family." Her expression stiffened slightly. "You didn't tell me that the preacher in town was your younger sister."

"I-I..." Carla stammered, surprised. "I was concerned that if you knew who she was, you would..."

"Might not want to help?" Betty completed the thought when Carla seemed too embarrassed to. "My name is Betty, and I work as a nurse. My role is to heal, not to pass judgment. I won't lie, it's difficult not to be bothered by what she's saying to me. But your sister is ill. She needs our help, not our judgment. It's really a shame that this new world seems to have no actual therapists."

"What about my grandma?" Carla asked, desperately wanting to move the conversation away from her sister.

"Sorry, yes, let me go back and talk to her," Betty remarked before vanishing back into the garden. Carla wanted to follow her, but she didn't have the strength to face Meredith right now. She watched them from a kitchen window. Betty squatting next to her grandmother asking questions. Pointing at different plants at times. Maria appeared to be responding to the woman's interaction.

Betty returned to the house a short time later, "Today is clearly one of her good days. She sounds forthright about her limitations. That is a difficult thing for most to admit."

Carla was a little surprised, given Maria's normal denial that anything was wrong with her.

"You're doing an excellent job on your own. But she is clearly deteriorating rapidly. I imagine the newness of the way the world is now is probably accelerating the progression. You've been doing everything right with the resources you've had. But I am sorry, it won't be enough for much longer. She'll need round-the-clock care before..."

The nurse couldn't quite bring herself to finish the statement. Carla, on the other hand, was hyper-aware of what was coming. She had imagined the scene a thousand times in her thoughts, as if to prepare herself for its eventual reality. She couldn't count on Meredith and knew she couldn't stay here herself all the time. What was she going to do?

Chapter Thirty-Four

The following night, Carla awoke to the sound of breaking glass.

"God, not again." She desperately needed sleep, but if Maria was at it again—then she considered the even darker possibilities and grabbed the baseball bat. Intruders or an attack on the house. Things like this were becoming more the norm with each passing day.

Creeping silently downstairs, she calmed slightly after hearing more breaking glass and shouting. It was coming from the house next door. The sense of dread came rushing back as she made out the two voices. Carson and Chelsea were going at it. She feared that she was the cause, but just didn't have the energy for this useless drama.

"You've got a lot of fucking nerve showing your face here!" screamed Chelsea.

"It's still my house, and they are still my kids!" Carson's voice was loud and desperate. Carla didn't recall ever hearing that tone from him. She'd seen him upset many times but nothing approaching this.

"You lost your right to see those kids the second you started screwing that whore next door!" Carla visibly winced at the words. Hiding there in the darkness, listening to the two of them, she was overcome with guilt over everything that was happening out there. It was because of her.

"You know what, I could have done a whole lot worse than Carla!" Carson gave a false laugh. "At least she was there for me, there when I needed someone. All you ever did was bitch and complain, always moping about the shitty life you had!"

"I had dreams of my own," Chelsea screamed back. "I sacrificed them all for you! For the sake of you and the kids! I chose to live in this shithole city with all these inbred fucks!"

"Oh, it's always somebody else's fault, Chelsea," Carson shot back. "You look down on people with your high and mighty nonsense, but there are good people here. And I tried to get you help. I begged you to see a therapist, anything to help you out of this funk! I could see how your attitude was affecting the children! Telling Rachel she needs to watch her snacking. Damn, Chelsea, she's just a fucking child!"

Chelsea remained mute, unable to respond. Carson's verbal attack continued. "To be honest, Carla is the only reason our kids aren't more messed up than they already are. She loves them more than their own mother does."

Carla grimaced. "Please leave me out of this," she whispered. She knew Carson was going to pay for every word he said to that woman.

"Get out of here," Chelsea yelled. "Get the fuck out of here before I do something I'll come to regret!"

"It's my house! I work my tail off to provide for you! For the children!"

"Well, you failed. We are all starving, and the kids are no longer your problem! I promise you this. You'll never see them again!"

"DO YOU THINK YOU CAN PREVENT ME FROM SEEING MY KIDS?"

Carla knew he had reached a breaking point without seeing anything. She heard a scuffle, and peeking cowardly through a window, she saw Carson stumble back into the street.

"In fact, why am I wasting my time arguing with you!? Shall we get the whore involved?"

Carla was stunned, fearing what was going to happen next. Carson's battle had spilled over into her world.

Seconds later, as expected, Carla heard the dreaded hammering on the door to her right. The pounding matched what her heart was doing inside her chest. She heard sounds of movement elsewhere in the house. The commotion was going to wake everyone up.

"OPEN THE DOOR, BITCH!" Chelsea yelled. "I KNOW YOU'RE IN THERE!"

Carla might pretend she wasn't at home, but she knew Chelsea knew better.

Carla reluctantly opened the door, bracing herself for the assault that was sure to come. As the door opened, she was met with a stinging slap across the face. Carla stood firm, saying, "That's the first and the very last hit you're allowed, Chelsea."

"I should fucking kill you," yelled Chelsea. "I should fucking burn this house to the ground!"

Carla strode outside, the cool night air damp on her face. She could see them only in silhouette, but she visualized snapping Chelsea in half as if she were a toothpick. Her own anger was rising, and she knew she had to separate herself from this marital mess.

"You leave me and my family out of this," she stated in a much calmer tone than she was feeling. "Your marital problems began long before I entered the picture."

"Shut up, bitch!" yelled Chelsea. "You are a snake, no worse, you are a monster! You do not have the right to lecture me about my family! You messed everything up for me!"

"That's enough!" Carson yelled, moving up between them, attempting to separate the two women. "You know we weren't happy together, Chelsea. Carla is not at fault for this. I tried everything. I tried ignoring it, I suggested therapy, mediation, and God help me, I even proposed a trial separation, but you always managed to find a reason to be pissed off with me when it came time to do any of those things. You have your own demons to fight, woman. I was never your enemy."

Carla wondered if Chelsea was paying attention to what was being said, or if she was just planning another attack.

Joshua tentatively poked his head out, then came out the front door in nothing but his boxers. "What the hell's going on here?"

Chelsea's venomous attacks were briefly silenced by the sight of Joshua. "Jesus Christ, she moved on quickly from you, didn't she?"

"We're not together," Carla stated emphatically. In the near total darkness, she didn't see the pain that remark caused Joshua. "I'll tell you what, Chelsea. I'm sad to hear about what happened with your husband. I am. But I have no control over that. Feel free to hate me, blame me...whatever you need, as long as it helps you move on. Face it, we all have bigger issues now than who is sleeping with whom. You have an opportunity to work on your marriage, both of you. I recommend that you try to do that or split up, but do something for the sake of the kids."

She reasoned that shouting insults at Chelsea would only enrage her. Chelsea, on the other hand, was suddenly deafeningly silent for no apparent reason.

Carson approached Chelsea, took her arm and led her away. "I'm sorry about this," he said, taking one final glance at Carla then Joshua before walking back to his house.

Carla went back inside and leaned against the front door as Joshua shut and locked it.

"Well," Joshua replied quickly. "That was dramatic."

"That woman needs to figure out her priorities," Carla stated. "The world has collapsed. Food is running out. Murderous mobs are on the loose. The clinic is closing, and she's more focused on what her spouse used to do with his dick?"

"She's upset," Joshua reasoned, attempting to stay objective. "Can you imagine yourself acting any differently?"

Carla let herself collapse; her body hunched in a ball against the base of the door. "I know, Josh. At the time, it all seemed like a lot of fun, just a distraction. We didn't consider the ramifications of our actions. God! What have we done to those kids? Carson is losing his children to a psychopath. That shouldn't be happening to him."

"It's brutal, Carla, I do agree on that. Carson is just as much at fault, but using kids as weapons is never right." Joshua looked away, his mind suddenly consumed by a question he'd always wanted to ask. "Do you think you might ever have any?" he asked, taking a seat next to Carla. "Kids, I mean?"

The sudden verbal transition threw her. But then she thought about the question. "People seem to think that because I was a teacher, I'm mom material. Personally, I've never been all that sure."

"Well, I think you are," Joshua said softly. His arm wrapped around her shoulder, pulling her close. "You're fantastic at taking care of people. But the real question is, do you want children?"

It took her a while to answer, her mind was still reeling with all the drama outside. "I'm not sure. I believe I do. But I'm not going to be stupid and just sleep with the first guy I see. I can't even think about anything like motherhood or even dating right now. Not with the situation the world is in."

She felt the man's embrace weaken slightly at the words. She knew it wasn't the response he was hoping for, but she needed some space and perspective on the bigger picture. What she'd told Chelsea was true. They had bigger problems to deal with.

Chapter Thirty-Five

Carla couldn't even bring herself to step outside the house for several days. She told herself it was because she couldn't bear the thought of leaving Maria and Meredith alone, and Joshua seemed to be spending more time away since that night. It was everything, the world, her grandmother's and sister's mental issues, her own guilt over the affair, and shooting Jenny. It was the world out there, and every day it changed a little more. Increasingly hostile and unrecognizable each time she walked out into it. In here, she felt a measure of safety, at least.

She ventured out only once in the middle of the night to place another box of supplies at Chelsea's door. As much as she hated the woman, she couldn't bear the thought of the kids going hungry. That was when she'd also noticed how quickly the shed's supplies were being reduced. They couldn't rely on Meredith's shed to keep them going, and the small garden only produced a handful each day. She needed to get to Lehigh to make a deal. That meant she would also have to try again with Mayor Cleveland. The very thought gave her the creeps.

Carla made up her mind, intent on getting past feeling like a victim. This was something she was going to have to do on her own. Carson needed to make peace with Chelsea. And if she had told Joshua, he would have tried to talk her out of it or insisted on coming. No... this was her mission.

She decided to make the trip on foot this time. She wasn't looking forward to it, remembering the last time she tried to get into Lehigh. She didn't think she would ever go down that road again. This time, she wanted to be smarter. Stupidity was what got people killed. She studied the few printed maps she could find, then made the decision to go through a few of the many farms to avoid the Vineland refugees. She figured it was doubtful that she'd run across anyone out there. The highwaymen were guarding the main roads, but it would still be risky. Carla also no longer had her service weapons, which hadn't helped her much last time anyway. Risk versus reward. If everything went well, she'd have what she needed for the immediate future. But if something went wrong, she'd be... well, she didn't really want to think about that.

Carla set out before the rest of the neighborhood had even gotten out of bed. She reasoned that she was less likely to get jumped at that hour. Nearing sunrise, she made it to the outskirts of the farming district. She was shocked by what she saw. As far as she could see the fields had been burned, nothing but lumps of blackened dirt left in place of the crops. Carla shook her head and began her lonely trek over the scorched earth. *Why burn something that could help keep us alive?* The stupidity just reinforced her sense of desperation.

As she topped a small rise, a shot rang out, and Carla dropped to the ground. Then there was another shot; this one hit something close by. Carla closed her eyes, convinced that this was the end.

"Get to your feet!" The voice came from somewhere on the far side of the field.

Carla rose to her full height, arms lifted, with little choice but to obey. *So much for this being the safer route*, she thought.

Soon enough the man came into view. He was alone, and from his appearance, she guessed he was a farmer. He motioned for her to keep coming. Her eyes could only focus on the huge shotgun he held, casually draping the barrel over one arm. "Don't do anything stupid. I promise you, the next one won't be a miss."

"Look, I'm not looking to cause any trouble," Carla said, attempting to talk her way out of this situation. "I was just looking for a safer way to get over to Lehigh."

The man motioned for her to stop about a dozen yards away. "Why? So, you want to join the rest of the parasites over there?" the farmer questioned her, raising his gun toward Carla's head. "We don't need any more of you over there. That place is already a cesspool." Carla awaited the blast that would end her life.

It didn't come. Instead, the man lowered his weapon and took a tentative step forward, then another. He cocked his head and looked at her strangely. "You're Meredith's sister, aren't you?"

Caught off guard, she fumbled a response. "What makes you think that?" Carla asked, unsure whether her kinship with Meredith might be a benefit or a curse.

"There is a strong resemblance. Both of you are striking women, and well...I've seen that girl up close a couple times lately over at the church."

Carla wanted to roll her eyes. Another one of Meredith's fans. But the man had a gun, and he didn't seem like a crazy end-times zealot.

"I'm Tom," the farmer said placing the gun against a tree and extending his hand. Carla took it cautiously.

"Is this a good thing, or should I start rehearsing my last words?" Carla asked.

"I'm sorry about that," Tom said, motioning to the shotgun. "We get all kinds of people out here. It usually takes a few shots to scare them away. But not so easy when they come in numbers, you know. Besides, everyone who knows Meredith Garcia is...well, a friend. Come with me."

Carla realized that there was something unspoken in his words. She struggled to keep up with him as he began to walk briskly across the field.

"So, please tell me..." he began.

"Carla."

"Carla, what's your business in Lehigh?"

"I'm looking to get supplies for San Antonio."

"San Ann? Haven't you heard; the city is a graveyard!"

"Well, parts of it aren't, and I'm just reaching out for help."

Tom paused for a time before saying, "You're not just trying to be coy, are you? I mean...you're serious? Young lady, Lehigh has no understanding of giving. It all comes down to taking with those people. Believe me, I know." He lowered his head.

"What exactly did they take from you?" Carla asked, already fearing the answer.

The man paused and slowly reached into a shirt pocket producing an old-style paper photo. "This is Anna, my daughter. She's a sweet seven-year-old." Tom's face was emotionless, but Carla could feel the sorrow he'd been through a thousand times.

"I know her!" Carla said. "She was Andrew Naismith's younger sister."

"Yes, she is," Tom sighed sadly. "Her brother couldn't wait to leave here. He stated that he did not wish to spend his life chained to an AgroBot. I wish I had paid more attention to him. J"pained the army tight after school. No idea where he is now.

"Why did they take Anna?" she asked, knowing it couldn't be anything good.

"I'm not sure. The militia or hired thugs simply showed up one day and snatched her away. She cried the entire time. I tried to stop them, but they beat the shit out of me." He looked away. "Pardon my language, miss."

Tom's inability to stop them or even go after her stunned Carla, but she saw the helplessness. She and her friends had been powerless against the mob just a few miles away in Vineland. Numbers and weapons count more than sheer determination these days.

"You couldn't have done anything to stop them," Carla offered. "Guys like that, they're on a power-kick these days. No rules, no law but whatever they say it is. Do you think she's still alive?" she asked, working up the courage to ask.

"I don't know," Tom admitted. "I'd have to believe that she is. After all, why would they take her just to kill her? But I shudder to think what they might be doing to my baby girl. I was told she was being held as security. In exchange for my child's safety, I was to keep my farm up and provide food regularly to Lehigh. All of the neighboring farms were forced to make similar deals. I'm not sure if they'll keep their word. But I can't take a chance without jeopardizing my daughter's life."

Carla felt humiliated as she witnessed the father's anguish. She had been about to join up with a group that could do this. Even with the demands of so many on her shoulders, she couldn't help the mayor. It was extortion and barbaric. Carla refused to even consider helping the evil bastards, even knowing what the alternative likely was.

"What if I go and try to find her?" Carla offered, her newly revised mission becoming clear.

Tom made a shaky motion with his head. "I'd advise you not to. Also, I'd beg you not to get my hopes up. I mean, you're just a girl yourself. I'd get her out of there if I could. But they'd never let me anywhere close. I've tried several times." He moved back and spat into the weeds. "How do you think you would do any better?"

"If I'm lucky, the mayor will let me walk right up to his front door."

This plan did not sit well with Tom. He figured it would be a suicide mission. But if there was even a remote chance of getting Anna back, he would be an idiot not to help the woman.

He dug behind his back and unloosed a strap with a sheathed

hatchet. "Take this, you never know when you might need it." Carla looped the strap over her own back.

She remembered what the girl looked like, so there was no sense in wasting time. She nodded, and he wished her luck as he gave her some advice on the best path to take. As she departed, her footsteps seemed a bit lighter, and she now had a renewed sense of purpose in her foolish mission.

Chapter Thirty-Six

The rest of the journey was uneventful, but Carla's stomach churned with the uncertainty in what she was planning. Still, rescuing Anna gave her a purpose. She began to see why Betty had come to help Maria when she was unable to help all those others. Sometimes you just need a win in order to keep on living. She reached the barricade outside Lehigh and showed her flimsy looking pass from the mayor. The guards waved her through with hardly a word, and then another man directed her to where the mayor was. It was not in the same location as days earlier.

The mayor had taken over one floor of the massive city museum. The space was solid, well-fortified, and much easier to defend than city hall. When she looked around, she saw the real need for such an elaborate space. Every spot was crammed with merchandise. From the mundane to the very exotic. A collection of brand name Smart-Comms, and several commercial food synthesizers, any one of which could feed a dozen or more homes, sat in shipping crates. Carla felt like she was entering a department store when she saw the new Holo-screen TVs all set up in a row. One section held case after case of unused P-cell power units. Other boxes with the logos from arms and ammo manufacturers ran down one entire far wall of the great hall. Then she saw, tucked into an alcove, a half-dozen of the precious, priceless autodoc treatment bays. How many people could these things save every day? The thought of all this loot being hoarded made her sick.

The gap between living in San Antonio or in Lehigh could hardly be greater. She was used to having to make ends meet with what she had, with even the most mundane objects quickly becoming a luxury, but here in Lehigh, they had all the technology and supplies they required. In San Antonio, a P-cell would have to last you for months. And here, one of the aides at a desk was handing them out two or three at a time, like candy.

"I know what you are thinking, Miss Carla," the mayor said, walking up and embracing her with his oversized, sweaty body. "It's no longer enough to simply survive. We must begin to rebuild the world. Everyone in Lehigh is dedicated to restoring their lives. That is where you come in. So let me welcome you to our little community. We are growing, making a clean start— however, we will be forced to make some slight alterations."

"Oh?" Carla asked, her gaze drawn away from a working BuilderBot that had moved inside the museum, its rubber treads squeaking on the polished marble floor.

"Yes, people need stronger leadership, they had far too few responsibilities in the previous world. So many of the populus and leaders, too, wanted something for nothing. A piece of the proverbial pie, but they didn't want to put forth any effort. Our society is filled with takers. We'd come to rely on robots, and the government to provide for our every need. It was time for a change, don't you think? When you think about it, it's surprising that the attacks didn't come sooner."

"But what about all this? Looks like you are a taker as well!" Carla said truthfully recalling those were Tom's words as well..

"I like you," he said, smiling. "You have spirit. Yes, we collected all the truly valuable assets and put them under armed guard because people are stupid. If left on their own, they would steal every last thing, whether they needed it or not. What they couldn't steal or use immediately, they would destroy. We didn't want Lehigh becoming another San An.

"So, you removed the temptation?" Carla asked.

"That's one way of looking at it. Let me break it down for you, Carla. Most people out there aren't going to make it. In three months, possibly eighty percent of the human population will be gone. Find a seat for that little fact. Oh, and those aren't my numbers, those came from the government think tank that met a few days ago. Almost everyone that you or I know isn't going to be around—that's the harsh reality. And yes, I'm an opportunistic asshole, but I had a plan."

"You letting me in on it?" she asked.

He turned to her and smiled a wicked grin. "I am. But trust me—you won't approve. My plan is to get us down to about twenty percent survivor level and do it as quickly as possible. That means most of the people still wandering around, eking out an existence will have to go. Then, and only then, we may have the resources to regroup and, in time, even thrive."

"And those who disagree?"

His smile looked almost feral. "They get invited to join the eighty percent on their way out."

"So, you're proposing sole leadership, kind of your way or the highway?" Carla asked dryly. She was likely being a bit too brave with her questioning, but she found herself genuinely curious. As draconian as it was, he at least had obviously thought it through.

"I prefer 'singular leadership.'" The mayor said it with a smile. "They said you were smart. Carla, I could use more people like you on my team."

Carla could see the hunger in the man's eyes as he got closer. He wasn't just a creep; he was a predator. Girls just know, and she had no doubts about what he really wanted. She forced herself to concentrate on getting to Anna.

He continued, "I've felt something of a connection with you since the first time we met, and I believe you would be ideal to help me rebuild this little corner of the world."

Carla had to use every ounce of control she had to keep her skin from crawling. She could tell what kind of relationship the mayor was really after. It made her feel sick just thinking about it.

"Thank you, sir, I'm grateful for the chance to work with someone as capable as you. I may not agree with everything you are doing, but I can see the logic, and honestly, no one else seems to have any plan at all." The very words left a bad taste in her mouth, but she felt sure appealing to the man's vanity would be the simplest way to get on the inside.

The mayor smiled. He fully understood she was stoking his ego, but he didn't mind. "I understand you used to be a teacher back in the 'before.'"

"I was," Carla said hesitantly, unsure where this was headed. "I've taught cultural awareness and history."

The mayor scratched at one of the fat waddles hanging from his chin. "I'll admit history was always a bit of a dry subject in school to me; so much time obsessing over things that might have happened. I've always felt that people should be looking ahead. When scholars write up the history of this period, it will be interesting to see what they write about us...about me."

If our society survives. Carla imagined the mayor would be a forgotten footnote at best. Just another in a long line of would-be warlord-dictators rather than the leader who saved them all.

She decided to change topics before she got herself in trouble. "Mister Mayor, in light of your 80/20 rule, could I ask about food supplies for San Antonio, or is that a non-starter?" After all, that was the public reason for her agreement to work here and truthfully, even just one of the commercial food synthesizers could easily feed her people. Not the whole city, but some.

The mayor waved his hand dismissively. "Oh yes, I wasn't lying about that, don't worry about it. Everything will be OK. Here In Lehigh, we work on a performance-based system. Since money is well...worthless, we've had to come up with alternative ways to reward, or at times, motivate. No one can simply come here to trade, or believe they can take what they want. We've gone to extremes to gather and protect the resources." He waved his hand around the room. "Not just what you see here either, other facilities as well. See, you have to be able to give back to the community. If you want your credits to help feed other survivors in San An, well, that will be your call. I may not agree, but I also won't object. I feel confident the numbers will continue to drop in spite of your good intentions."

"Coldly logical," Carla replied, dreading the prospect of what he might expect her to 'give back.'

"Teaching is a unique calling, perhaps more so than most people understand. Most schools have gone fully remote or just used AI instructors. You can't really get the full education from a holoscreen. Texas was right to keep people like you in the classroom. Now we must prepare the next generation of innovators and industry leaders. The world will only survive if future generations are willing to save it."

Hearing ideas that Carla deeply believed in articulated through the words of a guy she had every reason to detest was strange. This man was an evil pig, but many of his ideas were on point. She had to give him credit.

"You dislike me," he said coldly. "I get that, I probably would, too, in your shoes. I feel certain I am the last person you want to ask for help from or, worse, be working for."

Carla offered an unconvincing denial. "No, I've...we've just been through a lot out there. I'm not sure I trust anyone anymore."

He held up hands in a placating gesture. "Fair enough. So, tell me, would you be interested in teaching for us at a local school? We've had a few people step up to teach, but none of them have any actual experience."

"Of course," Carla responded. That would probably be her best chance to get supplies and locate the missing girl.

The mayor led her through the city unescorted by his usual cadre of armed goons. She took note of the mayor's lack of fear. If the rumors were true, he'd killed the previous mayor, or had him killed along with countless others, yet he acted impervious to any potential harm. Back home, she couldn't walk out the front door without fearing that each step might be her last. The mayor felt secure in his little enclave and possibly his own invincibility.

She also took note of the local security force and later a group of men walking towards the town barricades; they all wore uniforms that looked similar to the ones who had ambushed her in Vineland. She assumed they were working with the mayor, but it hadn't seemed like it at the time. If she found Anna, getting away might be even harder than she was expecting.

At the small school, they visited a classroom in session. "We're teaching them economics," the mayor said quietly.

Economics? Carla watched the students as they tried to concentrate on the lesson. They all seemed about seven years old. Most were way too young to understand the subject matter. She immediately saw other problems as well: some of the hand-drawn slogans on the wall and a list of homework assignments that included military drills at four each afternoon. She was witnessing brainwashing in action.

"Can anyone tell me what currency Russia uses?" A girl with long brown hair and a pink jumper nervously raised her hand in the air. "Yes, Anna?"

Carla's heartbeat quickened. She knew the face immediately. Carla recognized her as Tom's daughter. She wanted to grab Anna and flee from this place right then and there. Carla struggled to keep her cool. She was here on a mission. And she couldn't afford to become distracted. Turning to the large man, "When would you like me to start?"

The mayor raised a questioning eyebrow. "Your eagerness, Ms. Garcia, is a bit of a surprise. Not that long ago, you would have told me in no uncertain terms what I could do with my offer."

Carla tried hard not to reveal her anxiety.

"But then again, I suppose hunger and fear tend to make everyone desperate for a lifeline. Believe me when I say this, Carla, this is a lifeline—you get one chance at it." He whispered the final part.

"The classroom is my happy place," she said. It was the truth, but the nervousness in her words was evident. Maybe she'd pushed too hard to get close to the young girl. "Also, I've had to do some awful jobs since *The Fall*. Until now, I hadn't realized how much I missed the classroom."

The mayor pursed his lips and then nodded once. "Very well, let's get you settled in somewhere, and you can start here in the morning."

Seemingly satisfied, Mayor Cleveland went to handle other pressing matters. Carla was given a small room; it was too close to the mayor's residence for her liking, and she wasn't given a key. Carla was well aware that the mayor was not just wanting her for her teaching skills. He now saw her as his property, and he could take her whenever he wanted. She'd made a deal with the devil, but somehow, she would make it worth it.

Carla's new career choice began the following day, with a curriculum approved by the mayor. Despite, or perhaps because of, her original goals for being there, she quickly became enamored with all of the children. They had been partially insulated from the craziness out beyond the gate, and she wanted to provide them with the best education possible. That was challenging with the pre-approved curriculum, and she found herself going off script often. That wasn't good when the mayor's goons had a habit of popping in unannounced to monitor the lessons.

She approached Anna several times, as she did with many of the kids. She asked about her family and what life was like before the attack. The tiny girl was quiet on those topics, as if someone had scared her into not discussing them. When Anna did speak up, she was indeed a bright young lady. She had a fiery intelligence far beyond her years. Carla remembered the mayor saying something about preparing the next generation and assumed that was why Anna was abducted. Rather than having a parent or friend come to collect Anna and most of the other girls at the end of each day, she was escorted away by another one of Cleveland's men, an act that worried Carla and complicated the meager plan she was attempting to build.

Over the coming days, she found herself also becoming very attached to one little boy in particular. It wasn't that unusual; children are just little humans. Much like in adulthood, you find personalities that you prefer more than others. In every class she'd ever taught she would have a few favorites. It was inevitable, and Jackson quickly became hers here. Jackson was direct and seemed to hold a wisdom and possibly a sadness much greater than someone of his few years. His parents were gone, murdered, she later found out. She'd also been informed in no uncertain terms that he was the mayor's ward, so he was supposed to call Cleveland 'Uncle,' and get special treatment in class.

Carla didn't do favors, nor did the boy seem to want any. He was whip smart and seemed more interested in the other kids' success than his own. She wondered how or why Jackson's parents had been killed, especially when she learned they'd ran the local pharmacy. They probably didn't take kindly to the new mayor's acquisition rules.

Chapter Thirty-Seven

With all of the armed guards on patrol, it was tough trying to do anything discreetly, but Carla had finally seemed to earn a bit of trust from the mayor and his goons. She was frantic with worry about her family but had to believe that Joshua would watch over them. The note she left for him was both sweet and hopeful. Still, he was not much help against the mob. She had to get back there and check on them. That was part of her problem. Whatever actions she took here would likely get not just herself killed but maybe her family as well. Even if she got away, Cleveland knew where she lived. He would send guards there immediately.

A week after arriving in Lehigh, she learned where Anna was being held. Anna wasn't a prisoner, as such, but lacked any sense of freedom. Carla had already determined that sneaking her out during class was a non-starter. Armed guards surrounded the compound most of the day. Her evolving plan, if you could call it that, involved getting her from her room quietly and then making a break for the woods. Jackson had also given her a well-done hand-drawn map of the town as part of an assignment. It showed, among other things, the location of his family's drugstore. The store was another of the mayor's holding vaults with sentry guards at the door. The mayor had total control over what was given out. One of the school's instructors had informed Carla about a diabetic who required insulin. However, because she was only a Level 2 citizen, which Carla had learned meant part of the mayor's eighty percent, rather than the required Level 4, she was refused the meds and died a short time later.

One day, Carla was about to leave her apartment when the door opened unexpectedly. It was the mayor, who appeared slightly disheveled.

"I understand you've been avoiding some of my guards on the escort home," he remarked, and Carla could smell whiskey on his breath even from a distance.

He'd come alone. He didn't want an audience to accomplish this night's goal. "I don't always feel comfortable being surrounded by so many people," Carla managed to say. "I can take care of myself," she said nervously.

The door was blocked as the mayor moved closer. "Okay, I get it, Señorita. I've known many women who just keep their mouths shut and their legs wide open. That is one way to get by in this world. But you...you have fire, I see it in your eyes. That appeals to me in a woman. Someone who does not easily fold."

"Well, that's very good to hear," Carla answered, slowly backing away from the man. She needed to get out of here, he was screwing up her planning.

"You know," he continued, his words garbled slightly. "I used to be a bit of a softie. I was deputy mayor at the time. I used to have to take my level of shit from everybody. The old mayor saw me as his lackey, someone to make him look good and clean up his messes." Cleveland edged back and shut the door without breaking eye contact.

"When the attacks came, I realized that this might be my chance. "At first, I thought the old man might have been killed. He was over in his place in Apex towers when the bombs fell. Of course, I didn't get that lucky. I know there are rumors about what happened there, but he got out somehow." Cleveland removed his sport coat and threw it on a chair and began unbuttoning the sweat-stained shirt.

"Yeah, bastard survived. Not sure how, he was one of the few, but he came out with just a few bruises. I was sitting in his chair when he surfaced a few days later. I'd already organized the patrols, blocked the roads, and secured all the vital infrastructure. You see, while the mayor had been out shaking babies and kissing hands...or whatever, I was in charge of all the real shit. I organized a minor mishap that very afternoon to rid me of the mayor and his crone of a wife. They really should have shut the gas mains off on that street."

The news was supposed to shock Carla, but given the mayor's willingness to go to any lengths for power, it didn't. She knew where this was heading, though, and it was a price she was unwilling to pay.

"Look, I've got to go," she said as she approached the door, but the mayor grabbed her arm.

"You think you're something special, don't you?" The mayor scowled. All attempts at decency were abandoned. "Well, I remember you when you were a hungry girl hunting for food. I told you your value would depend on your service to the town, and by town, I mean me. Nobody, least of all Mexican trash, says no to me."

She was slammed against the wall and then the smelly man was all over her. Ripping at her blouse and feeling up her breast. "Get off of me!" Carla screamed in alarm. He supported her with one hand while struggling to undo his belt.

"So, you're just a simple rapist," she yelled. "That's your idea of leadership?"

She fought him off the best she could, but she was no match for the large man's brawn and determination.

"Best give me what I want, girlie. Otherwise, I might have to take one of your little students instead."

The image of Anna flashed through her mind, and she lost all concern for her own safety.

She stopped fighting the man and let him pull her jeans down, then her panties. She felt his fat hand grabbing at her vagina as she fought back the tears. She could get through this, she was tough. It would be over soon.

Her thoughts did not calm her. This wasn't something she could simply endure. She needed the food, the supplies, and had to get Anna away, but letting this man take her was not an option. It was, however, a scenario she'd thought about several times already, and she was not unprepared.

He leered up at her, then removed his fingers and smelled them before dropping his own pants.

She raised her hands in apparent surrender to the man. Then smoothly reached her own hand down the back of her shirt and yanked on the lanyard.

Her arm raised back up high as the mayor stayed focused on inserting himself into his prize. She swung down with ferocity, burying the hatchet into the back of the man's skull with a sickening thud.

Instead of falling, he stood straight, then staggered back in horrified disbelief, unable to conceive of what had happened. His eyes became unfocused, and he dropped to the floor in a crumpled heap.

"Welcome to the eighty percent, you fucking pig!"

She didn't know if he was alive or dead, but Carla was too stunned to do anything smart like check for a pulse. The bastard had been intent on raping her...then what?

Realization hit her with fury. A flood of emotions, anger, guilt, and fury. She had murdered a man. And not just any man, but the man who had complete control over everything in the area. Still, she had no regrets. Not like shooting Jenny. Ridding the world of this evil prick was a mercy killing.

"Fuck, fuck, fuck..." She quickly pulled up her clothes and watched the spreading pool of blood around the man's head. There would be repercussions for this. She didn't know who would be in charge now, and she didn't much want to wait around to find out. She had to speed up her plan, adapt, try and get the girl, but could she do it before they started hunting her? Her sister's premonition might just come true after all.

She went to the bathroom to get all the blood from her body, She removed her blood-soaked jacket and dumped it in the garbage. She washed her face and hands again, then pulled her hair back in a long ponytail. Slowly, she started getting her shit together, but she hardly recognized the woman staring back at her in the mirror.

She went back to the mayor's body and searched his pockets. As her fingers curled over a set of keys, she felt a wave of triumph. She made herself pull her weapon free of the man's body. She was repulsed at the bits of meat and bone clinging to the bloody steel. She cleaned it as well as she could and secreted it away once more.

The day before, Jackson had told her everything about the building that housed the other kids. It sounded like something out of a nightmare. It was an ancient basement, and the structure was deteriorated and beyond repair. The guards, according to Jackson, escorted them to and from afternoon military drills which were mandatory. They kept the youngsters under lock and key and when they brought them back later, they would have food and blankets, sometimes a few other supplies.

Carla estimated she had just over twenty minutes to get there and get the kids out. It was one part of her plan but shouldn't have been the first. Slipping out of her place was easy. The mayor hadn't even left a guard downstairs. She blocked her door as best she could so they wouldn't easily find the body, but that would only last so long. Someone surely saw him on his way to Carla's. She dashed over to the other building, her lungs on fire, knowing she was racing not just for her own life, but for the lives of everyone else.

It took her precious minutes to find the right door to the basement. Her hands were shaking violently. The adrenaline and endorphins flooding her system made it impossible to concentrate. *Calm the fuck down. Deal with it later.* She tried again with the rusted lock that finally accepted one of the numerous keys, having gone through several before hearing that click.

Carla swung open the door to discover all the kids inside a cramped, dusty room covered with cobwebs and smelling of feces. All of the kids were gathered together. She couldn't tell if this was for safety or comfort. They were all looking up to her, and she could feel the horror in their eyes as they imagined what would happen if they stepped out of line.

She had to get them all out. That hadn't been part of the plan. Not really, but in truth, she knew she had to. Every child here was being held against their will. What these people were doing to these children violated every fiber of her being. Carla meant to slip in quietly, grab Anna, and sneak away. Instead, she had a dead mayor and a group of children who suddenly saw her as a source of renewed hope. Carla swore at herself. She couldn't abandon them in this city.

The trance they were in seemed to break at once with many of them talking excitedly and yelling her name.

"Shhhh! Listen," she said emphatically. "We have to get out of here! Now!" None of them moved.

She lowered her voice to an ominous tone. "How many of you want to die down here?"

It was cruel, but she needed them to move their asses. "Let's go!"

The children stood up and began to exit. "Keep it quiet." Carla pulled Anna aside and said, "Listen to me, I'm a friend of your father's. I'm going to take you home, ok?"

She picked up the child and rushed past the others "Don't go for the roadblocks, instead go for the fields. You all grew up on the farms, right?" They all nodded. "You can lose them in the fields. You continue running, find your house and don't look back. The mayor won't be bothering your families anymore."

The kids nodded and hurried away in small groups. She desperately wanted to accompany them all and ensure their safety. But she had to finish what she had come here to do.

She went to the drugstore while carrying Anna. Carla should have been relieved that it was unguarded. She wondered if they were all waiting for the mayor's instructions. She dashed inside, opened her backpack, and began stuffing it with every anti-psychotic drug and sleep aid she could find. Carla was struck by the irony of the scenario. Jenny Harris had been in the same situation a few weeks before. Now, would she be executed for doing the same crime?

A sudden shriek brought an end to her shopping spree. It was the city-wide klaxon, the mayor's body... *had it been found so quickly?* She imagined the guards scouring the city for the murderer. Carla knew if she didn't go now, they wouldn't have a chance.

She and Anna dashed outside, only to find Jackson standing there with his own backpack.

"I figured you had a plan," he said. "So what did you do?"

Carla panicked, "Out of the way Jackson."

He shook his head, "I want to come with you."

Chapter Thirty-Eight

Carla felt the pressure, as if the universe was continually putting new obstacles in her path. The mission began as a simple job to earn some food and maybe get the meds her family needed. Then there came Tom and his desperate plea to find Anna. Killing Cleveland hadn't been part of her plan, but then again, neither was being raped. There were countless things in this town that she and her own community desperately needed, yet all she was taking were some meds and two small children. One of which was the mayor's ward—whatever that meant.

"OK," she responded, setting Anna down and taking the two kids' hands in hers. "Do you understand how you stay close to me no matter what?"

They both nodded, "Listen to me. If I go down, just keep running. Run until you get to your dad's Anna. Do you hear me?"

The little girl was crying now, but slowly nodded. Jackson gripped Anna's hand protectively. The three of them took off running. She was counting on most of the security to be massed at the common area near the school, so they avoided that. Carla knew it wouldn't be long before the men had the entire town covered. She slipped down an alley between shops and came up short as a guard stepped in front of them.

"Whoa! Where do you think you are going?"

Carla's mouth was frozen, she couldn't form words.

"She's our new teacher," Jackson said. " She doesn't know where the shelters are."

The man gave a near toothless smile. "Gotcha, yeah, it gets a little confusing."

Carla wanted to reach for her hatchet, but something made her slow-walk that idea. The man's posture was relaxed.

"What's going on?" she asked.

"Some ruckus off to the southwest toward the Space Force Base. It sounded like a war or something. Seems to be heading over toward us. The boss men are trying to find the mayor now to find out what he wants us to do."

The man told them to hurry to the shelters. Carla couldn't believe their fortune. So, they weren't hunting her...not yet. The trio dodged other people running in all directions, then edged past a gap in one of the walls and made their way unnoticed out into the burned fields. Carla noticed several of the school children vanishing into the distant line of trees. She wondered what would happen to them all and if she'd made the right decision in sending them off on their own. It was risky, but she imagined most of them making it to their farms, reunited with their families. She had to have hope, and it wasn't like she had any time to come up with anything better.

She heard shooting several times, possibly back in Lehigh, but like the man had said, it seemed farther south. They rushed through the fields, each of which was bordered by trees and fencing. They seemed to stretch on forever. She assumed guards would be unwilling to chase them all down, likely more interested in getting their share of the mayor's loot. Still, she felt sure some would come for them, they just had to be ready. Her legs kept trying to give out and more than once she felt herself falling, only to catch herself. She was not in a good place...not mentally or emotionally.

It was totally dark when Tom's farmhouse finally came into view. Anna quickened her pace. "Dad!" she exclaimed, rushing ahead, Carla and Jackson fighting to catch up.

Tom emerged from the farmhouse. He saw his little girl running towards him. He snatched her in his arms and held her close. "Dad," she wept. She'd never expected to see him again.

Carla held on to Jackson as they held back, giving the two as much space as they needed.

"My sweet, sweet girl," Tom said softly, clutching her close. After several minutes, Tom looked up at Carla and Jackson. Tears lined the older man's weathered face, "Thank you," he said softly. "I don't know how you did it, but thank you."

Carla offered a grim smile and nodded. "You...you're so welcome," she whispered, delighted to see something good come from the horror of the day. Truthfully, she wanted to savor the moment as long as she could, because she knew the feeling wouldn't last.

The farmer seemed to finally see the expression in Carla's face. "What happened, child?

She shook her head as the tears began to fall. She looked to the kids, and Tom seemed to understand. He approached Carla, innately sensing the trauma she'd been through. He pulled her close as he would have his own daughter.

They were both crying now, and Carla was surprised how much she needed this connection right now. She was surprised she would let anyone touch her.

"I am truly sorry, Carla. Please tell me you made him pay."

She sniffed and nodded but was unable to speak. A smell of food caused Carla's stomach to growl loudly.

Tom gently released her. "Come on. You've had a long day, you must be hungry," Tom murmured as he cradled his daughter in his arms. "Come on in, I'll make us some supper."

Carla, Tom, Jackson, and Anna sat down to a literal feast by current standards: roasted pork, potatoes, homemade bread, and simmering pots of vegetables. Carla loved the simple smell of home cooking.

"I tell you," Tom declared after the meal, "thanks to you, a lot of parents around here will go to bed a lot happier tonight."

His words made Carla feel good. But now that the adrenaline had worn off, she couldn't help but be concerned about the long-term ramifications of her actions.

"What do you think will happen regarding the mayor?" She'd told Tom everything, once the kids moved into a den to play.

He shook his head, "Hard to say," Tom said. "Guess there will be a power vacuum of sorts, and nature abhors a vacuum." Carla worried if Lehigh would turn into a pit of vipers or maybe vultures all squabbling over scraps. Then she considered the museum full of treasures, wondering if all those objects might end up destroyed, like Cleveland had said, or just wind up once more in the wrong hands.

"So, what happens now?" Carla asked, cautiously.

"Now?" Tom stated this with newfound zeal. "Now," he said with energy she'd not seen in him before, "we figure out how to keep you and your community fed. I have fields aplenty, and in time, you will have access to all of the food you need. I owe you, miss."

Carla was overwhelmed by the thoughtful gesture. "Are you certain, I mean you...you can do it? I'm grateful, but I've seen the fields outside; they're nothing but ash."

Tom gave a big grin. "I expected you to say that." He got up from his seat. "I'd like to show you something."

He led her out behind several barns to an enormous greenhouse. "This is constructed of Armorglass, the strongest stuff available. It cost a fortune to install and was a pain in the ass to even get, but given that it withstood a near miss by a tornado and then the missile strikes a few miles away, I'd say it was a great investment."

He proudly showed Carla row after row of beans, tomatoes, peppers, and more. Most were on large vertical trays that he could move down for picking or replanting. The entire thing was ingenious. "All grown from non-hybrid seeds, so we can replant, should be sufficient to help feed a small community, which is exactly what we will be able to do. I'll be able to send you some food back now. I know a farmer nearby who sells cows, so we'll be able to send you milk, cheese, and butter."

"In exchange for what?" Carla asked. Nothing in this world is free. The past twenty-four hours had driven that fact home like a dagger to the heart, or... a hatchet to the brain.

"You gave us more than just our children, hon, you have given us hope. That was something we didn't have before. This is the least we can do. In timem we'll work out a barter system or have you select people to come and help us out. Without the bots, managing this and the fields is going to be monumental." Tom's expression darkened somewhat. "How about the boy? Is it true, he's orphaned?"

Carla hadn't considered what she would do with Jackson. Like everything else she'd done today, she'd just winged it, it wasn't in the plan. She was aware that his family was gone, and he obviously had no desire to ever go back to Lehigh.

"He is, but he'll come home with me," Carla said, the idea just occurring to her, but she was confident she could take care of him. She literally turned down the idea of starting a family just a few days ago. But despite the horror and bloodshed, Carla now had a spark of something, maybe a belief that she could finally dream again.

She spent the night in Tom's spare bedroom. He said he had an old bunkhouse out back, but it needed to be cleaned out. Jackson had slept in a separate bed in the same room because he didn't want to be alone in case the 'bad men' came to take him away. Despite all the past twelve hours had brought, Carla got the best night's sleep she'd had in ages.

When they left the next day, there was a basket of food, and Tom promised to talk with the other farms about offering more supplies to her neighborhood. Carla was greatly relieved to know that she could help provide for her little corner of San Antonio. She might also be rid of the shame she'd felt over the stockpile of food in Meredith's shed. Still, they had to be watchful. The mayor's men probably knew where she lived. They might be waiting for them already.

Carla took confident strides back toward her house, the sun high in the sky, as Jackson grasped her hand tightly. Both seemed excited to see what the future held.

Chapter Thirty-Nine

Carla and Jackson got home a few hours later. They snuck through yards of vacant houses and surveilled the street and the houses before approaching. Carla had only been gone a little over a week, but it felt like much longer. She worried about her family and Joshua, too, if she were being honest. It surprised her how quickly all the concern over their issues had slipped to the background over the previous few days. Carla was constantly worried about Meredith having an episode or Maria losing more of her memory, but with everything going on, she'd barely had time to think about them.

She found Carson sitting on the curb, looking as deflated as she had ever seen him. "Are you all right?" Carla asked, still feeling sorry for him. But all those feelings now seemed to occupy a different place inside her. Maybe she was just no longer the same. Cleveland had robbed her of the last few shreds of youthful innocence. Honestly, she just didn't have time for the drama. People had real issues, and her neighbors' marital shit barely qualified.

"I've had better days," he said. "Chelsea hasn't completely shut me out. It turns out she does still like feeding her children and herself."

"So, what's the problem?" Honestly, she no longer cared, but it seemed like he was waiting for her to ask.

"Problem is, I am a lousy provider when I'm not with you. Everything has been stripped bare. I haven't eaten in days."

His eyes landed on the boy.

Carla held up one of the baskets of food Tom had given her, her conscience gnawing at her. "Well, maybe this will help."

Carson's mouth dropped open as he gazed up at the food. "My God, Carla, tell me I'm not hallucinating."

"That's my sister's department. I just get food." She said with a laugh as she slid the basket into his lap. "Does this feel like a hallucination?"

He shook his head. "What exactly did you do for it?" Carson asked. His gaze shifted toward Jackson again. The concern evident on the man's sunken face.

Carla refused to tell him, or who she had to killed in order to get it. She shook her head, "Maybe someday, but not right now."

"I can't accept this," Carson murmured as he pushed the basket back toward her.

"You are an idiot, Carson. Is there a reason why, or am I supposed to guess?"

"Chelsea will refuse anything from you."

Something snapped in Carla's brain. "If you're telling me that bitch would rather see those kids starve than accept any kind of help, she doesn't deserve to be a mother...or even to be alive."

"Whoa, whoa, whoa, OK!" Carson said this while holding out his hands and taking the basket again. "What's the matter with you? I've never seen you with that kind of fire before."

"Just be a man, Carson. Go be a dad." Carla was dumbfounded. All she had been through, and this spineless lump wouldn't do the very basics to keep his kids alive. Carla had been through much too much in Lehigh. She had changed, she just wasn't positive it was for the better. She was capable of brutality, vengeance...hell, anything that was required. Now she knew she was also intolerant of those who couldn't step up.

"I'll get this to the kids," Carson straightened up and returned his gaze to the window in his house. Rachel and Ryan were peering out the window, taking in the panorama. "You know, they miss you. They want to see you again."

She missed them, too, but worried that she was the reason their family was torn apart. "Yeah, I don't think so. Not with Chelsea around," Carla acknowledged.

"So, who is this?"

Carla saw Carson was looking at the boy. "He's Jackson, and he's going to be staying with us."

Carson looked bewildered but struggled to his feet. "We all were worried, I just... " Carson murmured, "I missed you so much." And before Carla could stop him, he held her tightly, and she didn't have the heart to push him away.

It didn't last long, but Carla broke the embrace when she saw Jackson standing behind her. The poor boy had been thrown into an entirely new world and needed someone to guide him.

Carla stepped back from Carson. "Don't ever do that again," she said. "Whatever you and I had is over. The world has changed. And so have I."

A visibly chastised Carson hung his head, then took the basket and silently headed toward home, where he would almost certainly face the wrath of his wife once more.

"Where do I fit in?" a tiny voice asked.

Carla smiled and knelt down to eye-level with Jackson. "You're coming to live with me," she stated. "I will look after you."

"Are you going to become my new mom?"

She'd forgotten just how direct he could be. The question nearly broke her. She didn't want to tell him that she would be a lousy replacement for his real mom, but she would do her best to try. Carla didn't respond, not with words. She simply hugged him, giving the boy the comfort and tenderness he'd been denied since the murder of his parents.

* * *

"Hey, everyone, I'm back!" she exclaimed.

Meredith descended the stairs, her usual frown dissolving as soon as she saw Jackson. "Hello!" she said with a smile. "Who's this?"

"This is Jackson, and he needs a family."

Joshua walked in, taking in the sight of the newcomer. "Whose kid is that?" he asked, his voice colder than normal.

"I brought him back from Lehigh," Carla said. "He's going to be living with us."

"I've got some toys he can have," Meredith remarked enthusiastically as she took the boy's hand and led him upstairs. Carla grinned. Meredith's childish nature would make her a perfect companion for Jackson. She'd always seemed to connect with children better than with adults.

"Lehigh." Joshua said in disgust. "So, we're just taking in strays now?" he asked, somewhat agitated.

"What's gotten into you?" Carla asked.

"What happened to me? Carla, you've been gone for over a week. It wasn't like I could call you and ask how you were doing! I had no idea if you were living or dead! Then you bring that kid home with you. We're already having difficulty feeding ourselves. We don't need another mouth to add to that."

"Quiet, Joshua!"

He kept talking, and she put her hand up. "Shut The Fuck Up!"

He shut up.

"I couldn't say no, Joshua. The mayor murdered his parents and then kinda adopted him, and honestly, if it wasn't for the boy, I would have never gotten away from there."

"Shit," Joshua mumbled, embarrassed by his callousness. "I'm truly sorry." Then self-preservation kicked in once more. "Wait, how do you know the mayor won't come after you and burn this place down?"

"He won't. Believe me." That didn't mean his guys wouldn't, but it wouldn't be the mayor.

"Carla, what exactly happened out there?" Joshua asked nervously. He also sensed that his friend, his crush, had changed. Something terrible had happened to her.

"It doesn't matter," Carla answered as she held up the bag with the drugs. "Just get these to Meredith and Maria."

"Jesus Christ!" exclaimed Joshua. "What exactly did you do? Rob a pharmacy?"

"Something like that," Carla responded, smiling at how right on the nose he was.

"Carla, I'm a bit concerned," Josh said. "How can you be sure the mayor won't show up here looking for these drugs or the boy? Does he know it was you?"

"It's not going to happen, Joshua," Carla said emphatically.

"How do you know, Carla? What would stop him from raining hellfire down on us?"

Anger flashed across her face, causing him to take a step back. "Because he's already dead!" Carla exploded.

Joshua turned white. "He's dead?"

Carla let out a sigh. "Yes."

"You?" Josh asked softly.

She nodded. "He didn't take no for an answer, so I drove an axe through his skull."

Over the next few hours, she eventually told him everything that had happened over the previous week, everything she had witnessed.

Joshua was astounded. "Carla Garcia, please remind me never to piss you off!"

Chapter Forty

"So, what will you do with the rest of the medicines?" Joshua asked. "I'm sure those two won't need all of these."

"I'm not sure, I hadn't actually thought that far, I was in a bit of a rush. Maybe give them to Betty so she can keep the clinic going a while longer," Carla replied. She knew they needed way more than the stuff in that bag, but it was a start.

"And then what? What are you going to do when they run out next time?" Joshua asked.

"God, Josh, you are exhausting. Complaining or asking a bunch of questions is way easier than finding a solution." She needed to think that her actions had resulted in some good and that things would improve, even if it was just temporary.

"So, how long is Jackson staying with us?" Joshua asked, his voice more subdued now.

His words this time were not unkind, but Carla saw through them just the same. "Us?"

"I mean...I mean, you guys. I know I'm just a guest."

"He will be here as long as he needs to be," Carla stated emphatically. "He needs to be with family."

"But Carla, you aren't his family."

"And you aren't ours, but we still love you, we still need your dumb-ass around. I may not be the boy's family, but he needs me to be."

Loud knocking on the door cut the discussion short. Carla rolled her eyes, wondering what Carson had done now.

But it wasn't Chelsea or Carson. Betty was there, but she was no less furious than Chelsea had been a week earlier.

"What have you done?" she screamed. Carla took a moment to register the woman was angry, with her.

"Come in," Carla offered, and Betty walked right past her. "What's wrong? What has happened?" She looked at Joshua. "Please go get Betty some water."

"Betty, can you tell me what happened?" Carla asked as Joshua handed her the glass.

Betty took a hesitant sip and nodded. She was calmer, but her face was still red and puffy. "It began last night. It had been quiet since most of the patients are gone now, and I was sleeping in one of the treatment beds. Anyway, I had an awful dream. I guess it really shook me up 'cause when I mentioned it to one of the other volunteers, you know, Nancy, the heavyset one, she said, 'The skies will rain down on us, showing us a thousand horrors to come, the likes of which have only been seen in the land of demons.'"

Carla was certain that was one of Meredith's standard bits about one of her visions.

"You can't be this upset over a...a bad dream."

Betty shook her head, "It was just a precursor. There was the sound of engines, the old kind. Then a crash outside. We feared the clinic was being attacked. Then gunmen stormed the building."

Carla's stomach sank.

"They came for what few medical supplies we still had. Everything, from the alcohol to the bandages to the mattresses and blankets. They left us with nothing. Our last doctor attempted to stop them but was beaten senseless. He still hasn't regained consciousness.

'Blame Carla Garcia for this,' they yelled before leaving. 'We'll kill her when we find her.' And just as quickly they were gone."

Carla was afraid she was going to get sick. She should've anticipated the far-reaching implications of her actions. Some of them knew she had helped out at the clinic. She should have known.

"What happened, Carla?" Betty asked. "What did you do to bring those thugs to our door? The clinic is gone now, completely."

Carla was at a loss for words. But she knew she couldn't keep it quiet for much longer. "I...I killed the mayor," she stuttered, like a parishioner going to confession. "I killed him and stole all the medicine I could find before returning here. I also set free a swarm of children he had kidnapped and was holding prisoner."

Carla was astounded by how cold it sounded. She was casually describing a murder of a man. One which had put their already feeble way of life in jeopardy.

This absence of emotion did not escape Joshua or Betty. "Do you have any idea what you've done?" Betty asked, her voice painfully weak. "Our last doctor quit because he didn't want to deal with those people ever again! Do you believe you've helped any of us? All you did was put a giant target on our backs!"

"Hold on," Joshua said. "Those men are beasts, Betty. You've heard about the mayor shutting down the clinics and hell, just about everything else just so he could be the one with the best toys at the end of the world. If they didn't screw us over today, they'd screw us over tomorrow. Carla has gone through a lot in the last few days. But she did it because she wanted all of us, including yourself, to have a future. Just like you, this woman has contributed to the survival of this community. She's had to make the hard decisions so that we don't have to."

Betty was still visibly upset, but she couldn't bring herself to curse Carla. She was weighing what the young woman had gone through in order to get some medication for her family and the clinic.

"So, what are we going to do now?" Betty asked.

"We fight...we live," Carla stated firmly. "That's all we have.

There are those out there who rely on us. We must keep them going. I've got some things going that should help. I'm looking into establishing some regular trading. It won't fix everything, but hunger should be much less of a concern."

Carla waited for a response as she felt the world just squeezing in around her more and more. One thing after another.

Betty stayed silent, contemplating all of their predicament. She suddenly tensed as she sniffed the air. "Are you cooking something?"

"No," Joshua answered. The two exchanged glances in the direction of the backyard. There was a distinct odor of burning.

Carla ran to the kitchen to look outside. "Oh, no!" she yelled, sprinting out to the garden, Joshua close behind her.

A pillar of black smoke rose into the air from a massive fire. The storage shed was the source, and none other than Chelsea was maniacally dancing around it, carrying a fuel can, almost in a trance.

When she turned back, Carla and Joshua were staring at her in disbelief. Chelsea, on the other hand, smiled broadly at their reaction.

"Do you think you can take my man and avoid the consequences, bitch? So, what do you think? You are free to have him. However, I'm not sure what you're going to eat. Your entire family is going to go hungry now, just like mine. And there is nothing you can do about it."

Chapter Forty-One

Not only were the shed and the stored food being consumed by fire, but it seemed like many of Carla's hopes and dreams were going up in smoke as well.

Chelsea was on the ground thanks to Joshua. She battled him like a caged animal. She screamed and scratched, one of her long nails cutting deeply into his cheek.

"For God's sake, knock it off, woman!" Joshua yelled.

"Let her up."

"Huh?" Joshua looked at Carla. "Seriously?"

Carla nodded. Her fury was white-hot now. What this woman had done was searing through her body, and she needed the bitch to pay. If she were honest, Chelsea had always intimidated her, but now, Carla saw her for what she was. A psychotic manipulator... maybe even a psychopath. Shit, you had to take a number in this neighborhood to try and be the craziest.

Carson's wife charged. Carla leaned out of her way, then drove her knee into Chelsea's thigh while battering her face with an elbow strike at the same time. The woman let out a shriek of pain as blood sprayed from her nose.

Carla dropped on top of the larger woman and pushed a forearm into her neighbor's throat. In that moment, she wanted her dead, but she saw Jackson watching her and imagined Carson's kids in the next yard. She released her grip and leaned over her prey. "You ever fuck with me or my family again, and I will end you, bitch. I will help Carson get his children as far away from your evil ass as I can."

Chelsea was ignoring her, so she grabbed her thick blonde hair on both sides and pulled her face close. "Are you fucking hearing me?"

The woman didn't answer immediately, so Carla twisted the hair in her grip even tighter.

"Owww. Yes, yes. Now get the fuck off me," Chelsea whimpered, trying and failing to retain some level of victory.

Carla stood angrily and looked at the shed, now fully engulfed in flames. She wondered briefly if she could hurry inside the shed and save anything. They had nothing to put out the fire. What little water they got each day was too precious to waste.

She looked back down where Chelsea was wiping her bloodied face. Then Carla drew back and kicked her in the head. Chelsea was out...or dead. Carla didn't care anymore. This was her own backyard. Not Lehigh or the downtown of San Antonio. Nobody had the right to fuck with her here. She felt the now familiar weight of the hatchet on her back. It was such a temptation, but she visibly pushed that hatred back down. Jackson, Maria, Carson's kids, she couldn't become more of a monster—not in front of them.

Meredith was the only one who seemed unaffected by the loss. Carla noticed the strangeness of her expression as her sister glanced down at Jackson. "I could see this happening," she remarked, talking to the young boy. "And so much more. Of course, no one believed me. They all felt I was insane and needed to be restrained and silenced. But if this doesn't persuade them, I'm not sure what will."

"For fuck's sake, Meredith!" Carla screamed, her patience with the craziness all but gone. She took a pill bottle from her pocket and hurled it at Meredith. "You're scaring Jackson! If you want to believe in this ridiculous nonsense, that's OK! But I'm not going to let you scare the boy! Take those pills and get the fuck over these damn hallucinations!"

"But they're not hallucinations!" Meredith screamed back. "They're premonitions! And you don't really want them gone because you have a constant need to save me! Besides, I know down deep—you're just jealous!"

"Are you serious?" Carla asked in disbelief. "And is this the time for this discussion?"

"I'm aware that I've always been the black sheep. You are the golden child. They loved you best."

"Who?"

"Mom...Dad. You never did anything wrong! But I was always unwelcome. Mom wasn't ready to have another! I was just an accident!"

Carla could see Meredith was spiraling out of control. It wasn't losing the supplies as much as coming to terms with her own self-worth.

"Even Maria hates me! She only wanted you when they died, not both of us."

"She's never hated you!" Carla spoke as she moved closer.

Meredith shook her head in denial. "You think I haven't seen how she looks at me? Maybe she's right, and I could have helped Mom and Dad. I tried though...I warned them. I've spent my entire life feeling like a fucking loser. I love you, but I know I'm just a burden. Carla, I'd like to do some good for once! But you won't let me. You don't believe in me."

"Meredith, all of this is not about you. Take the pills and go lie down." Carla eyed Betty silently pleading for help.

"What's going on?" Carson yelled as he came running toward the fiery scene, seeing the condition of his battered wife, who had regained consciousness and was again being restrained by Joshua.

"Your idiot wife decided to kill us all!" Joshua yelled as he struggled to keep the insane woman under control. "She set the whole damn thing on fire!"

"Chelsea?" Carson asked, stunned, as she trembled in Joshua's clutches with animal violence. "What have you done?"

"They have been storing food in the shed!" Chelsea yelled, spitting out blood and saliva. She wormed a hand free just as Joshua subdued her again. "They had loads of supplies in there, while the rest of us were left out here begging for scraps!"

Carla suddenly felt every eye on her.

"Is this true?" Carson asked, obviously confused by the twisting realizations. "Who did this to her?"

"None of your business, Carson, no one else's business, and thanks to your crazy fucking bride, it no longer matters. And I did that to her face, and I may not be finished."

"So, it is true." Carson said in disbelief.

"I was...we were going to tell you about it," she says, "but..."

"Oh really...when? After we'd all gone hungry?" Carson's voice was also now filled with bitter anger.

Carla stomped over and slapped her ex-lover in the face. "For the love of God, Carson, cowboy the fuck up. Maybe we wouldn't be in this mess if you remembered where your balls were instead of tiptoeing around your lunatic wife." Carla moved off a step and rubbed her eyes. "I suggest you collect your kids and find someplace to start over. You all need to forget this treacherous pile of human misery.

"And yes, you've been eating some of that food as well as your kids. Where does she think the mysterious boxes were coming from, the food fairy?"

Carson's cheeks burned, more with shame than the slap. He opened his mouth to say something, but Chelsea's frantic struggles stopped him, and he stared down at the woman. Joshua had snatched an old piece of rope from somewhere and was now binding Chelsea's wrists.

"Get her out of my garden, or I am going to plant her beside the beans," Carla growled.

Carson nodded and walked over to Chelsea, who appeared close to having a complete breakdown. "GET YOUR HANDS OFF ME!" she yelled as he forcefully drug her from the yard toward their own house.

Betty stood there, gaping at the spectacle. "I feel like I've just stepped into a soap opera."

"She's just overreacting because Carla slept with her husband," Joshua said as he stood up, seemingly surprised he had just said that out loud. "Shit, sorry..." he grumbled as he moved back to try and contain the growing fire.

Betty eased up beside Carla and took her hand. "To summarize, you've got a dead mayor, angry militia after you, a burning shed full of food, and now your role as the concubine is catching up with you, and your sister is an oracle of the future. Is there anything else you want to tell me?"

Carla was at a loss for words. Her entire world seemed to be collapsing around her. She'd felt so good coming home with Jackson, like finally they had a chance, a fresh start for everyone, but optimism seemed to be nothing but a curse in a world that wants you dead. She smiled at the woman and nodded. "That's about it."

They heard a loud thump in the distance.

"Jesus, what next?" Carla groaned.

Chapter Forty-Two

Carla felt certain that everyone in the area had seen the fire and would be drawn to it like moths to a flame. And with Chelsea's shrill voice carrying so far, it wouldn't be long before everyone knew about the Garcia's secret stash. The sounds in the distance were getting closer.

"What is that?" Joshua asked.

Carla shook her head. "I'm not sure, but it can't be good."

Maria had come outside during the fiasco. She seemed dismissive of the girl fight, obviously just concerned with her garden. The shed had scorched much of it already. "Betty, can you help me get her back inside?" Carla asked.

They did, and Joshua followed them in with Jackson. The boy tugged on her sleeve, and Carla knelt down. "I'm sorry you had to see that," she said, genuinely disgusted with herself and how badly the day had deteriorated. She wanted the boy to have a safe place to live...a better life. Yet, her home was obviously as fucked up as the rest of the world.

He ignored her apology but glanced out the window nervously. "We need to go."

The words stabbed at Carla. She'd promised to keep him safe, and already she was assuming that she might have to fight off neighbors tonight. They would have seen and smelled the fire. That was probably what was coming. They were probably all half-starved and would be pissed that she'd been holding out. None would accept that it wasn't even hers to give away. She was part of the patrol, supposedly someone they could trust. Someone who might help.

"Why do you think that, Jackson?"

"Bad men coming. I want to go back to Anna's house."

Carla couldn't help but be enraged, but not at the boy, he was innocent, but at herself and the world outside these doors. She had done everything she could to help her little piece of San Antonio. All the sacrifices she'd made, shit, the lives she'd taken, all for the sake of keeping others alive. To give them hope for a better tomorrow. And now she'd arranged a trade deal that could benefit everyone. Betty was right, though, everything she did just seemed to screw things up even worse.

Joshua moved closer. She saw him shake his head. "Don't doubt yourself now, Carla." In a whisper, he continued. "You're in charge, though. We do what you say."

That was just it, she had no idea what to do. She was the one putting them all at risk. If they went with her, they would all be targets, yet she couldn't just abandon them all. "Fuck!" She looked down and apologized to the boy.

Carla wondered whether she could persuade these people to see her point of view. This was home, none of them would leave willingly. Her top priority was to keep Meredith, Maria, and Jackson safe.

She heard Meredith yell out from somewhere outside. "They're here!"

Maria stared blankly, past Betty. "Was there a cookout? I smell a campfire."

Carla stood and eased over to the front door and cracked it open. What she saw terrified her.

"No...no...no!" It wasn't Cleveland's militia. No—the mob had found them. Many held lanterns and torches. The scene reminded her of villagers coming to blame the local witch for their bad luck.

They weren't attacking, though. They were not shouting protests. Mostly, they stood there in an orderly group near the edge of the yard. In the flickering light she began to recognize some of them. She'd seen them before, many of them from the church, all listening in rapt attention to her sister's ravings.

And there Meredith was, right in the center of the gathering, definitely getting the attention she apparently craved. Carla was slowly coming to terms with the fact that this really was her sister's mission in life. There was nothing she could say or do to pull her away from what she was doing. The crowd obviously loved her and needed to hear whatever Meredith was saying.

They are as crazy as she is. At least they didn't seem to want to burn them out of their house.

Joshua spoke up, "Yeah, she's been gone nearly every night you were gone. I heard she was, you know...doing her thing at the church."

Jackson had slipped out the door behind them. The small boy had wormed his way through the group to Meredith's side. He clutched her hand as if it were a lifeline, in the midst of the adoring mob as it shifted and moved like a living entity. Carla was thrown off by his attachment to her sister. They had obviously formed a bond in their brief time together. She knew he was very bright, but pairing up with Meredith didn't seem to fit. He obviously had no clue what was going on around him, but then again, neither did Carla.

She'd promised Jackson that she would take him away from the horrors of that town and offer him a more normal childhood. Instead, she had delivered him into the clutches of insanity. She pushed her way through the pressing mob. They all seemed to want to get closer and closer to Meredith, and the grunts and complaints as Carla moved toward the middle was nerve racking. The press of bodies, the smells, all of them in this rapturous fever dream. It was all just too much. Her hand finally reached the boy. He seemed frozen to her sister's side, but slowly he nodded and allowed Carla to lead him away from the group.

She took the child back toward the house, where Maria stood watching from the doorway. "Grandma, please get him back inside," she said. "Both of you go to your bedroom, close the doors, and don't open them for anything."

Carla wondered how clear-headed her abuela was right now. But the older woman looked down at Jackson and nodded wordlessly.

"Come on, Joshua," Maria whispered to Jackson as she led him upstairs, and Carla shook her head, understandably worried. "It's Jackson, Grandma. The boy's name is Jac..." She gave up and went back to the window.

Betty eased the exterior door closed, then turned to face her. "So, what now?"

"I don't think we can stay here," Joshua said. "Maybe my house for tonight, but after that..." He shrugged.

"I still don't understand why you brought all this on us," Betty said as she sat heavily on the old sofa.

Carla didn't want to explain herself again, but she needed them all to see the seriousness of the situation. "First of all, all that is not me." She waved a hand toward the street. "I have no fucking clue what that is.

"Secondly, the mayor, had to go. I'm sorry if it makes things worse, and it definitely wasn't my plan, but the man was evil. I'll admit that getting the food and medicine was my main goal. I didn't think things through, but when I saw everything that bastard was hoarding, I kinda lost it. He had several autodocs just sitting there collecting dust. Imagine what that could do for the clinic."

"And the only way you could get them was by killing the mayor?" Betty asked. "I understand you were thinking about us...about your family. But, if you hadn't killed Cleveland, the clinic might still be open."

"You already said you were closing; you were running out of everything."

"What we were in desperate need of was doctors!" Betty was adamant. "Do you believe they grow on trees? No one is going to step forward now and try to help if they believe they may lose their life as a result."

"Carla was trying to help," Joshua insisted, "Those guys would have eventually bled us dry. It was never a question of 'if' but of 'when.' They would have left us with nothing if we had given them enough time, Betty. And I think deep down, you know that. She definitely did some fucked-up shit, but I guarantee she did it for the right reasons. Yes, it may make it worse in the short-term, but she did a good thing, and it couldn't have been easy for her. She barely got away with her life."

"You know, I want to buy into that logic, but you don't need to take up for your friend. She is obviously very capable of that herself." Betty's words were dripping with sarcasm.

"Unfortunately, I have my own responsibilities," Betty continued. "People out there still need our help." As if on cue, a disjointed singing started from the mob. "People are going to die without real help. It will be your fault, Carla. If anyone dies because the clinic is gone, that is on you."

Carla refused to accept the woman's skewed logic. "I did everything I could to help people. That's something I won't apologize for. I'm working hard to ensure that we have a future worth living for."

"With what?" Betty yelled. "Your mission to set up some kind of trade with Lehigh certainly isn't panning out."

"I made a deal with a group of local farmers, so we will be able to feed some of these people in the meantime."

"And what about the mayor's private army?" Betty asked. "Do you think that just because you cut the snake's head off, they'll turn around and never bother you again?" Some asshole like him will always be out there. You take him out; another will step out of the shadows. And the next one will almost certainly be even worse."

She wasn't wrong, Carla knew that. "The other option is to roll over and give up, Betty. And I'm not going to let anyone put me in the ground without a fight."

Betty looked down at the floor and gave a grim smile. She did admire Carla's spirit in the face of adversity. "If I were you, sweetheart, I'd look to get your affairs in order. Those goons are coming. They will track you down, and by the time they're done, no one will be able to find what's left of you."

There was a loud noise outside. A sound they all assumed they'd never hear again.

Chapter Forty-Three

Carla knew of only one group that still had functioning vehicles. The soldiers from Lehigh.

She looked again outside at the large crowd making up her sister's cult. Why are they here? she wondered, as well as what they would do if the militia guys started shooting. They might support her sister, keep her safe, but she doubted it. More likely, they would flee in every direction. Carla needed to keep all of her family safe.

"CARLA GARCIA!" someone yelled. Carla already felt there was no way out when a masculine voice added, "If you don't come out here now, we'll burn down your house with you and everyone else still inside. You murdered our mayor, released all the brats, and now you are going to see how we treat traitors."

Betty had been right; they were after her. She had to hope that if she walked out there herself, they would allow the rest of her family to live. She wasn't about to do it unarmed, though. She had no illusions of living through this, but that didn't mean she wanted to commit suicide. Carla was about to arm herself when the realization hit. She no longer had her gun. She didn't have any kind of weapon, except the item hanging from her back still on the lanyard. It wasn't much, but it might help.

Betty walked up nervously and handed her something black and heavy. "You're going to need this."

Carla felt the weight, it was an old-style handgun. Stamped into the barrel were 'Glock' and '9mm.'

"Do you happen to have a cannon hidden somewhere?" Carla cracked a joke, trying one last time to be funny...to be brave.

"Sorry dear, it's all I've got," Betty said, shrugging. "You have eleven rounds in there, just pull the trigger. Make them count, hon. I'm...I'm sorry I blamed you. Your young man is right. I know you were just trying to do what was right.

"You can't seriously be thinking about going out there," Joshua yelled from his hiding spot by the window. "They will kill you on sight!"

"This is my mess," Carla said. She was attempting to get her nerves under control.

Maria appeared in the doorway with the boy just behind. "I thought I heard singing. Now, who's that yelling outside? Are the neighbors fighting again?"

"No one, Abuela, just go back to your room. Someone out there I need to talk to —that's all."

"Okay, honey. You sure?"

"Yes' ma'am." Carla went and hugged her grandmother tightly, knowing it was likely the last time. She had a lifetime of words she wanted to say, but instead, she just held her a moment longer and then directed her back up to her bedroom.

She then bent down to Jackson; tears filled her eyes. "This isn't what I had in mind for you. Look," she said coming up with a new plan for the child. "I want you to slip out the back and hide somewhere. Make it somewhere really good, okay?"

The little boy nodded. "If me or Meredith don't come find you, you may have to go back to Mister Tom's farm by yourself. I won't be able to help you anymore." The boy reluctantly followed her outstretched hand toward the back door.

Josh...if I, you know," Carla started, turning back to the others.

"Oh, no," Betty responded as she shook her head. "You're not getting off that easily. You've helped create this shitstorm, and you need to figure out how to make it right. And how can you accomplish that if you're dead?"

"And I'm right there with her on that one, Carla," Joshua said. "You don't have permission to die. Besides, I'm going with you."

The call for her to come out came again along with loud shots from some of the others. It sounded like her personal mob was ready for the lynching.

Josh had also produced a weapon. She'd never known him to handle guns, but apparently, he had one stashed away. Betty was soon holding a long kitchen knife. They were preparing for battle. "So, basically," Carla sighed. "A team of very pissed off heavily armed soldiers is pitted against two women and a gym teacher. And we're expected to be victorious?"

"I'm sure the odds could be worse," Joshua commented. "Besides, I was a very good gym teacher."

"Well, thank you, thank you, both. I would never ask you to do this, but I do appreciate it." Carla's legs refused to move, but finally, she took a step towards the door.

Joshua's hand blocked her path, "Wait! Carla, there's something I need to tell you before we walk out there."

Carla, knew exactly what the man wanted to say. Even though Joshua had never said the words aloud, she had always known.

Betty became aware of the situation. "Do you plan on making those your final words, Romeo?" she asked with a grin.

"Save it, Joshua," Carla said, clutching the doorknob.

"But...I might not get another chance!"

"That should motivate you to get us through this in one piece," Carla stated flatly. The man on the street yelled more urgently for her to come out. She could see firelight coming closer to the house. Her confidence faded as she turned the knob and slowly walked out.

The church congregation remained in the streets, protectively encircling Meredith and providing her with cover. There seemed to be even more of them now.

The military truck was parked in the center of the road, with the mayor's men positioned to the front and sides. They all held long guns, rifles, and shotguns, Carla guessed.

She stepped out, the pistol tucked behind her back, "Listen!" she said, taking a cautious step forward, arms raised high. "I'm the one you're looking for. You have no cause to harm anyone else here. Please let them go!"

The man leading the assault was leaning out of the hatch on the top of the truck. He remained stationary, his gaze fixed on Carla. "You don't get it, do you? It's not about what you did to the mayor. Look around you. Others will try to seize control. And obviously, you already have quite a following."

Carla wanted to correct him, let him know they weren't her people, but maybe this error could work in her favor. Meredith's people clearly outnumbered the armed men. The man whose name she finally remembered, Kincaid, kept talking.

"All these people may follow you. But that's the beauty of heroes. They make excellent martyrs." He leveled the rifle at her, and she began to reach for her own pistol when a bullet ripped through his shoulder. Blood sprayed in a wide arc, and his weapon clattered off the vehicle and into the street.

Carson was standing there, gun in hand, pumping shots downrange as fast as he could cycle the weapon. It was brave, but it was suicidal. Several more of Kincaid's men went down before they could even turn toward the gunman. Carla couldn't believe what she was seeing. Carson had stepped up to be the guy she had always asked him to be. Her own pistol joined in the fray and shot one man under the chin. He went down less than two yards away from her.

Then she heard her sister's voice and almost as one, her followers yelled a bloodcurdling battle cry and charged the soldiers. The crowd had not been unarmed, for now they all seemed to have machetes, sharpened tools, even one with a hunting bow. They were unified in their purpose, and the armed militia never had a chance. A few of Meredith's people were cut down, but they inflicted much heavier losses against the soldiers.

The battle had briefly swung in Carla's favor. Kincaid, who was now clutching the bloodied stub of his arm, blew a whistle. Headlights lit up the street farther down the block, and her heart sank as she saw even more troops heading toward them. As the streets were filled with the remains of followers, the soldiers' fury and sheer firepower began to tip the scales in their favor.

Carla had been firing and pivoting and hadn't noticed Kincaid had drawn a handgun and had leveled it shakily towards her. She swung hers up to shoot, but she was too slow. Before she got the man in her sights, she heard the shot and fully expected to feel the burning heat as it seared through her body. Instead, a bullet ripped the man's jaw clean off, and he fell onto the hood of the truck, gurgling blood out the gaping slash as he died.

Carla turned to see Joshua clutching the pistol. "I told you I'd have your back," he said grimly.

Along the corner of the house, she saw a small figure mostly in shadow. "Oh, God!"

"What?" Joshua asked.

Carla pointed, "It's Jackson. He didn't hide."

They were both taking cover behind the front of the massive truck now. The skirmishes had broken up into many smaller battles, but getting Carla was still clearly the main focus. "I got him!" Joshua yelled before sprinting off toward the boy. Bullets fell like rain, but somehow, he made it to the corner of the house.

Another shot rang out before Carla could protest. This time she felt the heat of the bullet as it grazed through the tender flesh of her neck. As a trickle of blood began to flow, she screamed in pain and clamped a hand to it. Her other hand shakily held the Glock, but nothing was happening. Her eleventh round had already been fired.

"NO!" Carson screamed as he raced towards Carla.

"We got her!" one of the remaining soldiers yelled. "We've got the bitch!"

Carla's scream had broken through to Meredith who'd been absorbed in the fight but not actually a part of any of it. "Carla!" she yelled. Despite the visions of Carla's death, Meredith couldn't bear to see another family member gone.

Meredith wasn't the only one who heard Carla scream. Maria was stumbling out of the house, seeming to have forgotten what Carla had told her. "Santina....Carla, darling?" she asked absently. "What's going on?"

"Grandma, get back inside!" Carla yelled as the firing began to subside slightly. She had no idea how seriously she was wounded but felt the blood seeping around her fingers. "I'll be fine," she reassured Carson, "It's not serious." In truth, the pain was firing through her like lightning, but she was ignoring it the best she could.

A lone soldier noticed Meredith racing towards Carla as she approached the front of the truck. He opened fire.

Meredith felt a brilliance coursing through her. She knew with perfect clarity this was the moment she had been anticipating her entire life. Tonight, she would die in order to preserve her sister's life. Her life's purpose was about to be realized. While she'd seen fragments of this night and told her flock about its inevitability, this part was new to her. She felt no sadness, only exhilaration. She understood that death would be what finally brought her the peace she so desperately wanted. As she ran, she waited in nervous anticipation for the life-ending impact... *that never came.*

Instead the round from nervous soldier missed her, but it did strike flesh with a sickening wet slap. Meredith fully expected to feel the impact and looked down curiously, then up to her grandmother. Maria had calmly stepped into the bullet's path. Then another shot burrowed deep into Maria's breast, snapping her backward onto

Meredith and sending the two crashing to the ground just feet in front of Carla.

Carson stood and fired. Carla was enraged and quickly swept the hatchet from her back and hurled it at the soldier. The razor-sharp blade cleaved his skull nearly in two. Carson moved in and pumped rounds into the man even as he fell.

"GRANDMA!" Carla yelled as she rushed over to Maria, who was on the ground clasped tightly in Meredith's arms. Her cotton nightgown was drenched in an expanding stain of blood.

"We've got to get her inside!" Carla was adamant before turning and motioning for Betty who still clutched the knife. "You're a nurse. Help her! Please!"

"Carla," Betty replied coming closer, "It's a GSW, mid-chest. Not even a trauma surgeon could help. I'm sorry, dear. There is nothing I nor anyone else can do."

"No! No, you have to do something," Carla cried. She'd imagined the day, the moment she would have to say goodbye to her abuela, countless times. But, of all the possibilities Carla had considered, this wasn't one of them. Maria lay on the street, dying in the arms of her granddaughter.

Maria glanced up at Meredith, her eyes momentarily clear and lucid, as if the lady who had raised them all these years had risen back to the surface for her last moments.

"I never hated you," Maria murmured, moving Meredith's hair away from her face with a shaky hand. "You have always been so precious to me, and you remind me so much of your mother. It hurt to see her in you, knowing how badly I failed her. You, though, will do great things."

She gave Meredith one last, reassuring smile before turning toward Carla, nodding slightly, then closing her eyes for the last time.

Chapter Forty-Four

Carla was numb. She felt dead inside and couldn't tear her eyes away from the body. This was the person who had raised her and Meredith. The woman who had been more mother than grandparent. She hadn't been perfect; she was hard, but that was how she'd been raised. Carla's head bowed over until it touched Maria's. She felt Meredith's hand resting on her neck. The three of them sharing one final grief-filled moment as family.

"I'm really sorry," Betty said, kneeling down beside them. Joshua, Carson, and Jackson also huddled around the two sisters, knowing no words that might comfort them. A few fights were still happening farther away, but no more shots were heard. "Carla," Betty murmured quietly. "We need to get inside."

"No," Carla murmured as the tears continued to fall. "No, we can't just leave her out here."

"We won't," Carson said nervously. "However, we don't know if they have even more troops farther back down the road. We need to get behind cover."

"How many people would they bring, just to get one woman?" Joshua asked to no one in particular.

Carson shrugged but kept looking around anxiously. The two men carefully lifted Maria's body and carried it inside the house, followed closely by the others. Jackson kept a watch out the door while they laid out a sheet to wrap the woman's body. Within minutes, no one was left on the streets but the dead. The young boy stood sentry looking for any signs of trouble, but it looked like the attack was over.

Meredith's anguish was overwhelming. Maria's final words to her seemed to have shaken her to the core. "I don't understand. It's not what I saw. It was supposed to be me. I said some awful things about her. I told you she wouldn't make it."

"I did this," Carla mumbled. "This is my fault. If I had listened...if I hadn't tried to play the hero."

Joshua had an arm around her shoulders and gently lowered her to the floor as she began to collapse. "Please don't," he begged. "Please don't beat yourself up. You've done everything you possibly could. If you did anything, it was to save us all in an impossible situation." He looked to Betty for confirmation. "Right?"

Even though Betty had blamed her earlier, she could not see Carla as trying to do anything but help make things better for others. She was brave, fearless even, and now it had cost her dearly.

"Right," she nodded.

"She will need a funeral," Meredith stated weakly, the words drained of all emotion.

Carla nodded. "Yes, we need to bury her.

Months ago, Cara had started planning a grand sendoff for Fiery Maria. She had even picked out music, some Bible verses, and flowers. She'd known there would be a crowd of people wanting to pay final respects to the tireless matriarch of the Garcia clan.

Maria had wanted to be buried, which was a rare thing these days. Carla had visited a beautiful cemetery a few miles away. It was set up like a garden with rows of gravestones overlooking a small lake. Now...she would be buried near her own garden in the backyard. No one would come. No one else would ever even know.

Carla grasped Meredith's hand, then pulled her younger sister tight. The sobs echoed through the house. Maria would have no flowers. She would likely only be remembered by the people in this room. Maybe now she can make peace with her own daughter. Guide her, Mom. Please give her peace.

"I failed everyone," Carla said.

"You didn't fail me," a tiny voice said from across the room.

Carla's tear-stained face shifted from Maria to Jackson. The two sisters motioned for him to come over. They held him tight. The boy had been through so much, suffered so much loss himself, yet he was the one consoling them.

"You can't stop now," he said.

Carla blinked back the tears, her heart nearly bursting with love for this newcomer. How could this wise little boy know what to say when none of the grownups could?

"You've been a superhero to me," he continued, "and superheroes never, ever give up."

Carla wiped her eyes, attempting to accept the child's praise.

"Even when the bad guys are winning?" she asked.

"Especially when the bad guys are winning," the boy said, grinning.

Chapter Forty-Five

Carla pulled the child into a fierce hug. She wanted to believe those words more than anything. But she'd lost too much. It wasn't just her grandmother lying there. A part of her had died as well.

Meredith had remained ominously silent since her earlier outburst. She looked down at Maria's body; her expression was one of great sadness and confusion.

"This wasn't supposed to happen," she mumbled again.

She obviously relied on her strange visions to guide her. In some ways, it was sad to see Meredith no longer buying into her own delusions, having invested so much of herself in them. "I failed her."

"No, you didn't," Carla said gently, once again stepping into the role of protector. Having been doing it for so long, she didn't think she could ever get out of the habit. "Maria loved you. And if it was her time to go, she would want nothing more than to do it protecting us...protecting you. That's just who she was."

Jackson moved over and hugged Meredith. The gesture resonated with her more than any words Carla could offer.

"What now?" Joshua asked.

"Honestly, I don't know," Carla replied. "I don't know what else we can do."

"I have to go check on my kids," Carson said, rising. "I left their mom tied up in the bathroom."

For some reason, that sentence caused them all to break out in muted laughter.

Carla just shook her head. An hour earlier Chelsea was one of her biggest problems. Now, the crazy woman barely registered. *What a day...*

"I think we should look at getting some sleep," Joshua said, beckoning to the street. "I think they have all left. Meredith's people, I mean. The rest...well, they will never leave."

Everyone was exhausted, having all lost something that night. Carson left, and Meredith took Jackson up to bed. Betty didn't love the idea of leaving with possibly more soldiers in the area, so she agreed to stay the night. Joshua was busy using a torn t-shirt on something. In the dim glow of the lantern, he handed it to Carla.

She felt the heft of it and knew what it was. The hatchet, he'd been cleaning the blood off of it.

"You handled that tomahawk well," he said.

Carla shrugged, as she looped it over her shoulder. She'd killed two people with it now. Just one more thing she owed that old farmer.

Betty went to sleep in Maria's bed. Carla went to the spare room and checked on Jackson. He wasn't asleep yet, so she tucked him in and brushed the hair from his face. Jackson had been uneasy about sleeping by himself in a strange house, but Meredith had given him a teddy bear that had been one of her most treasured toys as a child. He hugged it close, peering up at Carla from behind it. "Are you ever going to make me leave?" It was clear the question had been playing on his mind for some time.

"No, of course not," Carla responded, the question breaking her heart. "I brought you back with me to give you a better chance at life. Despite how today went, we will find a way. You and I are a team. Right?"

"Right." They bumped fists.

Carla stayed with the boy until she heard the beautiful, soft sounds of sleep overtake him. The moment pulled up memories from her own childhood of her mom staying up with her after a bad dream. She felt the tears come again. This time she did not try to push them away. She sat there stroking the boy's hair, fully remembering what it meant to be connected to others who love you.

Coming down later, she found Joshua was laying on the floor of the family room. He'd left the overstuffed sofa for her to use. Carla grabbed a light blanket to cover him. She briefly wondered if he was just pretending to sleep. Now, more than anything, she wanted to act on the feelings they'd tiptoed around for so long, but she knew she was just lonely. Her grandmother was gone, her body had been moved back to a far room for now. Nothing about that was romantic, and honestly, she knew they both were too drained emotionally and physically to say or do anything. Carla also had to come to terms with possibly investing in a relationship with him. She was no longer naïve in thinking she could just have fun with no risk of hurting each other...or others.

Life didn't work like that. Carson was next door trying to pick up the pieces of the disaster their brief affair had caused. Josh was a really good friend, but that didn't mean they would be a good couple. If they tried and failed, she knew that very precious friendship would be gone, probably replaced with a much darker emotion. Maria had wanted her to try with him, but any hope she might have had for the future had probably died with her.

Carla lay there for hours, her mind a tornado of conflicting thoughts, faces, paths. It was as though some unseen force was manipulating her to remain conscious, forever denying her that bit of a few hours of peace. She heard a sharp bump from her sister's room and used that as an excuse to go check on her.

Meredith was sitting upright in bed, trembling and drenched in sweat. Carla held her sister close. "It's ok, I'm here," she said soothingly. The two of them sat there in a quiet embrace. Other nights

Carla might have ridiculed her sister with irritation or anger. But Carla realized just how close she'd come to losing Meredith tonight. Also, it was thanks to Meredith and her followers that any of them were still alive. She didn't understand what her sister was going through, much less if she had an actual gift or not, but she still loved her more than ever. She never wanted Meredith to think she was unloved or second place in her life. In her own way, Carla knew she had been as cruel as Maria was to Santina in how she'd treated Meredith. That had to change.

"I saw something," Meredith finally whispered out. "It...it was bad."

"What did you see?" Carla asked patiently.

Meredith didn't respond right away. Unlike her other visions, this was obviously one she was reluctant to explore.

"We were in a field." Meredith spoke slowly, as though she was still having trouble making sense of it. "The entire field was blackened already, and there were bodies. I think it may have been us, we were all about to be killed. We had gone there thinking we would be safer. But it was only getting worse. They were coming for us." She then grasped Carla's hand. "And you must choose which one of us lives and which one will die."

If recent events had not worn Carla down, she might have been taken aback by this piece of information. But so far, it seemed that every choice she made resulted in someone dying. The image of the blackened field also hit close to home. Her sister's story and the fact of what had gone on tonight provided one other possibility. One that she had been reluctant to even consider.

What if there was some truth in Meredith's visions? Perhaps, she had tapped into something greater than herself, something ancient or spiritual. What if she wasn't crazy? The people on the street obviously believed her. Hell, they were willing to die for her tonight.

Carla saw the bottle of medicine on the nightstand. She picked it up and removed the cap. The foil seal hadn't even been broken.

"Sorry," Meredith said, "I couldn't. I wanted to, but..."

"But you were afraid the visions would stop. That you might miss something important," Carla said realizing for the first time her sister's own struggle. She hung onto the painful visions just in case they might somehow help.

"Yes." Meredith's head was bowed. "I need to be able to save you, Carla. You're all I have left."

"That's not true," Carla reassured her. "You have me, you have Joshua and now Jackson. If the last few weeks have taught us anything, it's that family is not just about blood. It's about the connections we make along the way. Besides, you have a unique fan club out there."

Meredith laughed and hugged her big sister.

Carla laid down beside her sister like they had when they were kids. Meredith finally calmed down and tucked up beside her. Carla had no idea if there was anything to the visions, but she vowed not to make her take the meds and not to act like she was crazy. Sleep soon took them both.

Chapter Forty-Six

They buried Maria in the back, near the garden she loved so much. It was a somber ceremony, with few words spoken. The girls just held each other and managed to tell a few stories about Maria. How awkward it had been when they first came to live with her. How many of the woman's rules they'd broken in those first few months. The early morning sky was streaked with pinks and oranges by the time they finished their goodbyes.

The still smoldering shed a few dozen yards away had a distinct smell of cooked meat. No one wanted to check it out, but Carla finally did. A partially burned corpse stared back at her. The skin peeled back from a blackened skull. She couldn't begin to guess the sex much less who it was.

"Dozens more out front," Joshua said unnecessarily. Already, crows lined the trees, and vultures were beginning to circle high overhead.

"Someone must have tried to grab the food," Betty said walking over. "To go into that fiery hell just for food. They must have been unimaginably desperate."

Food was an issue, no denying that. Carla thought about Chelsea rummaging among the garbage cans a few days earlier. Soon, that would also be their fate.

"We have to leave," Carla whispered slowly, in hushed tones.

"Leave?" Joshua repeated, unsure if that would be better...or worse.

"There's nothing here for us anymore," Carla said flatly. "And those soldiers know where we live. Where I live. This street will be a hot-spot for trouble. No one is coming to fix all this. It's up to us to make a better life."

"How many of them can there be? Must be a hundred bodies out there," Joshua stated.

Carla had an idea but knew it would have to wait. "There will always be more."

"But where will we go? I mean, correct me if I'm wrong, but we don't have many options. Are we just going to hit the road?" Joshua lowered his voice conspiratorially and said, "And then there's your sister. I don't know what kind of help we can be for her out there, you know... if she has another one of her episodes. It's the real-world, Carla. She's barely living in it, as it is."

Carla didn't believe she'd ever be able to fully understand her sister. But she knew that if she stayed here, someone would come for them again. She had only stayed in this house for so long because she needed to be near her grandmother. But, with Maria gone now, she had little else to cling to in San Antonio. That, and staying in Maria's house with Chelsea next door—no, it was time to go. Anywhere but here.

What she wanted was revenge, every fiber of her being was sparking with rage, but that would lead to more trouble. She had to tamp that fire back down for now.

"Yes...it's time for us to go," she said to her friend. "Meredith is stronger and smarter than either of us realize. It was she that had her followers show up last night. How did she know? She may not have all the skills needed to cope with the world the way it is, but shit...do any of us?"

Carla turned to face the nurse who'd been staring off into space. Obviously, her own demons were still torturing her.

"Would you come with us, Betty?" Now that the clinic was gone, Carla doubted the woman had many options.

"I don't know," Betty said after a long pause. She was stroking both arms which were folded across her chest, much like Maria's had been when they laid her in the grave. "I've always considered San Antonio home. My place—it's not much, but it's all I've got. I have to believe that with the time I have left, I can still do some good."

Betty had proven to be surprisingly strong-willed and resourceful in the little time Carla had known her. There wasn't much Carla could say that might persuade her. She appreciated Betty's determination to do good and wished her nothing but success.

"If it's any comfort, I think there's a good chance that any more of the thug soldiers will just come straight for me," Carla said, smiling. "You should be safe. Relatively so, but you do need allies...friends. Remember that."

"Thank you," Betty stated softly. "I will miss you, Carla Garcia." Despite their differences, she had developed strong feelings for the young woman. "You take good care of your family and yourself." She turned and began slowly walking away.

Carla ran over before she had made it too far and passed her something. "I almost forgot. Thanks!" It was the old pistol. "I found one more bullet that fit. It was in a cup in the truck out there. Just one round left."

Betty knew the significance and actually appreciated the gesture. "Thank you, dear. I may just pick up one of those rifles out front, too. I always hated guns...they do so much ..." she trailed off.

Carla suddenly had horrific visions of the medical ward and knew what the woman meant. She patted her arm and nodded, then pulled her into a quick hug. "Stay safe, don't die. The world needs you."

The rest of them were packed and ready to head out within the hour. Dawn was just breaking off to the east. They didn't carry much more than a change of clothes and a few family photos in their backpacks. Carla had also slipped the old SmartComms unit into hers. She'd never reached anyone but still tried every few days. "Get water, as much as you can carry," Carla ordered. That was one of the few things they had left in relative abundance. She saw Meredith pushing her teddy bear down into the boy's backpack. Their eyes met, and Carla noticed a surprising level of clarity in her sister. *Maybe this will be a good thing for her.*

She took one final look up at the house that had been her home for the past seven years before turning away from it forever. Carla didn't dare turn back around and look at it again. She knew she'd never leave if she did.

They, too, picked over the dead soldiers, retrieving weapons, ammo, and a few other items. It was obvious that others had come during the night to do a proper scavenge on the group.

Carla no longer saw the bodies of the dead as people, they were just things. Things that had been determined to get in the way of her surviving. She knew she had become much of what she'd originally feared but it was not a bad thing. She was adapting.

"Trucks are a no-go," Joshua said climbing out of the nearly antique vehicle they'd sheltered beside the night before. "The Jeeps, too. Motors are all shot to hell, battery packs are useless now."

"By the way, Josh, how did you get to be such a good shot?" Carla asked, still having trouble believing how quickly he'd killed that soldier, and who knew how many more he'd downed in the skirmish?

He shrugged. "When I was a kid, my father taught me how to hunt. He showed me all of the secrets. I just didn't much like hunting, didn't see the point, you know? Of course, I've never really needed those skills until now," Joshua responded.

They shouldered the packs and started south. They barely made it fifty yards when Carla saw Rachel, Carson's daughter, sitting outside. She was watching her little brother, Ryan. Carla was clearly upset as they looked up. "Hi, Miss Carla," Rachel said as her tiny hand waved.

Carla opened her lips to respond, but she was distracted by how thin and gaunt they looked. She hadn't seen the children in weeks. Chelsea had still seemed healthy enough yesterday, but the kids...damn.

"Rachel, honey, you and Ryan stay where I can see you," their dad called out from his yard.

Carla was surprised to see Carson, and she realized he'd not gone unscathed either. He was wearing a bloodied bandage around his arm. She wondered if it was from the soldiers or his wife's attack. Either was probably just as likely.

He'd been a huge help last night. Probably saved my life, she thought. Carson was always good in a crisis. He was a man of action —probably one of the things that had attracted her to him. She knew they were done, but still, a fire inside her just wanted to feel his embrace, to feel his lips on her one last time. Closure would have been nice, but it wasn't to be.

"You're leaving?" Carson asked.

Carla gave a slow nod, and that was all the proof he needed. Carla had hoped for closure after everything they had been through together. At the very least, the two should have a proper goodbye. Her opinion of him as a husband, a father, and even as a lover had run the gamut over the last month. Now she saw him from a different vantage point. He had a job to do, to keep those kids alive.

"Do you want to come along with us?" she asked, despite the fact that she already knew the answer.

"I can't," Carson said. His tone was one of total defeat. "I've got to stay for the kids."

"You know there's nothing around here for you," Joshua argued. "You should come with us, man. Not that I know where we're headed, but it has to be better."

"That may be true, but I have a family to care for. After all that last night, I'm surprised they even came outside. They don't want to leave their home. Therefore, I'm here."

"They don't look so good, Carson." Joshua whispered. Carla was glad he'd said what she was thinking. *Did the basket of food even get to them?*

Carson nodded, his eyes filling with tears. "We'll be okay. Good luck, guys." He hugged Carla tightly. "Find love...always."

That was the end of it. There was nothing else to say. The time for words was over, fate seemed to hold their future, not emotion, or logic. Carson looked longingly at Carla, his eyes going watery. He reached a hand up to gently touch the bandage on her neck wound, then slowly took Rachel's hand in his and led her and Ryan back inside.

Carla was worried about Chelsea's instability, Carson, and the children as well. It gnawed at her very soul that she could do nothing more to help them. She desperately wanted to believe they'd make it, but she couldn't deny the very real feeling that this was the last time she'd probably ever see them. Meredith met her gaze and gave a slow nod as if to confirm that feeling.

"You can't change their destiny," Meredith said softly.

"Do I even want to know what it is?" Carla asked. She'd slowly come to terms with how hateful Chelsea had been toward her sister, and apparently it had been going on long before the war started.

Meredith shook her head. "I'm sorry." She looked at the sunrise and offered a small, bitter smile. "That woman is caustic, Carla. Her hatred of herself will infect and destroy everything around her. She's going to take the kids and leave."

"What will happen to them? What about Carson?" Carla asked, anxious for any sliver of the truth. She didn't know exactly when she'd become a believer, but there was something to her sister's visions.

Meredith shook her head. "It won't be good. Chelsea won't be the only monster out here."

"Miss Carla?" Jackson asked, thankfully distracting her from the unpleasant discussion. She noticed he used the same name Carson's kids always had for her. "Where are we going now?"

Carla dried tears from her own eyes before answering. She wasn't sure. "Just somewhere away from here." Maybe there was an aid camp somewhere. Not Vineland, but somewhere official. Over by the Lackland Space Base might be an option. Then she recalled the sounds of battle that had come from that direction the night they'd escaped Lehigh…

"How about to Anna's?" Jackson asked. "They were really nice to us."

It wasn't a bad idea, and one she'd already considered, but hated being a burden to them. The man had agreed to a trade deal, not taking in refugees. Showing up unannounced was a bold move. But hell, every move felt like a gamble. Carla had earned Tom's trust, so perhaps he would be willing to return the favor.

Chapter Forty-Seven

Carla loved San Antonio, the downtown, the Riverwalk, all the trendy bars and cool eateries. Now it was all gone; no one would be living in this pile of steel and concrete anytime soon, maybe never.

"You see that building?" she asked Joshua as they quietly walked beside each other.

Joshua turned and glanced across the clutter of roads and wreckage to where she pointed. "The Apex tower?" he asked. It had been a towering symbol of the city for over a decade. The turquoise glass wall reflecting the rest of the city from every angle. The rumor was apartments went for over 150 million.

Carla nodded and gave a furtive glance at the lower levels as they passed. "I talked to one of the officers down at the precinct. He said no one got out of their alive."

"Holy shit, how can that be? There were thousands of residents in that building."

"And ten times that working in the offices and retail space. When the power went out, they were all sealed inside. The air stopped circulating, water, too. All the elevators stopped wherever they were at. That was bad enough, but the guy said the fire doors, you know, big heavy ones they must put on every few floors in high-rises, well, they all slammed shut and locked. No one could get them open."

"Come on," Joshua said. "There had to be other ways out."

She shook her head. "The exterior cladding is all Armorglass, unbreakable. There was no way out. At least for the top few floors above that final set of fire doors." She pointed to several darkened spots around the base of the building.

Joshua saw the blackened lumpy stains around the building and the street. "No!"

"Yeah, after a while they gave up and jumped."

The officials, or whomever was left in charge at that point, just wrote them off. *Faster to get to the twenty percent,* Carla thought morbidly.

They walked for hours through the rest of the city's wreckage until they'd left civilization far behind. They saw a few people obviously scavenging for whatever they could find, but the survivors seemed to be dwindling faster now.

"We're not going that way, are we?"

Carla looked where Joshua was pointing. Toward Vineland and much farther on, Lehigh. "No, we need to bypass all that. But we will have to get closer." In the distance, she could just make out the edges of the place they'd taken shelter after being attacked in Vineland. She wondered how the highwaymen were functioning now with the mayor no longer calling the shots.

"This is as close as I want to get to that place," she said a few hours later. Using the zoom feature on her nearly useless SmartComm's camera, she zeroed in on the highwaymen's barricade. It appeared unmanned for a change and also seemed to be scattered across the road in pieces.

She swept the view toward the forest to either side of the road and was shocked to see no people moving about. No cooking fires, nothing to indicate all the refugees that were there just a few weeks earlier. "Something's changed," she whispered. "I don't see any people." Something flashed through the screen, silver and small.

"Should we...you know, check it out?" Joshua asked, unable to hide the trepidation in his words.

A sound coming somewhere behind them spooked them into moving quicker. Carla had no intention of Vineland's fate becoming theirs.

She readjusted the straps on Jackson's pack. She knew it had to be getting heavy, but the kid didn't complain once. He was tough; they all would have to be even tougher to survive out here. That reminded her again of the previous night. She turned to her sister. "What about your...your followers?"

"What about them?"

Carla wasn't sure how to say what she was thinking. "Won't they miss you? I mean...what will they do if you aren't around?"

Meredith didn't seem concerned, or maybe she just wasn't accepting the fact that she had left them behind. Carla still wasn't sure of how Meredith was from moment to moment but, she was determined to accept her as she was.

"They'll be fine," Meredith said. "All I could do was point the way for them. It's up to each of them to do what is needed."

"They really helped us last night. Some of them didn't make it," Carla said. "We owe them ...everything, including our lives."

Meredith nodded. "They were faithful believers. Sadly, others will fall, but some...some will be around."

"I do need to tell you something else, Meredith. Where we are going..." Carla found herself suddenly tongue-tied.

"It's going to look like what was in my vision. I know, Sis," Meredith said with an eery calm.

Carla let it go. An hour later, they were into the first of the growing fields. Carla saw the lack of any beauty in the area. When she was younger, she often ventured out here to enjoy a place untouched by the rest of the world. These had not remained untouched, though. There were signs of a battle, a recent one. Not the destruction from the terrorist attack. But the burned-out vehicles mixed in with rusting Agrobots and more of the decaying dead was enough to make them avoid this area as well. This hadn't been the path Carla had used the previous day; she'd wanted to see the city once more and felt like this way might be safer. Now she was second guessing those decisions.

"What do you think this is?" Jackson asked as he moved up between Carla and Joshua. He was bent down looking at the ground. The boy touched his fingers to the blackened soil then rubbed them in front of his face. "It's purple."

It took Carla a minute to see what he saw, but then she noticed it everywhere. It was all around them. A thin layer of dust or pollen, but it was the wrong time of year for that. Also, it wasn't purple, it was more of a violet color. Lovely, but so alien. "I don't know, Jax."

The boy smiled up at her, "My mom used to call me that."

She knelt down beside him. "I'd love to hear all about your mom and your dad whenever you are ready to talk. I know they raised a very smart little boy."

He grinned and ran ahead a few feet, and she looked up to catch Joshua looking at her.

"What?"

"Nothing," he said, smiling.

The abandoned battlefield faded, and soon Carla found herself on more familiar ground. The countryside was dotted with fields and fences that stretched on for miles. "We're getting close."

"What do you know about these people?" Meredith asked. Carla had already told her that Tom had been to some of her services.

"Not people, not really, just a man and his young daughter. Honestly, I don't know much, the man is a farmer, I knew his older child from school. The wife is gone, youngest daughter is about Jackson's age. They are quiet, peaceful, but determined. I get the feeling they are good people."

"You don't think they will just turn us away?" Joshua asked.

Carla had been considering that possibility. It was front and center all morning, in fact. "They may, but I hope not. I know they need help to run the farm. You know, now that all the machinery is dead."

"We aren't farmers," Joshua added.

"Then we will learn," Carla snapped back. She wasn't sure Joshua had come to understand how completely the world had changed. *We have to adapt to it, not the other way around.*

"We could be bringing the threat to them," Meredith said casually.

Carla knew what she meant. Part of her, a very big part, wanted to sneak into Lehigh to see what was happening in the aftermath of Cleveland's death and the botched raid last night. He and Kincaid didn't have an unlimited number of enforcers. She hoped it was chaos, but she thought again of all the supplies and equipment they had stored there. It really was the best of what old San Antonio had to offer before it succumbed.

"Did you see that?" Joshua pointed ahead.

Jackson had dropped to the dirt as he'd been ranging a good fifty feet ahead of the rest of them. Carla only saw a vague shadow that looked strange. It was inside a narrow band of trees bordering the field they were traversing.

"What is it?" she asked, belly crawling up to Joshua.

"I have no idea." He was looking through the scope of his rifle. "Really hard to make it out. A man, I think, but it doesn't look right."

Carla assumed it was one of Cleveland's men. Maybe they'd been tracking them. She almost told Josh to shoot it, but what if it was Tom or simply another innocent trying to escape the gangs back toward town?

She heard her friend click the gun's safety off. Then watched as the barrel moved side to side in increasing arcs.

"Shit!" he said. "It's gone."

"Huh?" She looked back, and sure enough, whatever had been there in the shadows a minute ago was absent. Now it was just scrub brush and pines.

They rose as a group and cautiously began working their way across the field.

"I'm going to go check it out," Joshua said before veering off to where the man had been.

The others watched as he crouched low, his gun raised to high alert position looking for targets. He moved forward in ten-foot increments before dropping and scanning. Finally, he was at the spot. Carla saw he was staring down at the ground. His gun now held loosely. She started to go over, but he held a hand and stopped her. Whatever he was looking at he didn't want the rest of them to see it.

She watched as he knelt down and picked at something out of sight. Tall grass blocked most of her view, but she felt her pulse rising again. They weren't out of danger.

Joshua rejoined them minutes later and hurriedly got them moving away.

"What was it? Was it a man?" Carla whispered.

He didn't answer her, and she asked him again, noticing that the color had drained from his face. Joshua was scared.

"It's...it's something. I don't know. There was a body, part of a body. I think it was a person.

"You mean the thing died. Just like that?"

He shook his head, "Whatever we saw was gone, nothing but odd-looking tracks and a strange funky smell. The body had been dead a while."

Carla let that sink in. Something out there had killed it or maybe was feeding on it. Something in her friend's words made her think it was an animal instead of a person they'd been seeing. "I came through here yesterday, went right by those trees. There was nothing there."

The sense of unease grew as they neared the farm. Carla's senses were hyper-alert to strange sounds in the trees. Several times, they heard loud snaps, like firecrackers or guns firing. They held their newly acquired rifles even tighter. Even Meredith was carrying a gun now and scanning the surroundings.

Joshua stopped again to examine an odd-looking, purplish vine encircling a nearby tree. He was about to say something when he saw Carla crouching and motioning for him to stay quiet and get down.

Two figures were standing outside the farmhouse in the shallow valley below. She first assumed it was Tom and Anna. But the second figure was too tall to be his daughter. Then she noticed the truck sitting almost out of sight behind the barn.

"Shit!" They got here first, thought Carla.

She stood, ready to go down and help the farmer when Meredith grabbed her arm and pulled her back down into the cover of tall grass. "Don't," Meredith pleaded.

"We have to help them, Meredith."

"This is the place, you know...the one I saw in my dreams." She tugged on her sister's arm. "Please! It...it's going to be bad."

Another sound came from far back behind them, "Josh they're trying to box us in," Carla said, swinging her gun around in a wide arc. She wanted to remind Meredith that her visions had been wrong before, but she, too, had a bad feeling about this. Out of the corner of her eye, she glimpsed another vehicle moving slowly up the two-track trail toward the farmhouse. The beat-up SUV slowed to a stop, and armed men began pouring out of it like cockroaches when you click the light on.

"They're going to need our help," Carla said, motioning for Joshua to follow her down.

"You've got to be kidding," Joshua said in disbelief. "You know, when I said we weren't farmers, well, we aren't soldiers either!" He was still haunted by what he'd had to do the night before. Like the others, he was in no hurry to get involved in a replay of it way out here.

"I have to," Carla whispered. "That man down there agreed to trade us food, and that was after he gave me shelter and food even before he had any reason to help."

"Are you really going to have to kill those men?" Jackson asked, the fear evident in his shaky voice.

Carla's focus was several hundred yards away as her response caught in her throat. She'd once been an adamant pacifist, hated guns. The thought of killing another human had once seemed so barbaric and alien to her. Now, it felt almost natural.

"Yes, Jax. We may have to do it to save Anna and her dad," Carla said to herself as well as the group. "I'm not looking forward to it any more than y'all are. But this is the world we have. It's the wild west all over again. We must fight to survive.

"I don't know who these guys are, but I know the type. They are parasites, living off others. They won't stop until everyone is dead or under their control. If they saw us out here, they would massacre us. We can't give them that chance.

"Meredith, you stay here with Jackson. Joshua, you come with me."

"I want to help, too," Meredith argued. And Carla could see Jackson, too, seemed ready to join in. His superhero, drop-trooper t-shirt nearly swallowed him whole. She smiled, despite the tension in the moment.

"You are helping, I'm not sure we can take on that many and survive. You have to get away if we don't make it. Wait til its safe, try and get Anna out at least, then get as far away as possible. She leaned in and kissed her sister on the cheek. "I love you!"

"Love you, too," Meredith whispered, but Carla was already moving stealthily down slope.

She had two guns, and Joshua mirrored her, removing his second piece from the pack and winding his way down to slip in behind her. "I guess we're all in, right? I always wanted a hero's death, you know."

Carla turned toward him, her face a mask of determination. Her eyes had the same fire as the night before. He braced for a harsh rebuke, but instead, she leaned closer and kissed him. Once they separated, Carla looked at him. "You're such an idiot." But she was grinning when she said it. She rose to a crouch and ran. Joshua, who was completely at a loss, quickly moved to follow.

They proceeded along the field's border, their movements

shielded by the scrubby mesquite. The men's voices were easier to hear now. Some of those near Tom weren't adults. They were some of the kids she had rescued from Lehigh. She wondered what had gone on in the last twenty-four hours. Tom must have taken them in for some reason. Maybe they couldn't find their own homes, or, maybe there wasn't anyone left once they got there.

"What exactly do you want?" Tom was yelling and quickly motioning for his daughter to stay behind him.

Carla and Joshua worked their way closer, zipping between buildings and abandoned equipment to stay hidden.

"We need food and the girls. All of the girls," the spokesperson for the armed men said. "Give us what we want, we will leave you alone. Your choice, friend. Turn us down, and we take it anyway, and you'll not be around to make trouble for us ever again."

Carla and Joshua recognized the ringleader's voice. He was the one who knocked her out and robbed them. She guessed she knew what became of the people from Vineland now, although he and his men looked beat to hell. They all had bloody wounds, makeshift bandages, and strange cuts over much of their bodies. Their clothes were ripped to shreds, and some seemed be burnt.

This was not the first battle these guys had been in today. No, she was certain they were looking for a place to hide as badly as she was. Something bad had gone down at the refugee camp, something really bad.

Chapter Forty-Eight

No way the timing of this is coincidence, Carla thought. Maybe Meredith was right about fate, it kept putting Carla right where she needed to be. Whether she wanted it to or not.

"This is bad," Joshua said.

"Agreed," she whispered back. "They look even more desperate than before. We've got to be careful," Carla cautioned. "Otherwise, we risk getting all those kids killed."

Joshua was thinking the risk was even more personal but agreed with her. As they moved even closer, dipping behind a small earthen terrace, Carla saw Anna looking in their direction. But they ducked out of sight before she could spot either of them.

The ongoing talk between Tom and the leader was heating up to even more shouts and warnings. "We know you have plenty of food here," the man said. "And with all those seeds you've got stored back there, you'll never have to worry about going hungry. Shit, man, you're one of the luckiest men still living.

"But we know plenty of people who would *kill* for what you've got. And most of them are a lot less civilized than us. They know nothing about this farm...yet." The threat was more implicit than specific, but they all got the message.

"You know, on second thought," the man began, "maybe we should just set-up right here. There's some shit out in those woods that none of us wants to face again."

"No," Tom said with finality. "We might can work out something on the food, but my daughter will not go anywhere with you fucking animals."

The ringleader sighed. "Suit yourself," he said, signaling his men, who steadied their guns at the farmer.

"Wait!" Carla shouted, stepping up out of her hiding place before Joshua could stop her.

Oh, God! Joshua thought.

The mob immediately re-centered their weapons on her.

"You," the ringleader said, stepping forward. "I fucking remember you. I should have killed you when I had the chance. You're the one that took out Cleveland."

"Let this man and the kids go," Carla demanded.

"Are you always this stupid?" the man said, chuckling softly. "Boys, burn it all down. The farm is useless without Mister Tom anyway."

Several of the goons shouldered their long guns, lit makeshift torches, and headed for the fields; others went for the barn and house.

"You don't need to do this," Tom said.

The man flipped the power lever on the weapon. Carla realized it was one of the more advanced military pulse rifles. It fired a super charged lightning bolt of energy instead of a bullet. He raised it toward her head, "You're going to burn for this, darling. This thing will cook you from the inside out."

He held it dead center at her chest. Her mind went through all the emotions, then thought of Meredith's vision. This wasn't how she said the end would come. "Someone in Vineland must have really fucked you up, man," she yelled. "Ya'll look like you picked on the wrong people."

"It wasn't no fucking people that did this, bitch." The man smiled a nearly toothless grin as he squeezed the trigger.

The shot came before the man completed the pull. The fancy rifle fell from his grip and part of his head split away as well, as it was shredded by a round. The kids all ran for cover as the rounds began to fly.

Carla didn't need to turn around to know that Joshua had again come to her aid. Getting rid of the leader was all Tom needed to go into attack mode. He pushed Anna out of the way, down to the ground and began firing his own rifle at the mob. Many of them fell; torches dropped into the dry Texas grasses, which ignited at once.

"We have to get them all," Carla shouted over the gunfire. "If any get away, they'll come back with even more!"

Soon, there were only a few left standing. One fired a mean looking handgun at Tom; a bullet from Joshua connected with the shooter first, deflecting his aim, but the round still caught the farmer in the shoulder. He fell to the ground, and Anna was instantly by her father's side.

The fire was spreading quickly across the field, two buildings were already fully engulfed. Carla found herself thinking about Meredith's visions again, and as if on cue, a lone soldier came out from the woods.

He had Meredith and Jackson at gunpoint.

Carla had picked up the pulse rifle after both of her weapons had run dry. Now she and Joshua had guns trained on the man. But they could not get a clear shot. There was no way they could hit him without hitting one or both of his hostages.

"Let me go, and I'll release one of these two. I'll take the other one with me," the man said, holding Jackson and Meredith close together. "You might have enough time to kill me before I can do them both, but I don't think you can save them both. So, what do you say?" He ran his fingers creepily through Meredith's hair as he yelled his threats.

Meredith nodded slowly at Carla, who finally understood that this was the moment she would have to choose. Save her sister or the boy they'd adopted into their family.

It was an impossible choice. An impossible choice in a week of impossible choices. Carla couldn't bear to save one just to lose the other and she knew she couldn't trust the man to not kill them both. Life was meaningless to these people.

The man held the pair's heads together so that any shot would pass through both of their skulls to get to him.

Carla sighted down the advanced optics of the rifle, fingers rested lightly on the trigger; she felt the slight vibration of the energy inside the powerful weapon. It could take the asshole's head right off, but he was right, one...or both of his hostages would be dead as well.

Through the scope, she saw Meredith's mouth moving silently and somehow knew she was about to make the choice for them. Meredith had seen this all before. She was going to push the boy out of the way, drawing the wrath of the man. Carla would then have one shot to put the asshole down.

"No, no, no!" Carla saw her sister tense. "No, Meredi..." The words died on her lips as the shot rang out. But instead of her sister's head exploding in gore, Carla was shocked to see it was the man who pitched forward. His gun fired, too, but it narrowly missed both Meredith and Jackson, burrowing into the field.

He released his grip on the gun and stumbled forward. Carla unleashed a satisfying plasma round into his chest, and he sagged lifelessly to the ground.

The shooter emerged from the tree-line directly behind Meredith.

"Betty?" Carla said in total surprise.

She was walking down the small hill, clutching the Glock in one hand and her medical bag in the other. "You came after us," Carla gasped. "Why?"

Betty shrugged. "I guess I wanted in on that second chance. Been following you guys all day. Surprised you didn't hear me." She looked around at the flames that were already beginning to die down. "Looks like I got here at the right time."

"I'll say," Joshua said, grateful that another crisis was apparently over. "We need your help, though. The farmer took a round to the shoulder."

Betty patted Meredith and hugged the boy, then rushed down the field to Tom.

"How are you holding up?" she asked, digging through her bag for medical supplies.

Tom winced in pain from the wound in his shoulder as he pulled himself into a sitting position. "I've been better. But I'll survive. Maybe...just maybe we all will."

Meredith and Jackson ran down to Carla, and she held them both tight. "It didn't come true," Meredith breathed. "We're all still here."

Carla could hear Meredith's voice breaking. She believed in her premonitions, and even Carla had to admit, now that there was something to them, Meredith seemed relieved this one hadn't played out exactly as she'd seen.

"Sometimes fate gives you a choice, sister," Carla said grimly.

"I knew you wouldn't let anything happen to us," Jackson said, holding Carla tightly.

Chapter Forty-Nine

Carla helped Betty get Tom back inside. He shooed them away like fussy chickens, but the women persisted.

"Shut-up, you old fool," Betty said. "You always were a stubborn one."

It didn't register with Carla right then that Betty and Tom had a history. It would come out in time.

Carla worried that all the gruesome killing was going to be traumatic for the kids, but they were playing before she and Joshua had even hauled away the last of the bodies. Everyone, it seemed, we're all now conditioned to accept these horrors as normal.

"What do you think did this?" Joshua asked, pointing at a series of small but deep cuts on several of the corpses. The two of them had piled them on one of Tom's wagons like yesterday's trash.

She leaned in close; the cuts were all in a straight line and extraordinarily precise, almost like a surgeon. Most of them had multiple series of the wounds. "No idea, some new kind of weapon maybe, or maybe they just all ran into the same barbed-wire fence."

Joshua nodded thoughtfully. "Concertina razor wire could do it. Damn, had to be painful, though."

Carla thought back on some of the comments the guy had said. "They definitely were running from something. Whatever they'd encountered had taken them off the top of their game."

"Lucky for us," Joshua replied.

Several hours later, the homestead once again looked more like the idyllic farm it was. No sign of the would-be killers remained. Their vehicles were stored under tarps, and their weapons had all been cleaned and secured in Tom's makeshift armory room.

"Won't do for the kids to get a hold of those," he said, wincing as he turned to Carla. "In time, though, we're going to need to train them all on how to shoot, how to hunt.

As evening came, Carla sat on the front porch, watching her sister playing with the children. She couldn't tell what game they were playing, but she could see that her sister seemed truly happy and content for the first time in a long while. She couldn't remember the last time she had heard Meredith laugh like that. Maybe there was hope for her yet.

Tom had already made it clear they were welcome to stay there as long as they wanted. "Call this place home now, Carla Garcia. I owe you everything."

"Thank you for saving us," Anna said, huddled up next to her dad. "You're our guardian angel."

Carla laughed. "Don't say that around my sister. She'll think I'm trying to steal her spotlight."

"So, what happens now?" Betty asked, walking up and sitting beside them in one of the other old rocking chairs.

"I don't know," Tom said. "I guess we try to stick together and look out for each other. There are going to be other troubles out there. This thing ain't over...not by a long shot."

Carla knew he was right. She was already planning a recon trip to Vineland. She wanted to see what had happened at the refugee camp. "I think we should scout out Lehigh in the next few days. The mayor had some very useful stuff stockpiled there, and if I'm right, most of the security forces should be gone by now.

"Let's save that battle for another day," Tom said. "We need to heal up a bit before we pick another fight."

"So, all these other kids?" Carla asked a previously unspoken question.

Tom nodded glumly as he held Anna close to his chest. "Most of 'em got home to find nothing. Parents gone or dead. Homes destroyed or in the process of being overrun by squatters. They just started showing up here not long after you left. I couldn't send them away. Me and Anna did what we could to feed them, give 'em a safe place to sleep. This world has made orphans out of all of 'em. They've all had to grow up so fast."

He leaned back and sighed. "We have a large bunk-room, and all the kids automatically started helping out. I guess they had duties in Lehigh as well. The older ones even assigned chores for the younger group. So, we'll be looking at teaching them survival skills."

Anna gave Carla a playful nudge. "Maybe you could teach us a lesson or two, as well."

Carla hadn't imagined the world would still need teachers. But something about Anna's suggestion felt right. It was as though she was where she needed to be.

Joshua came out onto the porch to join them. Carla held out her hand for him to take it. They were going to get through this day and maybe the days to come as well. They would have to rely on each other even more. She missed her grandmother. Maria would have loved it out here, but that was history now. Tomorrow was what mattered.

"It isn't going to be easy," Carla said, already mentally turning to face this new reality. "It will be up to us to survive. But we've already made it this far. I don't see why we can't carve out a little piece of sanctuary for ourselves."

"It's something worth fighting for," Joshua said, clasping Carla's hand tightly. "I spent so long being afraid. Wondering if there was anything worth dying for... but now, I think we've got something worth living for."

Carla looked back to the ruins of San Antonio in the distance. Every day, it felt more and more like a wasteland and less like a city. An entire civilization wiped out. Just like the Mayan city of Caracol she'd told her class about. What would be left to remember of this place in fifty years, or a thousand?

Her mind also slipped back to Carson and the kids. They would have to go check on them, maybe in a few days. She had a feeling Meredith would be right again, and the kids would be gone with their mom. She didn't want to think about what else she might find. She did know with certainty that Chelsea would never know about this place.

There would be more battles, probably more killing, but Carla refused to let this be the end. Thanks to Meredith's gifts, maybe they could learn to see what was on the horizon, and then, with luck, they could live to rebuild the world.

Carla's thoughts of the future were interrupted by a flash high above. All of them looked up as a massive orbital ship shot across the western sky. Meredith looked up at the craft and then at Carla. And Carla knew something in that scene must be part of one of Meredith's visions. She wanted to know more about the future, and what else her sister could sense.

She also understood she might never get her head around Meredith's gift, or curse. They might never fully understand it, but perhaps they could use it, turn it into a tool to help guide them through this new and savage Earth.

About the Author

JK Franks is the popular author of numerous post-apocalyptic and near-future techno-thriller novels. He is an admitted tech geek, science nerd, cyclist, and storyteller. JK Franks' world was formed by a childhood growing up during the Space Age when he developed a love for books. He became an avid student of history and science and a regular reader of everything from reference books to dusty, old biographies. Once he discovered science fiction, he never looked back.

His work is mostly near-future thrillers, characterized by meticulous research, hard science, and a gritty, seldom-matched realism. "I hate stupid characters," states Franks. "Or even worse, smart characters, acting stupid." All of his work combines his passion for hard science fiction, well-crafted characters, and superb storytelling.

No matter where he is or what's going on, Franks tries his best to set aside time every day to answer emails and messages from readers. You can visit him on the web at www.jkfranks.com. Please subscribe to his newsletter for updates, promotions, and giveaways. You can also find the author on Facebook or email him directly at author@jkfranks.com.

Other Books by JK Franks

The Catalyst Series

Book 1: Downward Cycle

Life in a remote, oceanfront town spirals downward after a massive solar flare causes a global blackout. But the loss of electrical power is just the first of the problems facing the survivors in the chaos that follows. Is this how the world ends?

Book 2: Kingdoms of Sorrow

With civilization in ruins, individuals band together to survive and build a new society. The threats are both grave and numerous—surely too many for a small group to weather. This is a harrowing story of survival following the collapse of the planet's electrical grids.

Book 3: American Exodus

This companion story to the Catalyst series follows one man's struggle to get back home after the collapse. No supplies, no idea of the hardships to come; how can he possibly survive the journey? Even if he survives, can he adapt to this new reality?

Book 4: Ghost Country

Since the solar superstorm and CME almost two years before, the Gulf Coast town of Harris Springs, Mississippi, has suffered from gang attacks, famine, and hurricanes and has battled a crusading army of religious zealots. Now, they face their greatest challenge: outsmarting a tyrannical president and escaping an approaching pandemic.

Cade Rearden Thrillers

Book 1: State of Chaos

He's exhausted and brutally traumatized. Now, Spec-Ops Captain Cade Rearden must finally listen to the voices in his head...or everyone on Earth may die. If you like near-future technology, complex heroes, and high-octane action, then you'll love JK Franks' explosive new adventure.

Book 2: Midnight Zone

Nightmares are real in the cold, dark waters of the deep. National Security Agent Cade Rearden is used to secrets. Assigned to protect the ultra-dark-ops organization known as The Cove Project, he grapples with his role of defending a country still in crisis after a deadly super AI has devastated much of the U.S.

But when part of his team mysteriously disappears beneath the idyllic waters of the Caribbean, Cade finds himself thrust into a web of lies and mystery, at the heart of which lies an eons-old secret that somebody will kill to protect. Grappling with his inner demons and struggling to locate his friends, Cade stumbles upon a government cover-up...and terrifying creatures, hidden miles beneath the surface of the ocean.

The Fade Novels

The Night Gate

Since losing his daughter seven years ago, Pike Shepard has struggled to maintain a normal life for himself in the coastal community of Blackwater. It's a quiet life, until a beautiful scientist shows up on his doorstep with a desperate plea for help. Dr. Kate Cassidy has uncovered a new aspect to quantum entanglement: the ability to not just see the multiverse but a way to travel through it. Her device allows them to SideSlip between parallel dimensions that are at once familiar and quite bizarre, wondrous, and terrifying. Pike learns they aren't the only ones with this ability, and the others want them gone.

Savage Earth Series

Book 1: Nightmare Factory

In the not-too-distant future, a devastating global attack takes place and planet Earth is on the brink of extinction. In this sci-fi thriller, Master Sargent Joe Kovach has been through a personal hell as he struggles to adapt to his new enhancements. As battles escalates, so does his determination to uncover the group who triggered this brutal extinction event that has left the planet overrun by mechanical and genetic horrors.

Book 1.5: San Antonio

This isn't just the end of the world – it's a deeply personal story of Carla Garcia's fight to keep her family united and safe amidst chaos. After a devastating terrorist attack leaves society in shambles, Carla confronts dwindling supplies, haunting premonitions from her sister Meredith, and the slipping memory of her grandmother. In this close-knit struggle, where monsters lurk in the shadows and love is a rare treasure, every moment pulses with heart-pounding choices and the undying hope for a glimmer of light in the darkness.

Book 2: Eradication

In a world ravaged by a devastating attack, the remnants of humanity are barely clinging to existence. Months have passed since the enemy unleashed hordes of murderous creations that now engulf the planet. Amidst the chaos, One renegade group takes refuge on Earth's last remaining space vessels, orbiting above the desolate wastelands. They are Banshee Team, and they are alone beacon of hope in the face of annihilation. They are committed to uncover the truth behind the brutal attacks and lend their expertise to turn the tide of this merciless battle.

Connect with the Author Online:

** For a sneak peek at new novels, free stories, and more, join the email list at jkfranksbooks.com.

Facebook: facebook.com/groups/JKFranks/

Goodreads: goodreads.com/author/show/15395251.J_K_Franks

Websites: JKFranks.com or JKFranksbooks.coim

Twitter: @jkfranks
Instagram: @jkfranks1

Printed in Great Britain
by Amazon